MERCENARY REDEMPTION

DIANE MERLIN

TEASE PUBLISHING
www.teasepublishingllc.com

Other works by Diane Merlin

Mercenary Heart
Michael Angelo

Mercenary Redemption
A Tease Publishing Book/E book

Copyright© 2007 Diane Merlin
ISBN: 987-1-934678-11-4
Cover Artist: Stella Price
Interior text design: Stacee Sierra
Editor: Jenna Sherman

To everyone who read Mercenary Heart and harassed me about the ending. When you have a bunch of characters like the ones in these books, the story's never really over. You just move on to the next chapter. I hope you enjoy this piece of the pie.

I'd like to thank my grandson, Kyle, who is five. His innocent insistence that he wants to read one of NaNa's books makes me strive to do my best. One day my grandchildren will be old enough and will actually pick up something I've written.

Chapter One

Dashing tears from her eyes, Devona settled into the pilot's seat and hurried through her preflight check. She didn't intend to sit around and wait for Kevnor to come back for round two. *I am through apologizing for a heritage I wasn't even aware of before Umland spilled his guts. I am through listening to Kev lament our joining. I am through with him. Period.* "Damn you," she whimpered, ignoring the fresh rush of tears. She was a strong woman. How dare he reduce her to a driveling fool? How dare she allow herself to be brought so low?

Within moments, the Freebird lifted off the landing pad and its former first officer left behind her husband, her new home, and the only friends she had in the world. If they were still her friends, which was doubtful since she'd just stolen their ship. Friends were overrated anyway, she assured herself. It was much better if you didn't form attachments. They left you open to heartache. With that in mind, she laid in a course for Epsilon III. If you weren't too picky, you could pick up a crew there. Dev couldn't afford to be picky. In order to make a comeback as a mercenary, she needed to hire new hands for the Bird.

"Captain Devona." She said it out loud to see how it sounded. It had a nice ring to it. She complimented herself on her promotion.

The console signaled an incoming communication. She ignored it. It would be Kev, trying to talk her into returning to Bright's Planet; trying to convince her he didn't mean the terrible things he'd said. Closing her eyes she let the scene replay in her mind.

"You're a fucking what?" Kev had screamed. "Imani? You're a fucking Imani? My mate, the mother of my child, is my mortal enemy?"

"I didn't know," she'd cried, clutching at his arm. "Kevnor, I never even knew the Imani existed let alone that they were longtime enemies of the Bauxites. How can you hold that against me?"

He jerked his arm out of her grasp. "Sorry. That does nothing here." He thumped his chest over his heart. "To silence the voices of my slain family, crying out to me over this injustice."

She couldn't believe the cold, detached voice of her mate. "Kev, please, don't do this to us."

"Us? There is no us! I'll have the marriage annulled as soon as possible. You can deliver my child and turn it over to me, then go wherever you wish—as long as it's out of my sight."

He had turned his back on her, and the breath had left her lungs with a keening cry of torment.

There on the bridge of the Freebird, she felt the devastating pain again. Anguish gave way to anger. He would not have her child. Their brief joy had given her this child, and she would not let Kevnor Gaaus, or anyone else, take it from her. A hand wandered down to stroke her abdomen. Whatever it took, she would protect her baby.

***

Kev paced beside the engineer, a position he'd occupied for more than three hours.

"In the name of all that's holy, man, if you don't stop that pacing, I'll quit." Callus settled back on his heels and glared at his friend.

Holding out a placating hand Kev promised, "I'll go. Don't quit."

As soon as Callus leaned back into the engine compartment, Kev began to pace again. "That does it." Callus threw a calibrating wrench across the room. "I'm freaking out of here." He headed for the hangar door, his ugly face drawn into a grimace.

"No," Kev whispered to the spot where, moments before, his friend had been.

Zoë sauntered in. "You're not making this any easier."

"I didn't do anything," Kev assured her.

She raised her brows. "You need to find something to occupy your time. Those of us with tasks to complete cannot put up with your infernal badgering."

Flopping down in a chair Kev insisted, "I didn't do anything. Nothing. Honestly, Zoë I didn't say a word or get in his way."

"Let me ask you something," she said. "If you were working and I kept walking up and down and looking over your shoulder, would it irritate you?"

"Well, yeah, but..."

"I rest my case." Running her slender black fingers through his already tousled hair she tilted his head back so she could peer into his eyes. "Kev, get out of here. If you want us to get this ship in working order so you can go after Dev, you need to leave us alone so we can do what needs to be done."

Dark brown irises rimmed in red, Kev was the picture of self-loathing and recrimination. "This is all my fault."

"Yeah, it is." She didn't bother to argue with him.

"She's out there alone with a madman after her, and it's all my fault."

"All the more reason to get your sorry ass out of here so we can finish working on the Pelican and go after her." Twisting an ear she encouraged him to his feet and swatted him on the rear. "Now scoot."

Kev left the hangar, passing Callus as he returned. Thank the gods. Without the engineer's unparalleled abilities, the Pelican would never be able to track a fast ship like the Freebird. Moments later, Kev was in the jungle, the cool shade of the Hiberus trees offering a respite from the heat surrounding the complex that housed Ornithal Enterprises, the shipping business the collective crew of ex-mercenaries had recently purchased. Dropping down to sit on the ground, he leaned back against the spongy trunk of one of the giant trees and allowed himself a moment to rest his aching head. He hadn't slept a wink in the three days since Devona's departure. His lids felt like sandpaper as they closed over his eyes.

Devona turned to face the jackals that had been tracking her through the city. "Okay, you want me, you gotta fight me." A blaster in each hand she looked completely at ease—except for her hugely rounded stomach.

The three men confronting her laughed. "Lady, you must be kidding. A ten-year-old kid could take you down in your condition," one commented.

"Yeah. Just give it up and come along quietly. Save yourself the exertion," another added.

Sweat dotted her beautiful face, and Kev could see her chest heaving from the pace she'd been traveling. "You might win, but I won't make it easy for you." Without warning, she fired at the men. Two of them went down.

The third glanced at his dead companions and back at Dev. "I'm not human, bitch. Your blasters won't work on me." The bounty hunter stepped closer, and Dev screamed out Kevnor's name.

Coming awake with a jolt, Kev looked up to see Miklus Armstrong squatting beside him. Startled by the other man's presence, Kev crab-walked away before his brain made the connection that Mik was a friend and not one of the bounty hunters from his dream. "You startled me," Kev stated the obvious.

Mik grinned. "No shit. Did you have a nice nap?"

"Hell no. I was dreaming about Devona, and it wasn't a good one."

Mik stood and held a hand out to help his friend up. "Come on. It's almost dark, and there are some pretty unfriendly carnivores in these woods, according to our new neighbors."

Kev rose and dusted off the seat of his pants. Looking around, he frowned. "How long was I out here? I swear I just sat down."

Slapping him companionably on the shoulder, Mik steered him back toward the collection of metal buildings. "My best guess is four hours."

"Four hours? Impossible. I've got too much to do."

"Bullshit. You don't have anything to do but worry yourself into a decline. We're taking care of everything else. And you needed the sleep. From the looks of you, you haven't bathed or changed since Dev left."

Kev looked down at his rumpled clothes. "I don't remember," he admitted.

Mik wrinkled his nose. "Well my nose tells me you haven't. Why don't you hit the shower and then meet the rest of us in the mess hall. Shesshie has food on the stove for us so we can eat whenever we get a break."

Kev looked frantic. "I don't know…"

"Look, Dev has enough of a head start that she's going to be hard to find. We need a plan of action before we take off after her. To my way of thinking, you need to be in on this discussion and you need to be clear-headed. Go shower, change, and get your ass to the dinner table. We'll have a war conference while we eat."

Old habits were hard to break. Mik had been their leader since they were in grade school, so it was only natural for Kev to follow his directions now. Besides, he was too fucked-up to think for himself.

***

Once again the indicator light told her a communication was coming in. After so long they were becoming difficult to ignore. What had it been? A week? Her heart begged her to answer while her head told her to forget Kev and her old life. Tired of the internal tug-of-war, she slammed a palm down on the button to activate the holovid. She might as well get it over with.

"Greetings, Princess."

That was not the face she'd expected to see. Quickly she masked her surprise and glowered at the image. "Umland. What do you want?"

"I'm flattered you remembered me."

"I never forget an enemy. What do you want?" She gripped the arms of the seat to keep from touching her stomach.

"Why you, Princess. You. And I aim to have you sooner or later. Why not make it profitable for both of us?" His smile sent a wave of nausea coursing through her system. "If you cooperate, I'll cut you in for a percentage. Hell, I'll even sell you to the Imani instead of the Bauxites."

"You'll forgive me if I pass on that generous offer," she sneered and cut the connection. As soon as his image faded, Dev ran for the head and gave in to the nausea.

When she got back to the bridge, she settled into the communication station and tried to trace the call from Umland. Time after time she ran into a dead end. How the hell did Kev work the magic he did with the computer? Her head fell over, and she rested her forehead on the console. Tears of frustration clouded her eyes. What the hell was wrong with her? She never cried, or at least she never used to. It seemed like that was all she did these days. In frustration, she settled in for a good cry.

Once the pity party had subsided she pulled up her personal log and entered the events that had taken place. If something happened to her, she wanted a record left for Kevnor to find. She didn't doubt that he'd come after her eventually. Even if he considered her lower than a slimewort's belly, he'd come for the child. And he'd avenge them if Umland succeeded in capturing her. She had no doubt of that.

Thoughts of Kev soon had her reminiscing. Why right here in this very chair she'd opened his clothes and run her hands along his taut, bronzed muscles, tasted the flesh she'd desired for years and learned the best-kept secret of the Bauxite people. Closing her eyes she allowed her imagination to take over, pretending the hands that cupped her breasts were his not hers. Catching her lower lip between her teeth she eased one hand down between her legs, recalling the heat of Kev's long fingers as they touched her just so...

The strident peeling of the proximity warning system brought her feet to the ground and cleared the fog from her head. What now? Scanning the readouts she realized a ship was closing in fast. Dev smiled. For the first time since she'd left Bright's Planet, she smiled. "Come on over," she whispered and headed for the weapons station.

After engaging the shields, Devona enabled the pulse cannon and pulled up the targeting computer. "At last, something I understand and have control of."

The shield absorbed the first salvo. Dev checked the damage readouts and returned fire, taking out life support and engineering on the other ship. "Wanna fuck with me?" she asked rhetorically. "I'll cut off your dick." Her last shot disabled their weapons system. At last she felt like herself. There was something about the adrenalin rush of a good battle that settled her nerves.

She engaged the communications system. "Do you surrender?" she asked with audio only. There was no reply for several minutes. They must be working frantically to repair the damage she'd inflicted. She asked again.

"No, bitch, we don't," was the succinct reply.

"Okay." Dev's final shot ended the discussion. Blinding light flashed just before the area was flooded with space debris. Stretching, she peered out a nearby porthole. "You shouldn't have called me a bitch."

Chapter Two

Eb dished up a humongous serving of miner's stew. "This looks great, Shesshie," he complimented. "Just like my mom used to make."

Jim Darner rubbed his hand affectionately across the young man's head. "Leave some for us, squirt," he teased. At sixteen, Eb was eating everything in sight.

"You snooze, you lose, old man." The kid grabbed four rolls to add to his booty.

Just seeing Eb act like a normal teenager put a knot in Jim's throat. He'd come a long way in the short time since his liberation. Jim just wished he could erase from his mind the horror of the years the kid had spent as a sex slave. "Old man?" he feigned anger, "I'll show you old. I bet I can eat twice as much as you do."

"Now hold on, Doc." Callus used the affectionate name they'd given Jim. "The rest of us are hungry, too." Matching his words with deeds Callus also piled his plate with vittles.

Watching her sister watch the engineer, Shesshie prodded her with a hip. "Better keep an eye on your man, Marissa, or the rest of us will go hungry."

Blushing profusely Marissa denied, "He's not my man."

"But I'm working on it," Callus piped in.

Moving Tessa from her hip to the high chair, Shesshie placed a bowl of mashed-up stew in front of the baby. "Eat," she commanded.

"Eat," Tessa dutifully repeated.

"Look what I found wandering around," Zoë announced as she strolled into the room, an arm looped through that of each of the tall handsome men who flanked her. Not quite chest high to either of them, the petite black woman was in no way intimidated by them. "You just can't leave men unsupervised."

"Very funny," Mik disengaged himself to mosey over to his wife and child. "I don't get any respect these days." He kissed Shesshie and leaned over to kiss the baby. She flung a spoonful of food that hit him squarely in the face. Squealing, Tessa clapped her hands. "See what I mean?" He wiped at the mess with a napkin Shesshie handed him.

"Quit grousing and dip your plate," Shesshie told him.

"Or you might not get any," Jim warned. "Eb and I are having an eating contest."

That got him hustling. "Here you go, Kev." Mik handed over an already dipped plate.

"I'm not hungry." Kev pushed the plate away.

Shesshie pushed it back across the table. "Eat anyway," she advised. "You have to keep up your strength. You'll need it on your quest to find Dev."

"Speaking of which," Mik segued into the discussion of their imminent task. "How's the ship coming along, Callus?"

"Should be ready sometime tomorrow, Capt'n."

Mik eyed the engineer, taking note of the way his leg was pressed up against that of Marissa. "What can we expect from her?"

"She's not the Bird and never will be. But she'll do double what she could before, and she won't let you down when you need her," he promised. "Plus, I've made major alterations to her weapons system. You won't be caught with your pants down if you engage in a fight." Glancing down at his dinner companion he murmured, "Pardon the language."

Marissa smiled but said nothing. It was flattering to be treated with deference after the shameful life she'd led. She could love Callus for that alone, if she allowed herself. But a former slave to one of the most perverted men on Pagoda couldn't afford that luxury. Callus deserved so much more.

"We leave as soon as the work's complete on the Pelican. I want everyone packed and ready before you sleep tonight." Turning to his wife Mik asked, "Are you sure you'll be okay here? I could be gone for weeks, even months. We can't come back until we find Dev."

"Of course not. You have to bring Devona home to us. We'll be fine here. Doc and Eb will be with us, and Marissa and I are determined to get that extra hangar set up as a tavern. I have a feeling the locals will give us lots of business." She glanced at her sister, eyes twinkling. "Have you ever tasted their food?" Both dark-haired, green-eyed women burst out laughing.

Eb shuddered. "I have, and I thought I'd die before I could make it to the edge of the village to spit it out." As if to wipe the horrible image from his mind, he grabbed another roll and consumed it in two bites.

"You grow to that appetite, boy, and you'll be a giant one day," Zoë observed.

"That's the idea." Eb puffed out his chest.

Tessa clapped again, apparently approving of Eb's plan.

***

Dev docked at Epsilon III and filed her itinerary with the authorities. She didn't plan to be here long—just long enough to hire some crewmembers. Taking a last look in the mirror, she secured the Freebird and stepped outside. She hated to admit it, but she was a little nervous about taking on the role of captain. For years she'd told Mik she could handle his job, and now it was time to ante up. Squaring her shoulders, she headed for the Pirate's Den, a little club that catered to the less savory members of society. The blasters hanging on her hips gave her self-confidence a boost.

Dead silence greeted her entrance into the Den. The hairs rose up on the back of Dev's neck. Nodding to a couple of former associates, she strode to the bar. "Aurilian Ambergris," she ordered. Only the hardiest drinkers tolerated the thick, potent brew, and Dev used it now to reestablish herself as a bad ass. Back to the bar, she downed the drink without a break, wiped her mouth with the back of her hand, and swept the room with a defiant glare. "I'm hiring," she said and turned her back to the room once again. As if on cue, the noise level returned to what it had been before she stepped through the doorway. Her stomach roiled. By sheer willpower she tamped down the urge to throw up her toenails. If this bunch even suspected she had a weakness, they'd tear her apart like a bunch of Corgoni bone-pickers.

The mirror behind the bar reflected the room and gave her a few seconds to prepare for the massive grungy man who clamped down on her shoulders, spun her around, and pulled her in for a crushing bear hug. "Devona DiMetri, you are the ballsiest woman I have ever met."

Nose pressed to the pungent garments of the captain of the Siren's Song, Dev feared to breathe. His well-known lack of hygiene might send her racing for the bathroom. She'd barely kept down the Ambergris and didn't want to press her luck. Holding her breath until she was able to extract herself, Dev stepped back, grinned up at the middle aged man and said, "Harry, you SOB, it's good to see you." Indicating the bar, she offered, "Let me buy you a drink."

"Don't mind if I do, lass." The barkeep handed Harry a tankard filled with a bubbling green brew.

Dev felt her face take on a similar color. "Tell me what you've been up to." Surreptitiously she stuck her nose down in her empty glass and took a deep breath. "I've been out of the loop for a while."

"No shit." Harry lowered his voice to a whisper. "Last I heard you had a price on your head."

Shaking her head vehemently she told him, "No. That's been rescinded."

"Wanna bet?" He took a long pull of the noxious drink. "I just got an upgrade on the amount. I could retire with that many credits."

Dev frowned. This could be a major problem. "Harry, Mik and the rest of us liberated Pagoda and killed Simon Salacious. The paper he had out on us is no good."

"Hah. That pig was just a stoolie for a bigger pig: Umland. And he's put up major credit bounty on the lot of you, but especially on someone he calls the princess." He narrowed his eyes. "Know anything about that?"

A wave of dizziness caused her to grab the edge of the bar with white-knuckled intensity. She had to handle this with all the finesse she could muster. Obviously Harry already knew the answer and was waiting to see how she'd answer him. She couldn't afford to alienate what could well be the only friendly face in the place. "Well yeah." She forced a laugh past her dry, constricted throat. "It's me, according to that moron. He claims I'm some long lost heir to the throne of Iman. Imagine that."

Harry's gaze traveled the length of her. "I could believe that. You've always had a look about you."

Dev's palm slammed down on the countertop. "By the gods, Harry, you've known me for years. I've fought beside you, drunk beside you, and even slept beside you a few times." If you counted naps caught on a battlefield.

Harry chuckled. "You're right about that, but never without your damned sidekick Kevnor." Scanning the room, he asked, "Where is he, by the way?"

"Kev? Oh, he'll be along." She hoped.

"Too bad. When you said you were hiring, I was thinking maybe you'd decided to take a captain's berth for yourself." His gaze was speculative. "You deserve a ship of your own."

Dev shook her head. "I'm here on the Freebird." Let him make what he wanted to out of that. She glanced at the chronometer behind the bar. "Oh my gosh, look at the time. I need to get back and warn the others about the bounties. They could be walking into a trap here."

Harry moved closer. "Rumor has it you left your shipmates. A woman alone is easy prey. You could be in a trap here yourself."

She fingered the blaster on her left hip. "You've seen me shoot, Harry. Do you really want to do this?" Her total confidence in her abilities was reflected in her tone.

Sweat dampened his upper lip. "Not me. No, I didn't mean me," he hastened to say. "I just meant someone else could have spotted you. Someone who wasn't a friend and all."

"Ah. You could be right." She looked thoughtful. "Why don't you just walk me back to the ship, that way you won't be tempted to tell anyone else about the bounty and I won't have to kill you." Her smile was engaging.

"Sure," he agreed. "That's a fine idea."

She allowed him to clear a path to the door.

***

The Pelican eased out of orbit, her crew tense and quiet. Everyone knew the chances of locating Devona were not good, but no one voiced the obvious. Space was a very big place to try and find someone, especially if that person didn't want to be found.

"Coordinates, Captain?" Zoë asked.

Consulting the star charts Mik quoted her the location of Rekjavik. "Something tells me we just might be able to get a lead from the headmistress of a certain orphanage."

"My Lady of the Stars?" Kev asked. "What can the headmistress possibly tell us?"

"She can put us in touch with Umland and he, in turn, will have a handle on Dev's whereabouts."

"What makes you think that, Captain?" Zoë asked.

"Shesshie told me that bitch Olga was the one who arranged a ride for her on the so-called Med ship that attacked us. She's in on the whole slave thing right up to her armpits."

"I know none of us wants to think about it, but the fact is, Dev's been gone long enough to have gotten herself into trouble. My money says any trouble she might run into will trace right back to Umland." He huffed, "Besides, with the funds he has backing his search, he'll have resources not open to us."

"Mik," Kev's voice was hoarse.

"Yeah?" Mik glanced at his communications officer.

"The bounties have been reissued."

"Come again?" Zoë interrupted.

"Who issued them?" Mik wanted to know.

"Our pal Umland," Kev told them, "and the bounty has been raised considerably. Hell, our own mothers would turn us in for that much—assuming any of us had mothers."

No one said it, but they all knew what that meant. Dev was in much greater danger than they'd thought.

"I can get a bit more speed out of her," Callus offered.

"Then do it." Mik's lips were drawn in a tight line. "Kev, contact the Nest. Make sure Doc and the rest are informed of the bounty and the severity of their situation. Tell them to take no chances."

Kevnor knew the anguish his friend and captain was feeling. His wife and child were back on Bright's Planet, relatively unprotected, and he was out in space on a wild goose chase. But Kev's wife and unborn child were the goose in the chase. "Do you want to go back? I could drop you off and go on alone."

Mik nailed him with a glare. "Don't be an ass. Shesshie and the rest are on a relatively unknown planet and are well-armed. The immigrants from Pagoda haven't had much training, but they would guard their new home fiercely if they were attacked. Dev is one of us, and she's out there alone. We go with you." And that put an end to it.

Chapter Three

Harry delivered Devona to the Freebird, and she thanked him, tongue in cheek, for his kindness. As soon as the portal sealed shut behind her, she engaged the security system and leaned against the wall, heart pounding in her chest. Leaving her mate was one thing, getting her and her unborn child killed was another all together. As soon as her spaghetti legs would support her, she headed for the bridge. It was time to call in the troops. "Bird to Nest," she called. "Come in Nest." When she got no reply, she repeated herself. Still no one answered. What the hell? Could there be an emergency? What if they were all dead? She could be out here while her friends were massacred. Kevnor could be dead. Fear blossomed in her chest like Purnarian crystals. She entered the codes for departure. She was going back to Bright's. She had to know that they were all right. She had to touch Kev.

Outside the docking station, Harry keyed his wrist comm. "Did you blokes get it done?"

"Sure Harry. Disabling the communications system was a piece of cake. And planting the tracer was even easier." A slender man eased out of the shadows.

His companion confirmed, "That little lady won't ever know what hit her."

"Nothing better hit her." There was steel in Harry's voice. "She's worth millions alive and nothing dead. Now get back to the Siren and prepare to depart."

"Should we contact Umland, Capt'n?"

"No. Leave that to me." Harry watched his men depart and smiled. If there was one thing he was sure of, it was that the crew of the Freebird was tight. No way that little girl wasn't going to run straight back to her crewmates. He just might get to retire after all.

***

Dev paced the bridge till she was exhausted. Her communications was out. How had that happened? Mik always said nothing happened by itself. That meant someone had a hand in her communications going down. She narrowed her eyes. Harry had said the word was out she was solo. That being true, almost anyone could be trying to sabotage her ship. No. Not her ship, their ship. She plopped down in the pilot's seat. How could she have been so selfish as to run off with the ship? It was the backbone of their new shipping business. Having lost the Hauten on Pagoda, without the Bird, business would be cut down to nothing. And knowing Kev he probably took off with the Pelican, leaving no way for business to continue. Jumping to her feet again, she headed for the galley. She was starving. Five minutes later she looked at the food she'd prepared and almost threw up. She pushed the offending meal across the table.

"Kevnor," she whispered, "where are you?" His image rose in her mind's eye. Tall, broad shouldered and taut with well-honed muscle, her husband was a man among men. His black eyes could wither you with a glance or heat you to melting stage with a sultry look. He was perfect. So what if they'd had a little disagreement? He was always quick to anger and quick to get over it. She knew that, had known it for

~25~

years. Why had she reacted like a petulant child and run away from home at the first sign of trouble? He told her Bauxites married for life. She should have known he didn't mean it when he said he was getting an annulment. And even if he was serious, she should have stayed and fought for her marriage, her family. Kevnor and their child were her one chance at true happiness.

What was that about the Imani and Bauxites being at war? What was their problem? If her life was going to be affected by the feud that had raged for centuries, she was damn well going to find out what it was all about. Stepping to the communications station, she tested the availability of the web. To her astonishment, she was able to get online. Several hours later she rubbed her back where it ached down low and reheated the abandoned meal. This time she devoured it and searched the stores for something sweet. The whole pregnancy thing had her body acting like a stranger.

Returning to the computer, she looked over her notes. From what she could find out, the Imani were a matriarchal society while the Bauxites were patriarchal. The Imani women ruled their households with autonomy and were allowed as many husbands and concubines as they could afford. Male children of ruling houses were sequestered until they were of marriageable age while the female children received the best education and training available. Bauxites were monogamous. Though the males were considered in charge of the families, both male and female children were educated, and females could hold public office, though occurrences were rare. Dev snorted. Neither place sounded like paradise.

She wondered whether her child was a boy or a girl. What if she was captured and returned to the Imani and she had a boy? She couldn't bear to see him treated like a second-class citizen. She'd rather give him to Kev to raise than subject her son to such a life. Never see her son again? Her hand smoothed her still flat belly. How could she live without ever seeing him? For that matter, how could she live without Kevnor? She loved him so much. She'd loved him for years. He was the other half of her soul.

***

Kev, Mik, Zoë, and Callus entered the orphanage with a feeling of déjà vu. The damned places were all the same—sad, hopeless faces pressed up against windowpanes, wishing for a miracle to bring them a family, a home.

"This creeps me out," Zoë confessed.

"Me, too," Callus agreed. "It's like I'm suddenly back on the other side of the viewing screen. And with my ugly mug, I knew no one would ever pick me."

Zoë squeezed his forearm. "I'd have picked you."

"Thanks." He appreciated the lie.

A young woman came out to greet them. "May I help you?" she asked.

"We're here to see Olga," Mik informed her.

The girl's face underwent a transformation from happy and polite to cold and indifferent. "One moment," she said briskly.

Mik stopped her. "Miss?" She turned back toward him. "We're not friends of hers. In fact, I'm married to Shesshie Kosmato. We're here to settle a score."

"In that case—" She held out her hand. "I'm pleased to meet you. My name's Ann Marie Penne."

"Miklus Armstrong." Mik shook her hand. "Shesshie has mentioned you."

"I'm flattered." She blushed.

"Could you spare a few minutes to talk to me and my crew before we go in to see Olga?"

Ann Marie glanced over her shoulder toward the office. "Sure. I guess."

"Were you aware that Olga was associated with a slaving ring?" Kev asked her.

Gasping, Ann Marie assured them that she had no idea. "You mean she sells the children?"

"We think so," Mik replied. "What we're sure of is that she sent Shesshie off with a supposed Med ship that was really a pirate and slaver, and according to Shesshie, the same ship came here repeatedly. If you put two and two together, you'll realize Olga had to be in on the whole thing."

"It doesn't surprise me. Nothing surprises me where she is concerned. She's an evil woman." Ann Marie wrung her fingers. "What will happen to us if you take her away? I know how to care for the children, but I don't know anything about the funding."

"Not to worry," Kev assured her. "We've contacted the authorities. Within the hour an audit team and the Department of Orphanages will visit you. Be sure you answer all of their questions completely and honestly. And don't hesitate to volunteer information you think they need to know."

"Okay."

"And honey," Zoë added, "don't be afraid to leave this place. There's a great big universe out there."

Ann Marie smiled. "I'll remember that. Now if you'll follow me, I'll take you to Olga."

Sitting behind her desk, Olga frowned when her door opened without warning. She hastily shuffled papers around on her desk. "What is the meaning of this, Ann Marie?" she bristled.

"These people came here to talk to you," she said. "This one—" She indicated Mik. "—is Shesshie's husband."

That brought the robust woman to her feet. "Shesshie? That's not possible. She's..." Her voice trailed off before she said too much. "She's moved." Olga stepped out from behind her desk.

"Indeed, she has, no thanks to you." Mik stepped closer. Kev skirted both of them and eased in behind Olga's computer.

"I didn't tell her to leave. It was her idea." The woman's face was flushed.

"And was it also her idea to seek passage on a pirate ship bound for Pagoda?" Mik's voice had risen until he was shouting.

"I don't know what you're talking about," she bluffed.

"Oh," Kev interrupted, "I think you do."

Olga's head whipped around to see who was behind her. "What are you doing?" she asked him. "That's private property."

"Actually, no, it's not," Kev told her. "This is a public orphanage, and as such, all records are public. I have every right as a citizen to whatever information is on this computer."

Olga smirked. "You'll not find anything out of the ordinary on there."

"Want to bet?" Kev returned her smirk. "I am a communications officer, and I'm very good at what I do." He glanced back at the computer screen. "Looks to me like you've got several hidden files. Wonder what's in those?"

"They're password protected," Olga blurted.

"Nothing's safe from our Kevnor," Zoë bragged. "Just wait till the authorities get here. By then he'll have uncovered any secrets you've got."

Olga lunged at the smaller woman. Zoë sidestepped, tripped Olga and pounced on the other woman when she hit the floor. "Never—" She held a slender blade to Olga's throat. "—underestimate me, just because I'm small."

Callus chuckled. "That's the damned truth."

"I've got credits," Olga bargained, "lots of credits. I could split them with you."

"Oh?" Mik stepped closer. "Where have you got this money stashed?"

She started to squirm, but Zoë's blade changed her mind. "Let me up, and I'll show you."

"No need," Kev interrupted. "I've got that information for you, Mik."

Olga screeched, "Nooo!" Her body bucked, pressing the soft flab that hung beneath her chin into Zoë's blade. A thin trail of blood seeped into the creases.

Zoë pressed her knees into Olga's shoulders to immobilize her. "Hold up, bitch, or you won't live to face the authorities."

Mik stepped over so he could view the computer screen. "Well, well, well," he said, "looks like our girl has quite a retirement fund." He glanced at the members of his crew. "I don't think she needs all that, do you?" They all grinned and agreed with him. "Why don't you move, say half of each of the three accounts, into our business account? I think a donation like that would be a big help in feeding the immigrants we just brought back from Pagoda." His voice lowered to a tone that had put fear into many an adversary's heart. "Since the chances are good you are responsible for the enslavement of at least part of them."

Olga opened her mouth to reply, thought better of it and closed her eyes, resigned. "Smart move," Zoë told her.

"You know, Olga." Mik strolled back to stand over her. "My wife told me you had been dealing with the slavers for quite some time. In light of that, I can think of only one way to buy yourself some leniency from the court, and that's to cooperate with us." Squatting down he loomed over Olga, his jaw clinched in anger. "Tell us where we can find Umland and we'll put in a good word for you."

Her eyes grew large, but she shook her head. "No. He'll have me killed."

Mik glanced at Zoë and back to Olga. "We could kill you right now," he threatened.

"That's illegal," she blurted.

Everyone else in the room laughed, making her complexion pale. "We've made our living as mercenaries for years," Mik told her. "Think one more death would bother us?" She didn't have to know they would never murder anyone.

A commotion arose in the adjoining room. "Hurry," Mik prodded. "They're almost here. Last chance." As if on cue, Zoë put a tiny bit more pressure on the blade.

"Okay," she whined. "I'll tell you." Callus slipped quickly out the door, determined to delay the officials as long as possible. "He operates out of Maltoran. He has a secret camp there with lots of paid troops."

"And we can contact him how?"

"No need," Kev informed him. "The dumb ass has every code and contact in a file on her computer. I have downloaded all that info onto my portable drive and erased it from her computer."

"Excellent." Mik rose and Zoë pocketed her knife just as the investigative team burst through the door. "Charles," Mik held his hand out to the leader of the team. "Good to see you again."

"It has been a long time." The other man shook his hand and looked around. "What's going on here?"

"This piece of slime—" He indicated Olga. "—has been selling off her orphans to a slave ring."

"That's a pretty serious accusation, Miklus," Charles replied.

"You'll find documentation is all here, on her computer." Kev stood up. "I've managed to crack her security system and have left it open for you to see."

"Kevnor, you son of a Tumerian ork miner." Charles stepped over the prone woman to shake Kev's hand. "You still hanging out with this reprobate?"

Kev laughed. "Bad habits are hard to break."

"That's all right, just ignore me," Zoë chided.

"Zoë, damn girl, I didn't see you." He came around to hug her. "Is our entire graduating class here?"

"We all attended the military academy together," Mik told Olga. Her ass was grass, and she knew it.

"I thought you were a mercenary," she accused.

He shrugged. "We took different paths after a few years of service."

"I hate to interrupt the reunion," Kev said, "but if we're gonna find Dev we have to get moving."

"Dev? What's wrong with Dev?" Charles wanted to know. "I thought someone was missing."

"Know of a fellow named Draxor Umland?" Kev asked.

"Oh yeah. He's one of the most wanted men in the sector. Seems he's wanted for a variety of crimes, theft, assault, and murder among them."

"Well you can add slavery," Kev said quietly.

Charles frowned. "You serious, man?"

"And if we don't find Devona, kidnapping. He's after her."

Charles stepped back to clear the path to the door. "Good luck my friends," he said.

The three filed out to join Callus and return to the Pelican.

Chapter Four

She was so freaking stupid. Dev's fingers flew across the keyboard. How could she have spent hours on the computer without thinking of emailing? She hoped someone checked the email soon. She sent the same message to each person's individual email account as well as Ornithol Enterprises business account. *I'm returning to the Nest. All communications on the Bird are out. I just left Epsilon III where I learned the bounty on our heads has been reissued. Take all precautions. We each have a price on our heads, and the bounty is high. Stay armed at all times and trust no one. Dev*

Surely someone would reply soon.

How long had it been? Three freaking minutes? She slammed her hand down on the console and pushed up from the chair. She couldn't just sit here and wait. It was driving her even crazier than she already was. A shower and a snack were in order.

You've got mail flashed across the screen when she returned from the galley, roasted Hiberus nuts and cold Ickluk juice in hand. She couldn't seem to get enough of Ickluk juice these days. Strange, she'd never liked it before. Pulling up the incoming mail, she grinned at the reply. *Dev, I love you. I'm on the way from Rekjavik. Send me your coordinates and stay put. I love you. Kev* He loved her. That was a good reason to cry.

After a fortifying pull at the Ickluk juice, Devona checked her coordinates, emailed them to her spouse and set the Freebird's navigational controls to maintain her current location. She wondered how long it would take him to get to her. Another email came in from the Nest. It seemed they were in contact with the Pelican and knew the plan. Shesshie and Marissa wished her well. Doc groused about her leaving in the first place and reminded her that she was part of a family. Family worked things out. They didn't run away. Duly chastised, she consoled herself with more juice...and another trip to the head. It seemed like she lived in that place lately.

Wandering into her cabin, she straightened the bed, then lay down on it to rest a few minutes. Twelve hours later, she awoke to the proximity alarm's warning. She jumped up and nearly passed out. Pregnancy sucked sometimes. After her head cleared, she ran for the bridge. Not one but two ships were closing in fast. Draco! Just what she needed. She rushed to the communications station to email Kev. She hoped one of the two was her husband. She could deal with one ship, but two would be tough. She was good, but she was only one person. Navigating and manning weapons at the same time was pretty near impossible.

The computer told her one of the ships was almost upon her. Time was up. She headed for the weapons station. If Kev were on the ship, he'd know better than to approach her without her knowing it was him. Shields up, she took aim. Before she could shoot, her opponent took a volley from the third ship. Well this was interesting. She raced back to the computer. No reply to her latest email. She returned to weapons. "Computer, report," she ordered. "All systems normal," was the mechanical reply.

"Not us, damn it, the other ships." She couldn't believe she was yelling at the computer. Hormones sucked.

"One is registered as a class A frigate. She is ID'd as the Siren's Song out of Coregon System," the computer informed her. "The other is the Pelican, a freighter."

"Who took the hit?" Dev asked.

"Siren's song."

"Damage to the ship?"

"Minimal."

"Figures," Dev murmured. Taking aim with the ion cannon, she hit the Siren squarely in engineering. Just like that, she was dead in space. No one else had her affinity or skill for weapons. She didn't need the computer's analysis this time. She knew what damage she'd caused. The Siren would have to be hauled back to a starbase for an engine replacement. That is if they could get a tug to come out this far.

Lowering her shields she entered a message on the email. *Who taught you people how to shoot?* Her only reply was, *Baby, I'll be right over.* By the time she'd read Kev's message, he had launched a shuttle. She hurried to the cargo bay where he would dock.

Kev stepped off the shuttle just as Dev entered the bay. They froze for long moments, eating each other with their eyes. They never knew who moved first, but suddenly they were in each other's arms, lips welded and tongues entwined. Without a word they began to strip each other's clothes, pulling and tearing at the offending cloth. Kev toed off his boots, an amazing feat considering they were laced up over his ankles. Dev scored his shoulders with her nails as she raked his flight suit down to his waist. She dropped to her knees; her lips followed the progress of the fabric tasting the tang of his skin across his pecs, over his abs and down to the trail of dark hair that disappeared into his pants. She couldn't get enough of him.

"Oh, no, you don't." Grasping her gently by the upper arms he pulled her back to her feet, peeling her jumpsuit over her slender frame to reveal the coral tipped breasts he loved but trapping her arms in the process. "If you start that, I won't last," he rasped, "and I need to be in you." His head lowered and drew hard on an engorged nipple. Fire streaked from her breast to her groin. Writhing in his grasp, Dev was finally able to get one arm free, and she encircled Kevnor's head, pulling him even closer. She felt him smile against her breast and closed her eyes in ecstasy.

"Hurry, Kev," she urged.

With economy of motion Kev slipped her jumpsuit down to her ankles. Lifting one foot at a time he freed her completely and lifted her so she could wrap her legs around his waist. Her honeyed entrance welcomed him as he plunged deep. "I'm sorry." His voice was hoarse with emotion. "I'm so sorry about the things I said." A couple of steps had her back braced against the wall so he could pound harder. One hand wandered up to tweak a turgid nipple. "I would never let you go. Tell me you believe me. Tell me you forgive me."

"Yes." Her body trembled with the coming climax. Her ankles locked together, and she pressed him closer. "Yes." She held onto his shoulders with escalating need. Her hips tilted forward and back, forward and back, seeking the release they both desired. Her teeth nipped at his nipples, the pain soothed by her hot wet tongue. "Yes-s-s-s!" Release flooded her body at the same time Kev stiffened and filled her with his essence, his head thrown back in a triumphant roar.

Legs shaking from the exertion, Kevnor eased them both to the floor. He covered her face with a barrage of tender kisses, smoothed the fine blond hair back from her face. "Tell me you forgive me."

Devona sighed. "I suppose."

He pulled back to look at her. Her eyes twinkled with mischief. "I'll take that as a yes." Disentangling their legs he pulled free from her body. "We ought to contact the Pelican. They're probably afraid you killed me." He grinned. "And you damned near did."

"Just remember that the next time you think you might want to leave me," was her saucy reply.

"Oh, baby, I'll never leave you. You're as much a part of me as my right arm." He smoothed a callused palm over her stomach. "You and the baby. How's he doing?"

"*She*'s just fine. She misses her father."

The shuttle beeped. Kev laughed. "Might've known Callus would have some way to irritate me, even over here." Naked as the day he was born, Kev strode over to the shuttle and disappeared inside. "What?" he said into the mic.

"Took you long enough," Mik replied, laughing.

"Fuck you."

"So, have you had a chance to look at the communications problem yet?" Mik was a regular comedian today.

"Fuck you," Kev told him again.

"Guess not. Is Dev okay?"

"I am now," she answered, stepping up beside her husband.

"Give us a little while."

"Take your time," Mik told him. "You've got ten minutes."

"Gee, thanks." Kev disconnected and turned to ask Dev, "Any idea what they did to sabotage communications?"

"If I knew that, I'd have fixed it myself."

Kev grinned. It was good to have her back. "Let's have a look." He headed for the bridge. Dev trailing behind him had a good look, indeed.

***

"Communications are up and running, Mik, but I want to do a complete rundown of all systems before we head out. You might as well head back. I know Doc's got his hands full back at the Nest. Shesshie and Marissa are probably fit to be tied about the new bounties."

Mik wiggled his eyebrows. "Tied sounds good to me."

"Perv," Dev yelled over Kev's shoulder.

"Leave Marissa out of this," Callus said at the same time.

"Don't worry." Mik laughed. "Shesshie's all I can handle. You'll have to take care of Marissa, Callus."

"It's not like that," he mumbled.

Zoë harrumphed, "Not for lack of trying on your part."

"Hi Zoë," Dev said. "You'd better leave Callus alone. Someone might think to tease you about that guy back on Bright's...what did you call him? The Onyx God?"

His interest piqued, Callus asked, "Oh? What's that about an Onyx God? Come clean, little girl. Tell it all."

"Now look what you've done," Zoë complained to Dev. "He'll bug me all the way home. Besides, that guy had a lot more between his legs than he did between his ears, if you know what I mean." She shuddered. "Definitely one night stand material."

Kev feigned shock. "Is that the kind of stuff women usually talk about?"

Dev elbowed him. "Don't worry, stud. You've got plenty both places." Mik and Callus whooped at that comment.

"Seriously, you're sure you two will be okay if we go on ahead?" Mik asked.

"Yeah. No problem," Kev assured him.

The communication ended, and Kev turned in his chair, pulling Devona into his lap. "Hot and fast was great," he whispered, "but now I want slow and thorough." His lips nibbled along her neck and beneath her chin.

Chill bumps raised along her arms. She tilted her head to provide better access. "I thought you were going to run diagnostics on the ship," she whispered back.

"I am. Just as soon as I take my wife in every way known to man." He stood with her held against his chest and headed for her cabin.

Dev's heart thudded against his. "Were you taking notes back on Pagoda?"

Laughter rumbled out, deep and rich. "Hell no. I was too busy being tortured or fighting when we were there."

"Then maybe you don't know so many ways after all." She sucked on his earlobe.

"Honey, don't you remember all those years we were exchanging hot glances across the bridge?"

"Sure. I wore out many batteries during those days," she confessed.

"I spent my time on the computer studying; learning all the ways I was going to make love to you as soon as you made up your mind to commit to me." Once again, he nibbled her neck. "And you were well worth the wait." The doorway whooshed closed behind them, and he set Dev on her feet.

Dev glanced around. "This is Mik's cabin," she observed.

"This might be the captain's quarters, but right now you're the captain. And besides, it has the biggest bunk." He slid his hand along the closure of her jumpsuit, savoring the feel of her skin as he revealed it. "I want lots of room." His lips swooped down on hers, demanding, cajoling, tempting. Dev responded with lips and tongue and heart, desperate to show him how much she loved him, how grateful she was they were together again.

Chapter Five

Unbelievable fire coursed through his veins. Kev was sure his heart was pumping lava. The feel of Dev's soft breasts in his hands brought on an instant and throbbing erection. His balls drew up tight against his body, demanding release. He was not ready to give in to that demand. He needed to touch her, taste her everywhere.

Once he had removed every stitch of clothing, he turned her slowly around, noting the slight changes her pregnancy had wrought—fuller breasts, more width in the hips, the slightest rounding of her abdomen. All changes he approved of highly. His eyes smoldered with the fire she kindled. Urging her to sit on the edge of the bed, he knelt between her spread legs. "Let me look at you," he told her. "Let me touch you." She offered no resistance, so he ran a palm along her shoulder, over a breast and down her ribcage. "You have the softest skin," he praised. "I'll bet our son's skin won't even be that soft."

"Daughter," she contradicted, reveling in the riot of feelings his touch evoked.

His lips closed over a nipple. She jerked at the contact. Licking, nipping and sucking he finessed the honey from her body—honey for which he starved. "Watch." Lowering his head he ran his tongue along the seam of her labia. "Watch me eat you."

Dev's breath caught at the erotic sight—his dark head against her pale body, his hardness against her softness, all that made him male against her femininity. She whimpered and clutched his hair, lifting her hips closer to his mouth. He did not disappoint her.

Separating her folds with his thumbs, Kev plunged deep with his tongue, lapping at her juices, devouring her. Her clit throbbed with excitement, and he paid homage to it, laving, circling and stabbing it with his masterful tongue. When he closed his mouth around it and drew delicately, she found fulfillment, flooding his mouth. He raised his head and smiled at her, his face glistening with the proof of her pleasure.

Her arms shaking with the strain of holding her upright, Dev returned his smile. Her gaze had remained glued to the sight of him feasting on her body. She'd been unable to look away, even to lie back and enjoy the ride. Now, however, she collapsed. "Kev, that was the most incredible thing—"

"I'm not even nearly done." He flipped her onto her stomach and eased up against her body. "Raise up on your knees," he instructed.

The slide of his body entering her from that angle was amazing. He filled her completely. She was sure his penis touched the mouth of her womb. Dev arched her back, enticing him further. She clutched fistfuls of sheet, cried out each time his balls slapped against her clit. It was too much, too much. She went off like a rocket.

Kev held her up with an arm beneath her stomach, offering support until she was capable of holding herself up again. As soon as he was able, he began the ride again, pumping faster and faster, reaching beneath her body to pinch her nipples and stroke her clit. Twice more she came before he allowed himself to join her. Then he yelled her name as he felt the expulsion of semen, a hot endless stream, branding her as his.

Rolling to his side, Kev brought her with him cradled in his arms, their bodies still joined. Unable to speak, they luxuriated in the closeness, relishing the pounding of their hearts and the scent of their union. As breathing became more normal, Kev slid from her body, and Dev whimpered at the loss. He smoothed the fine pale hair behind her ear. "That was incredible," Kev told her.

"Hard to believe we were estranged just a few hours ago, isn't it?"

Rolling her to her back Kev leaned close, insisting, "We were never estranged. We have always been in love. You just have the misfortune to be married to an idiot."

Dev laughed. "That's hard to argue," she teased.

"The truth usually is."

"Well, what about me?" she asked. "I reacted like a child, running away instead of standing my ground." She shook her head in disbelief. "I still can't believe I did that. I wouldn't blame the others if they never wanted to see me again."

"Don't be absurd. They all understood perfectly. Trust me, they've given me hell since you took off." He shrugged one shoulder. "And I haven't been the easiest guy to get along with."

Laughing, she cupped the side of his face. "I'll bet. I've seen you when things didn't go the way you wanted them to."

Kev's brows raised in mock disbelief. "Me? I'm always an agreeable fellow."

"I know you are, sweetie—as long as you get your own way." Rolling off the side of the bunk, Dev headed for the shower.

"Oh, no, you don't." Kev was right behind her. "You can't hit me with a zinger like that and get away with it."

Dev squealed and ran, dodging his grasping hands. He caught her as she stepped under the water, tickling her until she cried uncle. Then he proceeded to convince her he was just as adept in the shower as he was in the bed.

***

Mik ran a hand through his dark hair leaving strands sticking up in a variety of directions. "I don't like this," he admitted to his crew. "I don't like this at all."

"Me neither, Captain." Callus scowled at the readout. "According to Charles, this Umland character has bounty on all of us that's high enough to tempt anyone but a saint."

Ducking between them Zoë whistled when she read the figures. "I'll say. I'm half tempted to turn you two in myself."

"Brat." Callus thumped her hair.

She hissed at him. "Hands off the hair or there won't be enough of you left to collect bounty on." Zoë patted the mass of intricately woven braids, her pride and joy.

"Doc and the ladies are sitting ducks back at the Nest. We need to get back to them." Collapsing into his seat, he sighed. "But I don't like leaving Kev and Dev alone either."

"They're tough," Callus reminded him. "And they've got the Freebird. It's not like when they were aboard the Hauten and that little bastard Reardon captured them. This time they've got plenty of firepower."

"I sure wouldn't want to go up against them," Zoë concurred.

Slapping his palms down on his thigh Mik gave up. "Okay, we go home. But I want to speak to them before we leave this sector."

"I'll ring them," Zoë offered.

"Well?" Mik asked after several minutes.

"Uh, there's no reply." Zoë hurriedly offered, "Let me try again."

"What?" Kev's disgruntled voice crackled over the comm.

Mik's mouth kicked up on one corner. "I guess you were busy."

"Ya think?" The communications officer's disgruntled visage materialized on the screen. His hair was wet, and he was not wearing a shirt.

"Oooh, honey," Zoë joked, "we need to put you on the stage at Delzora's on ladies night. You'd make a fortune."

Kev held up three fingers. "Read between the lines."

She couldn't let him get away with that. "That's the spirit. The feisty ones always get a G full of credits."

"Wrapped in a damp pink robe Dev bumped her husband out of the way with her hip. "Quit harassing my man," she told Zoë. "That's my job." Both women laughed.

Holding a hand up to his chest Kev told them, "You've hurt my tender feelings."

"I'm gonna hurt more than your feelings if you don't quit bullshitting and let me say what I've got to say," Mik threatened. "We need to get back to the Nest."

"Sorry, Mik," Dev soothed. "We're just feeling a little euphoric right now." She and Kev exchanged a look that even raised the temperature aboard the Pelican.

"Before you two go back into heat again, we wanted you to know the extent of the threat we're facing. Umland's put a very high bounty out on us. As soon as you two get back to the Nest, we're going to formulate a plan to take that fucker out. He's threatened my family for the last time."

"You'll get no argument from me," Kev assured him. He drew Devona close, draping an arm around her. "My family has been threatened as well. I say the two of us go get it done."

Dev pulled away. "I'm the one he wants. I'll be damned if I'll sit home like some delicate flower and let you guys have all the fun." She held up her right hand and wiggled her fingers. "My trigger finger is itching."

"What if you run into a problem? I wouldn't feel right staying behind." Callus obviously thought he was the only one who could solve a problem.

Zoë snorted. "Without me the entire bunch of you is liable to get lost." Her navigational abilities were legendary.

Mik shook his head. "You're a bloodthirsty bunch." A grin broke through, spoiling his tone.

"That's what I love about you. But I still don't know what we're supposed to do about the others. I don't want Shesshie and Tessa in the middle of this."

"Or Marissa," Callus interjected. Everyone laughed.

"You've got it bad, big guy," Zoë ribbed him.

His homely face flushed. "Well she's been through enough."

"Go ahead," Kev told them. "Get out of here. Dev and I will complete the diagnostic run and get some shut-eye. Then we'll follow."

"Don't delay too long," Mik warned.

"No, we won't." With the looks he'd been giving Dev, no one believed him.

***

By the time Kev had the autopilot set, the Pelican was off the screen. "What the hell?" Dev said, peering into the view screen. "I thought you were in the Pelican."

"We were." Kev was smiling. "Callus made a few adjustments."

"A few? I'd say he completely rebuilt the engines."

"That about sums it up."

"You know—" Dev shook her head. "—we're damn lucky to have him. That man can pretty near do anything."

"I know. I'll bet the governing committee on the Eurasian Megacontinent was furious when he took their funds, got his education and split." Kev grinned. "I would like to have been a fly on that wall."

Dev settled in his lap. "You might have been born into the ruling house of Baux, but you have the soul of a rogue, Kevnor Gaaus." She nibbled her way along

~48~

his jaw to the edge of his ear. Her smooth wet tongue traced the outer edge. "Aren't you hungry, honey?"

Kev slid her around to straddle him. The gaping edges of her robe afforded him tantalizing glimpses of her porcelain skin, mottled here and there by the abrasive contact of the stubble on his cheeks. Primitive thrill filled him at the sight. He had marked his woman. "I'm always hungry for you." His lips met hers, nipping and sucking, building the desire in them both. His hands parted the silky fabric that covered her breasts, bearing them to his view. "You are so beautiful."

Dev squirmed and eased back. Her breath was unsteady, but she pushed against his chest, clutching her wrap together with the other hand. "I meant for food. I'm starving."

Kev wore the dumbfounded expression of a wild bovine caught in the bright light of a hunter. "Food?"

"Yes. I'm dying for some Rumarian sour cabbage." Dev hurried toward the galley.

Kev let his clinched fists fall to his thighs. "Okay. I can deal with this." As he stood, he adjusted himself to a less painful position. "Expectant mothers have some pretty strange hormonal urges." He limped after his wife. "I didn't know you liked sour cabbage," he called.

"I didn't either." She met him at the door, steaming container in hand. "Want a bite?" Holding a forkful toward him, she didn't wait for his reply but shoved it into her own mouth. "Mmm. This is so good. You really should try it."

The noxious smell wafted toward him. His stomach lurched. "No thanks. I think I'll pass." He opened a cabinet. "Do we have any dehydrated meat packs?"

Dev shrugged. "Don't know. The thought of meat makes me puke. Literally."

"Thanks for sharing that." Opening the rehydrater, Kev prepared Cormorand stew for himself. Leaning against the counter, feet crossed, he eyed his wife. "Do you eat that stuff very much?" His nose wrinkled at the offensive smell.

"This is only the third time...today. I guess all the excitement of seeing you again got my mind off it."

"I see." He sure hoped she was as driven to brush her teeth as she was to consume the revolting green, slimy stuff.

"I've been doing some research," she told him.

"Yeah? About what?"

"Iman and Baux." She watched intently for his reaction.

"And what did you find out?" He was careful to keep his voice steady.

Licking the back of the fork, Dev threw the container in the recycle bin. "Mostly I found out that I wouldn't want to live either place. Did you know the Imani have a matriarchal society?"

Kev nodded, continuing to eat his stew with unnecessary attention.

"And that on Baux, while women are educated, they rarely hold positions of power or influence?"

He nailed her with a look. "Where'd you hear that?"

"I didn't hear it. I read it on the computer." Retying her robe she asked, "Want to see?"

"Yeah. I think I would like to see that." He wasn't finished, but the subject had stolen his appetite. He trashed the remainder.

Dev scampered before him, obviously excited about her findings. She couldn't be more wrong. Baux was a beautiful society where everyone was treated equally, and wise leaders gently but firmly guided the masses.

Or not.

The information from the intergalactic information highway contradicted his memories quite a bit. He had been twelve when he was orphaned, and he never returned to his home world. But his parents had gone everywhere together, and he and his brother were always differed to. Yet the computer said the society was heavily male dominated, though females were allowed and even encouraged to apply themselves academically. So why were there only two women in the senate? And only thirty-four women were listed as physicians. No lawyers were female. He frowned. "This can't be right."

"You think that's bad." Dev pulled up another site. "Look at Iman. The men are pretty much slaves there. They are kept in isolation until they are wed or contracted as a concubine. That's the most disgusting thing I've heard of since we left Pagoda." A hand rubbed her lower belly. "If we had a boy on Iman, he'd have a horrid life."

Kev frowned. "And if we had a girl on Baux, she wouldn't be much better off. I wonder if my mother was unhappy?"

"I doubt it. Not if your father was anything like you." Once again she climbed onto his lap, pulling his mouth around for a scintillating kiss.

Draco! The woman would drive him insane. She didn't want sex when he was hornier than a two-peckered gormarant, then she did when he was completely involved in something else. Peeling back the edges of his fly she reached in to fondle him, stroking until he was once again hard.

"Know what I was thinking?" she asked.

He sure hoped it wasn't about Rumarian sour cabbage. "No. What?" His voice was getting ragged.

"I was remembering that time when we'd just picked up Shesshie and we were both on late duty." She slid to her knees in front of him.

By the Gorthan Nebula, he sure hoped she was remembering the same time he was thinking about. "Yeah..." he encouraged.

When she worked him completely free from his trousers, she bent her head to taste him. "Thank the gods."

"What was that?" She raised her head to ask.

Damn. He hadn't intended to say that aloud. "I said thank the gods I have such a wonderful wife." Tangling his fingers in her hair he urged her back to finish what she'd started.

The proximity alarm went off with a vengeance, shrieking while the computer calmly announced the arrival of five cruisers.

Chapter Six

Kevnor was an even-tempered guy. He really was. But even he could only take so much. His curses began as a low murmur but increased in volume and intensity; his fists balled into damage-inflicting threats, until Dev sat back on her heels and stared at him in awe. Unlike the rest of the crew, he had been twelve before he was orphaned and had always had better manners than the rest of them. She hadn't realized the depth of his cursing ability.

A smile blossomed across her face. "I'm impressed."

Sitting there like temptation come to life, her breasts bared and her lips red from pleasuring him, Dev's sincere comment sent a surge of blood straight to his already painfully engorged penis. Her brow rose at the extra length added to his erection. "In more ways than one," she amended.

His body thrumming with need, aching with desire, he drew on unknown depths to calm his raging spirit. Make that redirect his raging spirit. Someone was going to die for interrupting them. "Pull up the targeting computer," he snapped. "Let's get this over with so we can finish what we started."

Rising with inherent grace, Dev retied her robe and took her place at the weapons control station. "Come on babies," she talked seductively to her guns. "Momma has a little job for you."

Fearing permanent damage, Kev didn't even try to close his pants yet. He turned away from the stimulating sight of his wife finessing the tools of her trade. He'd never lose the erection if he watched her. "Computer, identify approaching craft."

The computer complied.

"Shit. Did you hear that, honey?" Kev shook his head. "Our old pals are now our enemies."

"So it seems." Dev sighed heavily. "You'd think they'd have better sense than to challenge the Freebird. They all know how well she's equipped." Completely confident in their abilities, she continued, "It's going to be a drag, killing former friends."

"We have a message incoming. Shall I take it?" Kev asked her.

"Why not? Maybe they have some last words."

"You are wicked," her husband complimented. "Here goes." He engaged the comm.

Johan Reardon's face filled the screen. "We know you're alone Devona," he began, "so we're willing to offer you terms."

Kev exchanged a glance with his wife. This was the scumbag who'd captured them the last time, turning them over to be tortured. Revenge was going to be sweet. "I'm afraid you've been misinformed," Kev told the younger man. "My wife is definitely not alone." Looming over the camera to block out his scantily clad mate, Kev hastily secured the closure of his pants.

The look on Reardon's face was priceless. He was obviously not expecting the kind of threat a fully manned Freebird offered. Kev intended to make sure he didn't find out there were only two of them. "Gaaus," he replied. "We were informed she was alone." His Adam's apple was visible, bobbing as he swallowed. "But we're still willing to offer terms. My benefactor is willing to drop the bounty of the rest of the crew if you hand her over."

Incredulity suffused his face. "Hell no," Kev yelled. "Unlike some people we've associated with in the past, this crew is loyal to one another."

The young man apparently got the dig, because his face flushed red. "Believe it or not, we're working out of friendship."

Kev couldn't believe the gall of this guy. "What a crock!"

"No, really. If Devona doesn't give herself up, all of you will end up dead. Every person old enough to tote a blaster is looking for the lot of you. This is the only way you're going to stay alive." Warming to his subject he continued, "And we're ready to assure her safe conduct to Iman."

"Iman," Kev spat. "What possible demon could have infected your brain that you think I'd turn my mate over to those bunch of lunatics?"

Reardon shrugged. "Your choice. Check your readings. There are five well-armed ships surrounding you. And all we'd have to do is send out word that we've spotted you to get dozens more here within mere hours." He leaned in to the camera, his face filling the screen. "Face it, you've lost. Avoid any damage to the ship or her personnel and hand over the princess."

"I'm not a fucking princess." Dev nudged Kev out of the way. Clad now in a black jumpsuit, she addressed the young upstart. "But I am one hell of a warrior, and I'll blow your sorry ass out of existence. This is not the same scenario as before, kid." Her lip curled in a sneer. "We are far from defenseless this time."

Reardon bristled at being called kid. "Your call," he said. "We can shoot your ship to hell if that's what you want." His image winked out.

"Shields up," Kev ordered.

Dev returned to her station. "How the hell'd they find us?" She frowned, thinking. "First Harry, now these guys." Looking over at Kev she admitted, "Something's not right here."

"Tracer," they said at the same time.

"Draco." Dev shook her head. "I went to Epsilon III like some kind of a green recruit. That bastard Harry kept me occupied while his men sabotaged my ship and put a tracer on it." Hot tears stung her eyes, and she blinked them back. "For all my bragging, I am not captain material."

Heart aching at her comments Kev reassured her, "It could've happened to anyone. You were alone, looking for a crew. You had to take a chance. Besides, you didn't know about the new bounty, right?"

Mollified, she shook her head. "No. Not until Harry told me. But still, I should have been more careful. Mik would have been."

"Mik's been doing this for a long time. Since we were children, really. He's always been in charge. Don't beat yourself up, honey."

The first volley of fire hit them. "Minor damage to the shield on the port side," the computer informed.

"Fire at will," Kev said unnecessarily. Dev had already returned fire on the offending vessel.

"Direct hit on the ship at three o'clock. Damage to shields." The computer kept them appraised.

Dev placed her shots like the master strategist she was. Kev maneuvered the ship to give her maximum advantage. With damage to their port side, Kev kept the Bird pivoting left so the starboard took most return fire. That worked for a while, till the shields to starboard began to weaken. Dev's maniacal firing had disabled the crafts at twelve and eight o'clock and the other three maneuvered slightly to compensate. The ship at three moved to a one o'clock position, and the craft at ten moved to nine. Incoming fire was nonstop. The Bird was fighting a gallant but losing battle, and everyone knew it.

"If I do nothing else, I'm taking out Reardon's ship before we surrender," Dev promised. "Where'd that little bastard get a cruiser of that caliber anyway?" Ion cannon fire breached his forward shields, and she followed quickly with photon torpedoes. "Gotcha!" she yelled as she destroyed Reardon's bridge. "Hope you died, you bastard," she yelled.

"Navigation inoperable," the computer announced. "Port shields down."

"Shut the fuck up," Dev snarled. "I hate a smart-assed computer."

Gentle hands came to rest on her shoulders. "Honey, they've got us," Kev said quietly. "If we don't surrender, they'll demolish the Freebird and us along with her."

Abandoning the controls, Dev clutched her belly with both hands. "I will not raise our baby in that hellhole." Devona DiMitri, the ice queen of their graduating class at military school, unflappable fighting mercenary, disintegrated into a mere mortal in Kev's arms. "I won't give you up," she whispered, clutching him around the neck, burying her tear-streaked face in the hollow between his pecs.

"No, sweetheart, you aren't giving me up. And our child will not be raised on Iman." He soothed her with tender kisses and ran his big capable hand down her fine hair to rest on the indentation of her waist. "I swear I will follow and rescue you." He pulled back to make eye contact. "No force in the universe will keep me from you. Do you believe that?"

She nodded, dashing the tears from her cheeks. Ashamed of her behavior she straightened, squaring her shoulders. "I can do this," she told him. "You know I'm strong. I don't know what came over me."

Kev placed a hand over her stomach. "I think our child came over you. Hormones," he suggested.

"I guess." Sniffing she asked, "Got a plan in mind?"

"I suppose the first thing we have to do is contact Reardon." He moved to communications and hailed Reardon's ship. At first there was no reply; then the soot-streaked face of their former pupil came into view.

"Damn, you're good," was the first thing he said. That mollified Dev's ego somewhat.

"Terms," Kev said succinctly.

"We transport over and pick up the princess. You go free." Reardon shrugged. "Simple."

"Not so simple. I won't allow your men to board our vessel," Kev replied. "I will bring Dev over in a shuttle. When I'm assured of her safety, I'll return to the Freebird."

"No," Dev interrupted. "I'll take myself over. You stay here to guard our ship." She had no intention of placing Kev in the position of being captured, too. What was to stop Reardon from throwing him in the brig for bounty, too?

As if reading her mind, Kev nodded. "Agreed." He hated the idea, but he couldn't rescue her if he, too, was incarcerated. Neither could he contact the Nest for reinforcements. To Reardon he said, "Give us half an hour to clean up and pack some clothes for her."

"Make it a quarter hour." The screen went black.

Running shaking fingers through his thick black hair, Kev turned to find Devona had already left the bridge. He hurried to follow her, setting the Bird's controls to maintain position. The sight of her nearly caused his heart to break. Standing beneath the hot jets of the shower, Dev leaned against the glass wall, her face contorted with grief, her hands clutched over their child. Shedding his clothes, Kev joined her, pulling her close. They had no time for sex, but someone forgot to tell his dick, who jerked excitedly at the full body contact. Dev moaned, pulling his mouth down to hers.

"Please," she whimpered, raising a leg to rest on his hip, "one last time, please."

Lifting her with both hands beneath her ass, Kev slid home, filling her repeatedly with frantic thrusts. Tears washed away by the steady stream of water, they came almost immediately. "Not the last time," he vowed. "Just the last time for a little while. I will find you. I will rescue you." Never so determined in his life, Kev shook her gently. "Do you believe me, Dev? Do you promise to wait for me?"

She knew he was a ruthless warrior, feared on the battlefield, but she'd never seen him like this. The look on his face made her breath catch. Her lover was a very dangerous man. "I believe you and I'll wait—as long as it takes."

"That's my girl." He kissed the end of her nose.

***

Maltoran was a very inhospitable planet. Draxor Umland had spent billions of credits establishing a base there. But the view was worth it. Standing in front of a wall of windows, he looked out at the ever-changing landscape of endless volcanic activity struggling to produce stable landmasses and a viable atmosphere. Slightly distorted by the plasma dome that encapsulated his entire base, the sight was mesmerizing. "Amazing, isn't it?" he asked the Imani delegate. Stunningly beautiful, she stood his exact height and wore the tiniest of skirts and an abbreviated halter-top. Suede boots came up to her knees, and a matching belt hung low on her hips, securing several interesting weapons.

Shrugging her shoulders, the woman was unimpressed. "What is amazing to me is that you spent the kind of credits this must have cost when you could have purchased enough weapons to—"

"You see," Umland interrupted, "that is the trouble with you Imani bitches. All you think about is war."

Gritting her teeth, she refrained from commenting.

"Here I have created something unique. Something that will be my legacy." Turning, he asked her, "What will your legacy be? A demolished planet?"

~60~

"That is not your concern, is it?" Her hand came to rest on her sidearm. "Your concern is the price of our princess, and I have that. I presume you have her or you would not have brought me here."

"Relax, Aldora, I've got her. I just thought we might enjoy a few minutes of pleasure before we got down to business." The woman was a fine looking piece of ass.

Her bark of laughter surprised him. "Spending time in this bubble that could burst at any moment, killing us all, is not my idea of pleasure."

"Plasma shields are the latest technology. We are safe here." He allowed his eyes to roam over her muscled body. Though lean and taut, she had all the right equipment in all the right places. He'd always lusted after the Vancourans, but that was before he got a look at the Imani. "Safe enough to spend some time exploring each other's proclivities." He stepped closer, drawing a deep breath through his nostrils, searching the air for an indication that she was as turned on as he.

Basically a good-looking man, Draxor had let his body go to fat. Aldora was repulsed. "I think not. You wouldn't last ten minutes in my bed."

"Oh, I wouldn't bet on that."

She ran a finger suggestively over his shoulder and down his arm. "Have you studied Imani sex habits, Umland?"

He raised one brow. "What's to study? Sex is sex."

"Let me show you," she whispered. In a flash she had him flat on his back on the floor while she stood over him. "Remove your clothes," she ordered.

"It's a little difficult with you standing over me. Not that the view isn't nice." Her boot heel came down on his inner thigh, perilously close to some very important flesh. "Hey, watch out."

"Shut up. You are not allowed to speak."

"Bullshit. This is my..." Aldora pulled a small quirt from her belt and brought it down across his cheek.

"Men on Iman are our playthings. We can do anything to them we wish. My particular pleasure is inflicting pain." She squatted over him, legs spread to give him a view of her bare crotch. Excitement overcame him at the sight. Her words quelled his desire. "My personal record is three days with a lover. Of course, he died from his injuries before I was fully satisfied." She rose again, kicking him in the side. "Get up and summon the princess before I forget my honor and take the hide from your bones."

Eyes narrowed, Draxor pulled himself to his feet. He needed the funds or he'd have Aldora tortured. Oh well, if there was one thing he'd learned through the years, it was that if you waited long enough, things came full circle. He'd have his chance at this bitch eventually. Depressing a button on his desk he spoke, "Bring in Devona."

Moments later, two armed guards arrived dragging an unconscious woman between them.

Aldora was incensed. "What is the meaning of this, Umland?" She stepped over to Devona's prone body where it had been deposited on the floor. "Is this how you treat a valuable hostage?"

"She was uncooperative," one of the guards replied.

Grinding her teeth, Aldora told Umland, "Get them out of my sight or I won't be responsible for my actions."

A wave of his wrist sent the guards back the way they'd come. "Don't go on so. She's alive. That's all you stipulated."

"You'd better pray to whatever deity you worship that she is unharmed." Positioning a portable anti-grav sled beneath Devona, Aldora turned back to Umland. "Or I will personally return to see just how long you would last beneath my knives and whips."

Unconcerned, he reminded, "Uh, there's the little matter of the credits..."

"I will deliver the credits to the pilot of the shuttle that delivers us safely to my ship." She glared at him. "You don't actually think I'm stupid enough to hand the money over to you here in your domain do you?"

He smiled, spreading his hands in a conciliatory gesture. "Can't blame me for trying."

Turning her back, Aldora steered the sled toward the door.

Chapter Seven

Not waiting for the ships to clear out of the quadrant, Kev set a course for Bright's Planet and slammed the Bird into hyperdrive. He was lucky she didn't rip apart. It was probably a testimony to Callus' magical engineering abilities, but he didn't take time to marvel about it this time. He was just too damn stressed. All the while he fiddled with communications, which were out again. It made him wonder if they had ever been fixed at all, or if the temporary restoration had been another aspect of the sabotage. He'd have to look into it some day. But not today. Meanwhile, he was barreling head-on into a situation he knew nothing about. He prayed Mik and the rest had arrived okay. He was going to need them.

In desperation he resorted to Dev's method and emailed Doc at the Nest. While he waited for a reply, he scanned for information on Maltoran. What he found was not encouraging. The place was a tectonic nightmare. How could anyone establish a base there? Even an underground facility was out of the question. Leaning his forehead against the consol, he fought encroaching depression. There had to be a way. Intellect had never failed him before. Or if it had, his muscle power had been enough to tip the scale in his favor.

The screen flashed an incoming mail warning. He scurried to retrieve it. It was from Doc, sure enough. The crew hadn't arrived yet, but he'd just been in communication with them. All was well at the Nest.

He'd alerted everyone to Kev's plight, and they'd be brainstorming until he got there.

Already Kev felt better. Together, they could figure something out. They always had. The crew of the Freebird was an awesome opponent, if he said so himself. Except they were short one member. Pain shot through his chest like a blast from a pulse rifle. The ache filled his heart, numbing him to the depth of his soul. Rising from the comm, Kev made his way to the gym, stripped to his briefs and activated the Kum Chen video opponent. For the next two hours, he battled the holovid, fighting for his sanity and his life.

Mik was at the bottom of the ramp when he debarked the next day. "Hurry up," he snapped as soon as Kev appeared. "Everyone's waiting."

Kev frowned. "Has something happened?"

"No. And I don't intend to wait around until it does. I want Devona safe."

Holding a hand up for Mik to stop, Kev turned to face his best friend. "Look, I know Dev's your first officer and all, but she's my wife. I will plan this mission, and I will command it."

In all the years they'd known one another, Kev had never expressed any desire to lead. Oh, he was more than capable; he just didn't seem to have the desire. This was apparently a different kettle of fish. Brows drawn together, Mik asked, "What brought this on?"

"My wife. My problem. My decisions." Rubbing the back of his head nervously, Kev blurted, "If for some reason this doesn't go down right, I will shoulder all the blame." He caught Mik's gaze and held it. "I need to be the one."

Nodding, Mik continued toward the main hangar. "I agree. Now, have you got any plans made yet, or did you want us to kick it around as a group first?"

"I have some thoughts, but I want everyone's input as usual. Ultimately I will formulate the plan, but we have always worked as a team. We work best as a team."

"I'm glad to hear you say that. I'd hate to have to see you try to whip each and every one of us before you left on this quest." Opening the door for him, Mik waved Kev through first. "And you'd have to. We all love her, too." Mik ushered Kev to stand beside the holoboard, where a holovid of the galaxy wavered. "Just so we're clear on this," he addressed the others, "Kev is in charge of this mission." Mik sat down with the others.

No one said a word. They just waited for Kev to start. Honored by their acceptance, Kev had to swallow past a lump in his throat before he could speak. "Dev was taken by Johan Reardon." Several groans were heard. "And I am not happy." That was an understatement. His black eyes radiated anger. "I will personally remove the beating heart from his chest once I have Dev home safe, but right now that revenge is secondary. From what we learned aboard the Bird, Umland has contracted with Iman for Dev's return to her home world."

Callus snorted. "Home world? She's never been to Iman in her life. This is her home."

"I couldn't agree more," Kev assured him, "but the Imani people don't. They think some freaking tattoo makes her the savior of their world."

Zoë chuckled. "The Imani might just get more than they bargained for. I've seen that girl mad, and it ain't a pretty sight."

Marissa spoke quietly, "How can we be sure the bounty has been removed from you all? It seems to me you're going to have a much more difficult time if you're dodging bounty hunters all the way."

"Good point." Kev nodded. "As soon as we're finished here I'll get on the computer and see what I can come up with."

"I've been working on the Pelican already," Callus told them. "She's even more beefed up than before. She'll be a worthy ally to the Freebird in any fight."

"I appreciate that." Kevnor took a deep breath and bit the bullet, so to speak. "There's something I need to tell you all. Something you don't know and didn't matter until now." Squaring his shoulders he announced boldly, "My father was third in line for the Baux throne."

No one said anything. They just sat there, waiting for the punch line. "Well," he prompted.

"Damn," Zoë quipped, "you think you know a guy..."

"I'm serious here. I'm pouring my heart out to my friends, and you guys act like I'm joking."

Mike shrugged. "I guess we're waiting for you to make your point."

Kev stood slack jawed for a moment, and then he burst into laughter. "You guys could care less. I just told you I'm royalty, and you act like I just told you I have black hair."

"I guess one's about as important to us as the other," Callus remarked.

Kev sat down. "All those years we scrimped and saved and pooled our money to buy the Bird and get set up in our own business and I could have furnished as much money as we needed and then some. I thought you'd all hate me."

"Kev, you don't question family," Jim Darner said quietly. "You just accept them as they are and stand by them. Like we did with Devona. Like we'll do with you."

Grinning like a fool, Kev told them, "Then you won't mind if I call on my relatives for a little support."

Mik was on his feet. "Now wait a minute, Kev. Accepting your royal ass into our midst doesn't mean we want hoards of your relatives telling us what to do. That's why we left the military in the first place."

Kev spoke quietly, but from the heart. "I know. But I just don't see any other way. I've been researching Iman, and our chances of getting her off that planet are next to none. Men are completely subservient there. If we tried a covert op and got caught, we'd be as bad off as we were on Pagoda."

"Surely not," Shesshie said. "They don't have slaves, do they?"

"Oh, they don't call them slaves, but they're slaves nonetheless. Males are not allowed to be educated, nor are they allowed a career. They are kept sequestered until they enter puberty, and then they are married off or offered up as a concubine."

Shesshie shook her head. "Well, what if Zoë, Marissa and I went there?"

Callus and Mik jumped to their feet at the same time. "No," Callus said at the same time Mik declared, "Absolutely out of the question."

The women exchanged glances. "And just who will stop us," Zoë asked, "if we choose to go to Iman?"

"Come on, little girl," Callus cajoled. "Don't take that tone. This isn't about throwing your weight around—" All ninety-two pounds of it. "—so to speak."

"I just don't like being underestimated." She was angry.

Mik raised a brow at his navigator. "Believe me, no one here would ever underestimate you."

"Oh." Shesshie, too, stood. "So it's me and my sister you think can't hack it?"

"Now, Sweet, that isn't what I said at all." He looked to the other men. "Help me out here, guys."

Kev crossed his arms across his chest. "You don't need any help," he assured the other man. "You're kicking yourself in the ass just fine all by yourself."

"I'll remind you of this next time you need me," Mik threatened. Turning to Shesshie he placated, "Honey, it's not that you and Marissa aren't smart capable women, it's that with only three of you against an entire planet of warrior-women, the odds aren't good enough to risk it."

"Four. There would be four of us. Dev's already there," she reminded him.

"Not yet," Kev broke in. "Right now she should still be at Umland's place on Maltoran."

"Well there ya go." Jim Darner smiled. "We'll go there and get her. Umland's place can't possibly be as hard to work with as this Iman place."

"That's where you'd be wrong, Doc," Kev said. "Umland's base of operations is a new planet. The place is a tectonic nightmare. Volcanoes popping up all over the place, geysers, lava flows...you get the picture. I can't figure out how he's doing it. A place like that doesn't even offer the option of underground facilities."

"Plasma dome," Callus said.

"What?" Kev was mystified.

"Plasma domes are the latest technology, specifically designed for colonizing inhospitable terrain." Callus' eyes lit up like a lad at his first strip show. "Remarkable, really. The entire area is contained in a sort of bubble that blocks the native atmosphere and allows artificial environments to be contained within."

"How big are these things?" Mik asked.

"Depends of the number of credits you want to turn loose of." Parallel lines formed between his brows. "I read in an engineering periodical that one company had encapsulated an area big enough to house an entire continent."

"And you get in and out of this bubble, how?" Zoë asked.

"There's the rub, I'm afraid." Callus sighed. "You have to be invited in. The bubble not only keeps out the surrounding environment, it also seems to repel any and all weaponry tested against it. And ships can only enter if provided with the genetic code. I'm not medical, mind you, but what I read said the ship actually becomes like a virus or something, infiltrating the plasma. Then, when it leaves, they reverse the code, making the plasma expel the ship, like fighting off a disease." Dimples creased his cheeks. Callus had dimples? "After we tie this up, I may take some online classes to learn more about this."

"Great idea." Kev nodded. "But not helpful now, I'm afraid." He looked around at his friends. "I just don't see any other way but to go to Baux for help. I will not leave my wife and child on that heinous planet."

"I think we're all in agreement with the last part," Mik told him. "I just wish we didn't have to involve anyone else. When you start asking for favors, you inevitably end up having to grant some." It was a testimony to the devotion the crew had to one another when he said, "You're in charge. Do it."

***

"What the fuck do you think you're doing?" Dev came out of her unconscious state instantly. The hands probing at her belly were attached to a middle-aged woman.

Smiling, the woman straightened and said, "I was just trying to determine how far along you are."

Dev sat up too quickly and had to close her eyes for a moment against the dizziness. "Why didn't you just ask? I don't like to be pawed, especially by strangers."

"I am no stranger. I am your aunt. Your mother's sister." Tall, graying blonde hair, green eyes bracketed by laugh lines, the woman was attractive in an oh-my-god-the-woman's-wearing-a-loin-cloth sort of way. "So, how far along are you, Princess?"

Steady now, Dev stood. "First off, let's get this princess thing straight. I'm not your long lost princess. My name's Devona DiMetri, and I am first

~71~

officer of the Freebird, formerly a mercenary ship, now a freighter." Draco! She didn't have a stitch on. Refusing to be intimidated, she held herself tall and straight, resisting the urge to cover her body.

The unnamed woman nodded. "Yes, you are all of those things. But you are also our princess." She held a mirror out to Dev, who took it automatically. "Look and see for yourself."

Glancing at her image in the glass, Dev did a double take. Not only was she completely without clothing, she was also without hair. In shock, she ran her palm over her now bald head. "Bitch," she accused. "You shaved my head."

"Yes. I'm afraid we had to, to insure your identity. Look closer at yourself, Princess. See what was revealed beneath your hair."

An intricate pattern of tribal symbols interspersed by small delicate flowers covered most of her head. Dev frowned at her reflection, touching the tattoo gingerly. "Has this always been there, under my hair?"

"Yes, my dear. The moment you were born, artisans were waiting to assure your identity. All females born into the royal line are identified in such a way." The woman reached out to touch Dev's head, but Dev pulled back, frowning at her. Sighing, she continued, "At the time of your birth, there was much unrest on Iman. Not only was the ongoing battle against the Bauxites a concern, but rebellious factors here on Iman made it necessary to secrete you away— for your own good."

"Secrete me away? In an orphanage? That's a bit extreme, don't you think?" Dev clearly thought the woman was lying.

"Persis, please, you have to believe me."

Dev was losing patience, fast. "Who the hell is Persis?"

"You are Persis. That is the name you were given at birth. You were entrusted to a member of the royal guard. She was to take you to a safe haven and guard you until the civil rebellion was quelled." Tears filled the older woman's eyes. "But she was a spy, planted by the rebels. She took you away from us, and we have searched the universe for you for years. Now your mother lies dying, and there is no other heir. All her other children were males, sadly."

"Sadly? Why sadly? What, she doesn't like boys?"

The woman looked shocked. "This is Iman." As if that said it all.

"Okay...what's your name, anyway?"

"Nambia."

"Nambia, right. Okay, Nambia, assuming I am this lost princess, what exactly is it you want from me?" Dev needed answers if she was going to be able to plan an escape.

"To assume the throne, of course."

Dev looked around for a robe or something. "Do I get clothes, or do I have to run around buck assed naked?"

Nambia clapped her hands and two young boys appeared, eyes downcast. "Yes, ma'am?"

"The princess requires clothing. Please fetch the blue garments laid out in her room." Nodding the boys retreated.

"What was that all about?" Dev asked.

Nambia was obviously not tracking. "I sent for clothing, as you asked."

"I meant with the boys. What, were they just standing outside the door, waiting for you to clap?"

"Of course. They are domestics in training." Nambia smiled. "They will be your personal servants."

"I don't want any servants. I'm used to doing for myself. And I sure as hell don't want a couple of little boys underfoot all the time. They should be out playing, or better yet, in school."

Scandalized, Nambia drew in a shocked breath. "But they are males."

"They are human children, just like females. They should be treated the same as the girls."

Her mouth drawn in a tight line, Nambia remarked, "You obviously need to be indoctrinated into Imani customs."

Dev had a sudden epiphany. If she could make these dames decide they didn't want her as queen after all, they'd let her go. She smiled, feeling confident for the first time since her capture. "No, I don't think so. If I am to be queen, I'll be making some changes. I can't abide the thought of small boys as servants. Get rid of all of them."

Eyes rounded in shock, Nambia asked, "You want them killed?"

"Draco, no! I want them to go do something else, like play or go to school. I want them to go be children."

Soundlessly, the boys slipped back into the room, holding several lengths of blue cloth across their arms. In addition, one held a pair of blue leather short boots. They just stood there, eyes downcast, waiting for the woman to tell them what to do next. It broke Dev's heart. In her mind's eye she could see her own boy—Kev's son—in a similar role. Over her dead body! She lifted one's chin with her index finger. "What have you got there?" she asked him.

"Your clothing, as commanded, ma'am," he replied.

She felt like a perv, conversing naked with a couple of kids. But they didn't seem to notice. "Thank you," she said softly. "Put the stuff down and run outside and play, both of you."

"P-play?" The smaller boy's lip trembled. "I don't understand, ma'am."

"Really, Persis," Nambia remarked, "you're confusing the child. How do you expect him to obey a command he doesn't understand?"

Looked like the plan to make herself undesirable was going to be harder than she'd thought.

Chapter Eight

Shesshie smiled down at her daughter. "Good night, Tessa. Mommy loves you."

"Lo'you." The tired baby was asleep before Shesshie could get the bedroom door closed.

"How's our girl?" Mik asked, slipping an arm around his wife's waist.

"Perfect." She hugged him back and laid her head against his shoulder as they walked toward their own room. "Of course, I might be slightly prejudiced."

Mik feigned a shocked look. "Not you!"

"Guilty." Stepping over to her dresser, Shesshie fiddled with the assortment of knick-knacks that cluttered the top. "Mik, I'm afraid. I know you have to go save Dev—and I want you to—but I have a bad feeling."

Bending to place a gentle kiss at the back of her exposed neck, he reassured her, "Oh, sweet, it's just the thought of having to wait and not know what's going on. The few times I've been out of the thick of things, I've had those same feelings. All it means is that you care."

She turned, tilting her head back to look up at him. "Maybe you're right. Still, I expect frequent communication."

"I promise I'll contact you as often as possible. But you do realize I can't stop to send emails in the middle of a mission, don't you?"

"I'm not an idiot," she scoffed.

"Of course not. I never implied that you were. You're just new to this whole lifestyle, and I want to make sure we're on the same page here." Mik suddenly realized that his wife's shirt had tiny little buttons all the way down the front. Never one to run away from a challenge, he started working on the damn things. His big fingers did not have an easy time of it.

"As long as the page you're on says you're coming home to me and the kids in one piece, then we're on the same one." Shesshie's small fingers eased under the edge of his shirt to stroke along his washboard abs.

Concentrating on his task, it took several minutes for what she'd said to sink in. When it did, Mik found himself frozen with emotion. Did she mean what he thought she did? Slowly, relentlessly, his eyes rose from the tantalizing glimpse of skin he'd bared between her breasts to the sparkle of mischief in her eyes. "C-children?" His voice was barely audible, so he cleared his throat and asked again, "Did you say children?"

Raising her brows, Shesshie teased, "What do you know, you were paying attention after all."

Dropping to his knees, Mik laid his lips against her stomach. "You're pregnant." It wasn't a question.

"Almost two months," she said proudly. "It must have happened almost immediately after you got the implant removed."

The intrepid warrior's hands shook as he pulled his wife's clothing aside to stare at her stomach. "My baby's in there." Awe laced his words.

Shesshie ran her fingers through his thick dark hair. "Our baby is in there. I debated telling you before you left, but I decided I wanted you to know just how important it was for you to come back, whole and healthy." Overcome by tenderness, she bent to kiss the top of his head, hoping he wouldn't notice the catch in her voice.

Of course, he noticed it anyway. "Honey, don't cry." He stood again and drew her into his arms. "I'll be back. I promise. Now I have not only my two beautiful girls waiting, but a new baby as well." His chest hurt with the swell of pride. "I'm going to be a father."

She tickled his ribs. "You're already a father."

"I know. And I couldn't love Tessa any more if she was my own, but I never expected to find anyone who would want to have my baby." His palm curled protectively over her abdomen. "You have no idea how much this means to me. How much I love you for this gift." Lifting her in his arms, Mik strode to the bed and laid her down. "And now I'm going to show you just how much."

Her husky voice tickled his ear. "Are we going to play helpless hostage rescued by the virile mercenary?"

Mik burst out laughing. "What have you been reading, woman?"

"Lots, and I've got the goodies to prove it." Pulling a box from beneath the bed, Shesshie dumped the contents out. Purchased before they left the space station where they were married, she proudly displayed blindfolds, silken ropes, an assortment of feathers, and a few items she couldn't identify. But Mik would know what they were...and before the night was over, so would she.

***

Skeptically, Dev held up the end of one length of cloth. "And I'm supposed to do what with this?"

"I will show you the proper way to wrap it," Nambia offered, taking the cloth and looping it around Dev's hips and between her legs. When she knotted it in front, the ends hung down between her knees. She looked like a freaking barbarian from some outer rim world, breasts bared and loincloth in place. A bark of laughter escaped, almost giving away the hysteria she was desperately trying to subdue. She was on a freaking savage planet. Undaunted, Nambia continued her ministrations, fashioning a halter-top from another length of blue cloth. Well, at least she wasn't going to be gracing the cover of Galactic Geographic. Thank the gods for small favors.

Bending at the waist, Dev slid her feet into the surprisingly comfortable shoes. "These I can figure out for myself." She wiggled her toes. "Perfect fit."

"Of course. The were made for you." Nambia tossed the remaining cloth into a nearby basket.

"Huh?" Dev must have misheard her. "Did you say they were made for me?"

Nambia nodded.

"How's that possible? I just got here."

"A cast was taken of your feet when Aldora first carried you aboard her ship. The specifications were sent ahead so we would be prepared."

Dev couldn't believe she'd been that out of it. "Was I unconscious for long?"

"We felt it best to keep you from worrying during your journey. A chemical sleep was induced."

"You drugged me? I'm pregnant, you moron! It could have harmed my baby." Furious, Dev took a threatening step toward the older woman.

Nambia squared off. "We would never harm you, Princess," she said formally. "But neither will I allow you to dominate me. I am your maternal aunt, and as such, I demand the respect of my position, if not your affection."

Frustrated, Dev reached out and kicked the wall, leaving a big hole. "It's not me I'm worried about. It's the baby."

"If you are not harmed, the child is not harmed."

"I hope you're right," she mumbled to herself. "Kev would never forgive me if I allowed our baby to be hurt."

"Who is Kev?" Nambia asked.

"My husband."

Horrified, Nambia repeated, "Husband?"

"Yeah, you know, permanent mate, father of my child, lifelong companion." Surely the institution wasn't unknown to these wacky women.

"You have pledged yourself to a man?" Nambia was clearly horrified.

You'd have thought she'd just announced she had purposefully sliced off her own right arm. "Yes. We are very much in love." Dev looked down her nose at the older woman. "And you can expect to meet him, because he will be coming to take me home."

"You are home, Persis. Iman is where you were born and where you will die." There was finality in Nambia's voice.

"You don't know Kevnor." Dev thought she'd leave it at that.

Nambia shrugged. "If he does come, we will just assign him to the stable of one of our citizens."

Dev saw red. No one else was touching her man. "Let me make myself clear," she ground out. "Assuming you manage to capture Kevnor when he arrives on this planet, he will be in my bed—and no one else's—every night. If another woman touches him, I will kill her." Her body language must have convinced the other woman she was serious because Nambia took a step back. "And don't think I can't carry out my threat."

A slow smile spread across Nambia's face. "I believe you," she said simply. "And I honor your right. You are indeed Imani." With that she exited the room.

Dev wasted no time searching the room. It was clean. No potential weapons, no escape routes, not even any real clothing. Dejected, she sat back on the bed to wait for whatever happened next. She didn't have long to wait. The two boys she'd spoken to earlier entered and stood on either side of the door. Just stood and stared at the floor. "Boys," she asked quietly, "what are you doing here? I thought I told you to go out and play."

The taller of the two, presumably the older, whispered, "We don't know how, ma'am."

"Well I'll show you," she blurted before she thought about it. How the hell was she supposed to teach them? She had never played as a child either. Except war games. Shrugging she motioned them over. "I'll show you how to spar."

"Spar, ma'am?" the little one asked.

"You know, fight. I'll teach you some fighting moves." Pleased with herself, she stood up and circled the lads, sizing them up, trying to figure which techniques were best for which boy. "I think the first thing you need to know is a basic stance. Stand with your feet slightly apart, relaxed." Dev demonstrated. "Be sure your weight is balanced, so you can move any direction you need to."

"Like this?" She glanced over at the younger one and bit back a smile.

"That's perfect." Bending she readjusted his feet. "Just a tiny bit over, like this."

The taller of the two mimicked her perfectly. She winked encouragement at him over the little guy's head. "What are your names, boys?"

Both froze, looking warily at each other. The little one took a fortifying breath. "Tim. They call me Tim."

"My name is You," the other boy whispered.

"You?" Dev smiled, thinking he was joking.

"I think so. The house mistress always says, hey You, when she talks to me." He stood straight and tall, looking her in the eye. Dev knew he was using every bit of courage he had to look at her. She'd dealt with male egos before.

"That's a nice name. Rather unusual, but nice." She elbowed him playfully as she passed. "Now come at me as if you're going to hit me."

The child hit the floor, kneeling with head bowed almost touching the gleaming hardwood. "Mistress, I cannot."

"You," she said. Draco it felt funny to call the child You. "This is just for fun. You're not really going to hit me, because I'm not going to let you." She raised his chin with a finger beneath it. "I am a trained warrior.

You are a little boy. There is no way you could hurt me unless I allowed it. Now stand up."

Tears fell silently down his cheeks. Dev's heart broke. Gathering him in her arms she kissed the top of his head and smoothed the hair back from his face. "I didn't mean to make you unhappy. I was only trying to have some fun. You don't have to do this if you don't want to."

Tim stood at attention; his large brown eyes round with fear. She pulled him into the embrace, too. "Boys, where I am from it is what little boys do, play at being warriors. I didn't mean to scare you."

"Boys get to fight?" Tim was impressed. His face had become animated again.

"Yes, they do. And girls do, too," Dev assured him.

"Well, girls do here. But boys don't." You was coming around. "I wish boys could fight, too."

"And read," Tim added.

You got caught up in the excitement. "And write, and get a job." His lip trembled. "I don't want to be a concubine." A child that age shouldn't even know what that was, let alone fear becoming one.

"Well, why don't I just keep you for myself. Then I can do what I want with you." She ruffled the hair on both their heads. "I'll teach you to read and write myself. And when my husband comes to rescue me, I'll take you with me."

They stepped back from her. Their expressions said clearly they thought she was insane. "Yes, ma'am," they agreed in unison. Silently Dev vowed to free these boys...and all the others trapped on this fucked-up planet.

Chapter Nine

A soft tap sounded at her door. Marissa glanced at the clock. Seven o'clock. Running a palm over her shiny, dark hair she opened the door. "Callus, you're in danger of becoming predictable." Stepping back, she invited him inside.

A frown marred his dear, ravaged features. "I'm sorry. Would you rather I—?"

Petal soft fingers pressed against his lips. "I was just teasing you," she admitted. "Your visits are the highlight of each day." His beatific smile transformed his face. The phenomenon never ceased to amaze her. Callus Vukovik was not an attractive man...until he smiled. Then the beauty of his soul was released, and the sight always made Marissa weak in the knees.

"Would you like to go for a walk?" he asked, just as he always did.

"I'd love to," she replied, just as she always did. Grabbing a shawl, she led the way.

"We leave tomorrow." There it was, the announcement she had been dreading. She knew they had to go after Devona, but selfishly she had hoped Dev would return by herself before Callus and the rest had to search for her. "Forest or desert?"

"Forest tonight I think." That was unusual. She always loved the clean lines of the desert landscape, so different from the cluttered oppressiveness of Pagoda.

"Okay." Callus ambled toward the trail that led to a secluded lake. "That's different." He reached over to take her hand, twining their fingers.

"I know. But tonight I think the concealment of the trees would be welcome." A carpet of vines and fallen leaves muted their progress as they walked. Silence was not an uncomfortable presence between them. Marissa and Callus knew how to enjoy each other's company even without benefit of words. "How long do you think you'll be gone?" she asked after a time.

"I have no idea. Kev has this crazy idea of asking his relatives on Baux for assistance. Just negotiating that will take a while. The logistics of the rescue will take still longer. Then we'll have to execute the plan." Sighing, he pulled her closer, slinging an arm across her shoulder. "I'm afraid it will be a long campaign."

They had reached the lakeside, and Marissa stopped, turning to face the man she very much feared held her heart. "Will you be able to contact me?"

"At least at first. Once we reach Iman—" He shrugged. "—who knows."

Marissa had learned through extreme circumstances how to mask her emotions. This time she didn't even try. She allowed her feelings to show. Callus cupped her cheek with a large, work-roughened hand, tilting her face up to catch the moonlight. Could he trust the love, the longing he saw there? His body burned for her, but he had promised months ago not to push the issue, not to add a physical element to their relationship. He may have leaned toward her, he wasn't sure. "Marissa, I think I'll die if I don't get to kiss you before I leave."

Dimples flirted at the corners of her mouth. "We can't have that, can we?" She closed the distance between them, touching her lips to his, a gentle brushing of flesh. They both waited, terrified that her horrific memories would surface and destroy the tenuous pleasure. When no ghosts assailed her, she leaned in again.

Callus was an engineering genius of cosmic renown, but his body was simply that of a man. The fire her touch ignited raced through his veins, rendering his legendary patience a pile of smoldering ashes. With her head cradled gently in his palm Callus angled her for his carnal reply to her timid advances. Lips firm but full sealed over hers, ravenous for the sweet succulence of her mouth. When his tongue begged entrance, Marissa opened gladly, overwhelmed by the rush of desire. Only once before in her sordid life had she experienced sexual ache— when Callus kissed her on the floor of the gaming room at Simon Says. She had almost convinced herself that earlier kiss was a figment of her imagination. In fact, it was just a prelude to the symphony of longing that was playing in her heart now. Her heart raced, her nipples became acutely aware of the hard-muscled chest they pressed up against, and her thighs clinched against the gathering need. She moaned.

Callus disengaged, stepping back. "I-I'm sorry, Marissa. I shouldn't have rushed you. Please, forgive me."

Dazed, Marissa watched his mouth move, but it was several minutes before her brain registered what he said. "No. Oh, no, Callus. Don't apologize." Tears filled her eyes, accentuating their crystal green color. "Please don't be sorry for the single most wonderful experience of my life."

Now he was the one dazed. She couldn't possibly mean what it sounded like she was saying. "Huh?" A very un-genius like comment.

Raven curls danced when she shook her head. "Don't talk. Just kiss me again."

He didn't need a second invitation. Ravenous for the affection freely offered, Callus devoured her mouth, exploring with tongue, lips and teeth. Never in his life had he known love. Not from a parent, not from a sibling, not from a woman. Though he tried to curb his excitement in deference to her delicate sense of worth, his long-bridled affections overpowered his good intentions. Callus pulled her close, wrapped her securely in his powerful arms, and offered her all that he was.

Marissa responded like she never imagined she could. After the years she had endured as a sex slave on Pagoda, she thought true affection was beyond her damaged soul. She couldn't have been more wrong. Callus' love—the thing she had feared—was the thing she had needed most. His love was magic, healing her from the inside out. Tentatively, she ran a hand across his broad chest. He sucked in air. Tensing, she asked, "Did I do something wrong?"

He laid his hand on top of hers where it rested against him. "No. You could never do anything wrong, not with me. I just don't know how much control I have right now, and your touch is quickly dissolving what little remains." He drew a shaky breath. "I have dreamed of this moment for weeks now. I don't want to ruin it with my clumsy manners."

Marissa leaned her forehead down to rest just beneath his chin. "I, too, have dreamed. And dreaded.

I was afraid I wouldn't be able to respond like a normal woman. I was afraid I'd disappoint you."

"You could never disappoint me." He smoothed her hair with a tender touch. "I want our first time together to be special. Not outside without the comforts you deserve."

"I don't want comforts," she confessed. "I don't want to be reminded of the lavish boudoirs of Pagoda. I want this clean, honest environment—" She swept a hand to indicate their surroundings. "—to witness our first time. I want our joining to be something new and special, nothing like what I endured before."

It made a kind of sense, he supposed. Wow, he had not been expecting this when he left his quarters earlier. He glanced around, searching for a likely spot. Without comment Marissa handed him her shawl. Laughter crinkled his eyes and rumbled from his chest. "You planned this. When I picked you up, you knew you were going to do this, didn't you?"

"Well, I had hoped..."

Spreading the shawl over an outcropping of clover, Callus knelt beside it, holding out a hand to her. Marissa knelt before him. "I'm more nervous than my first time," Callus told her.

"As far as I'm concerned it is the first time...for both of us." Marissa reached out to smooth the fabric over his shoulder. "Tell me what to do."

Emotion clogged Callus' throat. "Whatever you want." His gravelly voice sent shivers down her spine.

Marissa smiled and began to unfasten his shirt.

***

Kevnor stood before the monitor screen awaiting connection. When it finally came, his knees nearly buckled. His Uncle Zedne looked the same as he had eighteen years ago when Kev last saw him. Nodding his head and tapping a closed fist over his heart, Kev greeted the man in the traditional Bauxite manner, "Greetings, Zedne."

Squinting and leaning in toward the monitor, Zedne said, "Klaus?"

Apparently he resembled his dead father. "No, Uncle Zedne. It's Kevnor." Though the Bauxite culture dispensed with titles once a person reached adulthood, Kev slipped back into the role of nephew.

"Kevnor?" Sitting abruptly, Zedne began to smile. "Klaus' son Kevnor?"

Relaxing somewhat, Kev grinned back. "Yeah. It's me, Kevnor."

"I cannot believe it. After all these years...I feared you were dead."

Guilt washed over Kev. He should have communicated with his extended family long ago. "No. I'm well."

Brows drawn together Zedne cut to the heart of the matter. "Obviously not. You haven't felt the need for family in many years, yet now you contact me. What is wrong?"

"Now I remember why you eschewed politics," Kev teased him.

"Never had the stomach for all that pussy-footing around."

"Exactly why I called you instead of anyone else." Taking a fortifying breath Kev forged on, "My wife has been kidnapped and taken to Iman."

"So, you married. That's great news. How many children do you have?" Kev expected an explosion of hatred. The old man surprised him.

"None yet." Pausing for a moment to let that sink in, Kev continued, "So you can imagine my concern. If I can't get to Devona, I'll lose them both."

"You've been away a very long time," Zedne hedged. "Things aren't the same here as when you left."

"What is that supposed to mean?" Kev's heartrate picked up along with the hairs on the back of his neck.

"Jacton is on the throne now." Zedne stood to pace the floor. "And his policies are a lot different than what we old timers are used to." Hands on his hips Zed blurted, "The plain fact is we've stopped all aggressive action toward Iman." There. He'd said it.

"That's wonderful. Perhaps we can negotiate a release for Dev." He tried not to get his hopes up.

"Doubtful."

After a lengthy pause Kev prompted, "Because..."

"The Imani recently acquired their long lost princess. According to Imani legend, this woman will lead them to victory over us, and we will be enslaved. Since her return, those crazy women have become berserk. Their aggression is such that we have pulled back into a defensive mode. Much of our fleet has been damaged or destroyed."

Kev joined his uncle in pacing. "That's impossible. She hasn't been there that long."

Thinking he misunderstood, Zed asked, "What? What did you say, Kev?"

"I said she's only been there a few days at best. How can all this have happened in that short a period of time?"

"No. Your information is mistaken. For six months the princess has been back on Iman."

"Zedne, I don't know where you get your information, but it's faulty. The princess was with me until a couple of weeks ago." Sucking in a fortifying breath, Kev calmly announced, "The Imani princess is my wife."

Zed sat again. "I think you need to repeat that, nephew."

"Devona, my wife, is the Imani princess. She was raised in an orphanage and sent to the military academy I attended as a child. I have known her since before my parents died, and I can assure you she had no idea who or what she was. Anyway, my friends and I were on Pagoda leading a rebellion when she learned of her heritage. By then, we were already mated." Kev scowled. "But it wouldn't have made any difference. I would have mated with her anyway. I love her very much."

"If she wasn't leading the planet's military, who was? Probably that old bitch Nambia." Staring at Kev he asked, "Do you think your mate capable of leading the Imani military?"

Kev snorted. "Oh, yeah. She's very capable. But she won't. From what I've learned about the Imani society, Devona would be the last person to aid them in their attempt to conquer another planet. In fact, she's much more likely to sabotage their efforts."

Zed smiled. "Then we have an ally in the enemy camp. All we have to do is figure a way to get to her."

"Do you think I can depend on Bauxite support?" Kev asked.

"How soon can you get here? I'll begin putting out some feelers. We'll need to approach this from just the right angle." Grinning again he assured Kev, "Yes. I believe you can rely on Bauxite support."

"We'll be leaving in the morning."

"We?" Did Zed's voice have an odd ring to it?

"Yes. I thought I'd mentioned my shipmates would be with me." Kev frowned. "Is that a problem?"

"No," Zed said quickly. "Not at all. I presume you'll stay with me? How many should I tell my housekeeper to prepare for?"

"That's very generous of you. There are only four of us. The others will remain behind to keep the business going."

"Very well. I'll tell her." The ghost of a smile played around the older man's mouth. "I can see my dull life is about to be rejuvenated. Until we meet." The connection ended.

"Until we meet," Kev echoed, though there was no one left to hear the traditional parting. His mind whirring with possibilities, Kev paced his quarters. His uncle had seemed supportive, yet there were things unsaid. And he hadn't liked the gleam in the old man's eye when he realized Kev was bringing the crew along. They would need to keep their guards up and their eyes open once they reached Baux.

Chapter Ten

Nambia's nostrils flared. "Persis." Her tone dripped venom. "If your proclivities run toward young ones, you need to secure your pleasure through proper channels. These boys are of good breeding and are designated house staff."

Sitting back on her heels, Dev glared at the older woman. "Don't be insulting. These children needed comforting. That's all." She rose and patted each boy on the shoulder. "Go back to your stations," she commanded. Returning her gaze to her aunt she continued, "I have decided to keep these two. They will remain near me at all times. Is that understood?"

Eyes narrowing, Nambia replied, "Yes. Of course." She obviously expected more of an explanation from Dev, but she wasn't going to get it.

"Was there something you wanted?" Dev was getting good at affecting an imperious tone. She grinned. Kev would tease her about that.

"Your mother, the queen, has asked to see you." Nambia snorted. "If it wouldn't be too much of an imposition."

Squaring her shoulders, Dev indicated Nambia should precede her. "Not at all. I would like to meet the woman who thought I would be better off in an orphanage than at her side."

"I explained that." Nambia was losing patience. Good. Dev intended to make a lot of the locals lose patience.

"Yeah, yeah. Whatever." Dev's heart lurched when Nambia clinched her jaw and balled her hands into tight fists. This just might work.

Queen Lila was not what Dev had expected. Frail and emaciated, her pale skin blended into the linens. Her eyes, however, were still sharp and missed nothing as they swept from shaved head to leather boots, sizing-up her grown daughter. "So." Lila's voice was as dim as her physical self. "You survived. That's good."

"No thanks to you." Dev was inexplicably angry. She didn't know this woman, and she'd long ago given up thinking about a reunion with her absent mother. "Nice place." Dev glanced around the room, pretending an indifference she didn't feel. She wished her mother were well and strong...so she could beat the hell out of her. How dare the woman give her up to strangers? She would never give her child up to anyone. Unable to stop herself, she rubbed a palm soothingly over her belly.

Slight though it was, Lila caught the movement. "Nambia tells me you are pregnant. Any chance it might be an heir?"

Stepping closer, Dev hissed, "No child of mine, female or male, will stay on this piece of shit planet long enough to be the heir. Do you understand me?"

Nambia inserted her body between them. "I told you not to start anything. My sister doesn't need to be overly excited."

Dev backed up a step. "What's wrong with her anyway?" Hell, Lila could be contagious, and she hadn't even thought about it. And didn't that make her great mother material?

"We have no name for it. She began to waste away several years ago. Now she can barely move and must be tended at all times." Pride laced her voice as she continued, "But her mind is as sharp as ever. She has led the planet from her chamber, through me."

Dev smelled a rat. A big, fat stinky rat. "How convenient for you, auntie."

"Save your sarcasm. I am as devoted to my sister now as I have ever been." Did the old bitch actually feel affection for someone?

"So you say," Dev commented. "Was there a purpose to this little family reunion? I have things to do."

"I wanted to see you," Lila whispered. "To see the daughter I gave birth but never held, never talked with or trained with. I thought we might have some sort of relationship before I die, but I see now I was wrong." Laboriously she turned her head toward the window. "Get her out of here, Nambia."

An ache rose up in Dev, an ache that settled in her chest, hard and hot. "Wait," she said before she could stop herself. "I'm sorry." She took a deep breath. All her life she'd wondered about her mother. Here was a chance to find out some of the answers to questions she'd asked. "May I sit for a while and talk?" Catching her aunt's eye she promised, "I won't upset her."

A slight nod from the queen had Nambia stepping away. "Very well, for a few minutes." Patting her sister's hand she promised, "I'll be just outside."

Dev couldn't believe it. Did they expect she'd spring on the mostly dead woman and finish her off? Geesh. She dragged a chair up beside the bed and parked herself in it. When Nambia closed the door behind her, silence filled the room. For several minutes they just sat there. Finally, Lila asked, "Was your life horrible?"

Dev considered that for a little while, thinking back over her childhood and the friends who had become her family. Thinking of the man who was her husband, lover, and friend. "No. No it wasn't," she admitted. "Well, parts were bad, but I have some wonderful friends and a husband who would do anything for me. He'll come here you know. He'll come and take me home."

The animated eyes of her mother snapped with green fire. "He'll wish he hadn't. Our warriors will capture him. We don't tolerate men who are not properly docile on Iman."

Dev burst out laughing. "From what I've seen you don't have any real men on this rock at all. Think what you want, but my Kevnor will come for me, and you will not be able to subjugate him or the others who will accompany him."

Lila smiled. "We will see." Dev didn't like her attitude.

"Why did you let them take me away?" The question surprised Dev as much as it did her mother.

"For your safety. You were the heir. I couldn't let personal feeling interfere with my duty."

"If you or anyone else on this wretched planet have any feelings at all for anyone, I have yet to see evidence of it. How could grown women allow little boys to be kept from learning and playing? How could any sentient being divide the population by gender and think it was natural or pleasing?" Rising to her feet Dev warmed to the subject. "Women fought for centuries to escape the yolk of men only to turn around and perpetuate the same despicable conditions in reverse here on Iman? And you expect me to embrace my kinship with such barbarity? I think not." She strode to the door.

The quiet words of her mother followed her, "I would like to have held you, at least once."

***

Kevnor sat in the galley staring at the glass of juice sitting in front of him. Orange strands of Ickluk pulp drifted around in the chartreuse liquid. Revolting. But it made him feel closer to Dev. Tossing back the revolting mess he screwed his face up against the sour taste. How in the hell could she drink that stuff? He poured another glass.

"What are you doing in here all by yourself?" Mik's voice preceded him. As he rounded the corner into the small room, he observed, "From the looks of you, you could do with a lot more sleep." He twisted a chair around and straddled it, draping his arms across the back. Leaning closer he squinted at Kev's glass. "What the hell is that?"

"Ickluk juice." Kev swirled the glass, stirring up the pulp. "Nasty shit." He tipped the glass up and drained it.

Mik stared in horrified fascination. "Then why are you drinking it?"

"It makes me feel closer to Dev." It was a pathetic admission, one Kev would not have made to anyone but his best friend. "Lately all she does is drink this stuff and eat Rumarian sour cabbage."

Mik drew his head back as if the very mention might contaminate him. "You aren't eating that gross mess are you?"

Kev grinned. "Even I am not that desperate."

"I'm glad to hear it." Mik nodded. "I don't want to be around you with that stuff tainting either end of you."

"So says the fart king." Callus joined them.

"Hey," Mik protested, "I'm not the worst one around here."

"Yes, you are," both men insisted at once.

Kev eyed the engineer. "You look mighty pleased," he observed.

"I am mighty pleased." His craggy face looked out of place sporting a constant smile.

Mik and Kev looked expectantly. Callus said nothing more. He just sat there smiling.

"Well?" Mik prompted. "Are you going to tell us why you're smiling like a resident of the Thelian lunatic colony?"

"Nope," he replied.

"That's all right." Zoë strolled in to lean against the counter. "I'll tell you."

Callus scowled. "There's nothing to tell."

"Um hum. That's why you and Marissa left to go for a walk over two hours ago and just returned, rumpled and grinning like fools. Not to mention you couldn't keep your hands off one another." She raised a brow and glanced around for effect. "That adds up to only one thing I can think of. How about you, gents?"

Kev stood and leaned across the table, hand extended. "Congratulations, man. About time she fell for all that sweet-talkin' you've been doing."

Callus shook the proffered hand. "I'm not admitting to anything."

"You don't have to." Mik slapped him on the back. "And we wouldn't want you to. We're just glad the two of you have finally reached an understanding. I trust she will no longer try to hide the fact that you're holding her hand with the folds of her skirt?"

"Who knows?" Callus' smile gave way to a frown. "I can never figure that woman out."

"Welcome to my world." Kev poured another glass of juice.

"Is that Ickluk juice?" Zoë asked. "Can I have some?" She reached into the cabinet for a glass.

Shuddering, Kev passed the one he'd just poured. "Here. Be my guest. I don't think I can stomach another drop of this stuff."

Zoë shrugged. "Suit yourself. I think it's delicious."

All three men watched, open-mouthed, as she drained the glass, then grimaced when she licked her lips. "What?" she asked.

"It must be a female thing." Mik nodded sagely.

Zoë bristled. "What's that supposed to mean?"

"Settle down, little girl," Callus teased her. "We just think the stuff is foul, but you and Dev both think it's good."

"I think it's more a question of good taste rather than gender," she huffed.

"Would somebody explain to me why we're all sitting around here instead of getting some shut-eye?" Callus asked. "Aren't we leaving in about four hours?"

"Yeah." Mik stood. "You're right. Let's all turn in."

"I'll be along in a little while," Kev promised.

"Nope." Zoë linked her arm through his and drew him to his feet. "You are coming with us. If we leave you here, you'll be right in that chair when we board in the morning."

A haunted look crossed the big man's face. "I can't sleep. Every time I lie down and close my eyes, I see Dev." He looked to his shipmates for support. "Just let me sit here."

Tenderness softened Zoë's eyes, and she patted Kev's arm consolingly. "I know, sweetie. But if you're going to be any good negotiating with your relatives, you need to be sharp, and that means you need more than four hours of sleep out of ninety-six."

Knowing she was right, Kev allowed her to steer him toward his cabin. Sleeping on the ship did offer him a better chance of actually falling asleep than their bed in the compound. He fell face first onto the bunk. Thirty seconds later, he was asleep. Three minutes after that, the nightmares began. By daybreak Kev dragged his weary body to the shower in an attempt to revive his exhausted brain. When the rest of the crew boarded, he was already on the bridge, monitoring the computer for any unusual activity.

"Permission to come aboard," Mik called.

Kev shot him a bloodshot glare before turning back to his computer.

"I see you slept well. Have you eaten?" Zoë asked.

"No. I'm not hungry," Kev told her. "Mik, come look at this." Mik leaned over Kev's shoulder so he could see the monitor. "This article is from the most recent edition of Intergalactic Times."

"Hey, that's Umland," Mik observed.

"Yep. Read on. It gets better." Kev slid over in his chair so Mik could see better.

Mik's scowl deepened as he read. "Son of a bitch."

"What?" Zoë wormed her way between them. Moments later she echoed Mik. "Son of a bitch."

"There's an echo in here," Callus quipped, then asked, "What's got your panties in a wad, little girl?"

"That subhuman freak, Umland, has been lauded for his humanitarian efforts."

Callus raised his brows in disbelief. "Son of a bitch."

"That's what I said," Zoë reminded him.

"Let me look at that." The powerfully built engineer wedged his shoulders between his shipmates and squinted at the screen. "*Through the humanitarian efforts of entrepreneur Draxor Umland*", he read, " *a temporary truce between longtime enemies Baux and Iman has gone into effect*...you've got to be kidding. What moron would call that flesh peddler a humanitarian?"

"There's more." Kev switched screens pulling up a holographic news clip. The four of them stood mesmerized while the image of an Imani warrior gave an impassioned speech thanking Umland for returning their long lost princess.

"Draco." Mik ran his fingers through his hair. "That bastard has got to be eliminated."

"He's hard enough to stop as a criminal. If he gains public support, there'll be no stopping him." Zoë's voice was hoarse with emotion.

Kev spun in his seat. "The bounty on each of us has risen yet again, even though he already has Dev. It seems obvious he won't rest till all of us are out of the picture." He looked at his friends and knew what they were thinking. Hell, he thought the same thing himself, but he couldn't seem to bring himself to say it.

"Kev," Callus said quietly, "you know what we have to do. We have to get Umland. Now."

His face pallid beneath four days growth of beard, Kev nodded. "I know. There's no other way. But I can't leave Dev alone on Iman any longer than I have to."

"You're in charge," Mik solemnly told him. "We'll do whatever you say." Callus and Zoë nodded.

The total support of his comrades gave him strength. Sucking in a deep breath he released it slowly through his nose. "Here's what we're gonna do." He paced the bridge. "You're going to drop me on Baux; then you're going to Maltoran and blow that fucker back to hell where he came from."

"I'll be in my quarters," Callus said, "studying up on plasma domes."

Zoë moved over to the navigation post and activated several stellar maps. "With a little creative plotting," she mused, "I can shave off several days of travel time."

"Guess that leaves me weapons." Mik grinned. "I'll just go inventory our resources."

Kev glanced around. Looks like liftoff was up to him. Seated in the pilot's chair, he fired up the engines and turned to face his navigator. "Which way?" he asked.

Grinning, she entered the coordinates. "Second star to the left and straight on till morning," she quoted one of the books in Shesshie's ancient children's literature collection. She thought Peter Pan would have loved to travel with this crew.

Chapter Eleven

Devona stretched and reached for Kevnor. When she felt only cool empty space, her eyes flew open. Then she remembered. She was on Iman, and Kev was who knew where. Sitting up she glanced around the strange bedchamber. She'd never been anywhere more luxurious or less appealing. Groaning, she rose to go to the bathroom—for the third time—and nearly stepped on You. The poor little fellow was curled up on a woven mat beside her bed. Gingerly she stepped over him and took care of her needs. When she returned, she spotted Tim lying just inside the threshold to her chamber. Anger, her usual frame of mind these days, simmered in her veins. The boys were subjected to child abuse, pure and simple. If she weren't afraid of hurting her baby, she'd lift them into her bed. She consoled herself by removing two pillows from her bed and placing them beneath the boys' heads.

Her balcony offered a spectacular view of the city and the lofty peaks of distant mountains. Opening the glass door she stepped out into the crisp night and studied the constellations, wondering if Kev was in the same sector. Closing her eyes, she called up his image: brooding dark eyes, thick black hair and chiseled features softened by full sensual lips. She could almost feel his capable hands sweeping surely over her, warming her blood and causing her passion to rise. She longed for the comfort of his strong, muscled body and the joy of his company. She could barely remember when he wasn't part of her life and didn't want to contemplate a future without him. She had to find a way to aid his rescue efforts.

As she turned to go back inside, she caught a glimpse of something out of the corner of her eye. Stepping to the rail, she leaned over watching the compact sleek ship that landed on a small, personal pad at the edge of the palace grounds. Moments later a woman dressed in warrior garb emerged, glanced about furtively and motioned for someone inside to follow. Swathed in a hooded cape the figure kept close to the warrior. Together they disappeared into the south wing, her mother's wing. Perfect brows drawn in contemplation, Dev stepped back inside and drew the door closed silently behind her. Now there was something worth investigating.

As she neared the bed, moonlight revealed You sitting silently in the dark. "What's the matter?" she asked, ruffling his hair.

"Nothing, ma'am." His voice trembled slightly.

Dev perched on the edge of the bed and patted a place beside her. "Come sit here and tell me about it. Did you have a bad dream?"

Barely touching the edge of the thick mattress, You nodded.

Draping an arm over his thin shoulders she urged him to sit comfortably. "Everyone has bad dreams," she assured. "Sometimes it helps to tell someone."

"I-I can't." His voice was barely audible.

Thinking he was shy she prodded, "Why not?"

"When I was little and first came into service, I had a lot of bad dreams. I missed my father." As though it was a deep, shameful admission he added, "I cried."

Unsure what to say Dev simply made a sympathetic noise and the lad continued, "I got in a lot of trouble. The housekeeper told me if I ever bothered anyone with my silliness again he'd have my tongue removed." A shudder traveled through him. "And I believed him."

The acid burn of anger boiled up in her throat. "Surely he was just trying to frighten you."

You shook his head vigorously. "No. Tamun, the scullery boy, had no tongue." Huge tears streamed silently.

Closing her eyes against the sight of his terrified young face Dev drew the child into her arms and hugged him. "To the extent of my power I will protect you and Tim. I promise." Smoothing his hair back she kissed his forehead. "Now tell me about your dream."

Wiping his nose on the back of his hand, You whimpered, "It was a big scary man wearing a hood. I thought he was going to kill me. He had a sword."

The coincidence was too much. "Tell me, You, have you ever seen such a man?"

"Once, when I attended the queen's sister."

"My aunt, Nambia?" she asked.

"Yes." The boy obviously knew more. She'd have to be careful to ask the right questions if she expected information.

"Did he threaten you?"

The boy nodded. "I woke up because I had to go to the bathroom. I was very quiet, but I disturbed them, and the man jumped out of bed and threw on his cape, swearing at me and waving his big sword around. He said if I breathed a word of his presence he'd cut me into little, tiny pieces and feed me to the Prima

Lizards." Grasping Dev's hand, You confided, "Prima Lizards love to eat meat."

Dev was at a loss. She didn't know how to comfort a child. She couldn't very well reassure him when she was so unsure of herself. "Tell you what," she said after a while, "why don't you climb up here and sleep with me? That way if you have another bad dream you can wake me up and we'll talk about it."

Shocked, You backed away from her. "No." His voice was loud in the cavernous room. Tim shifted in his sleep. Softer, he pleaded, "Please, ma'am. I'm too young." His bottom lip was trembling again.

Dumbfounded, Dev jumped to her feet. "Oh, honey, I didn't mean...that is I don't want...I would never..." She sucked in a deep breath. "You, I don't want to do anything. I just thought we could sleep beside each other because we're both a little scared. Sometimes it's nice just to have the company of another person beside you." Her palm rested protectively over her abdomen. She had to get the hell out of this place before her baby was born. "I have a husband, a grown man. I love him very much. We are going to have a baby." She smiled tentatively. "Maybe it will be a wonderful little boy, just like you and Tim."

"You would want a boy?" Incredulity tinged his voice.

"Of course. In fact, I'd rather have a boy. I know a lot more about boy stuff than girl stuff. When I was a child, I grew up in an orphanage. Do you know what that is?"

"No," he admitted.

"It's kind of like a school, only you live there all the time. It's a place for kids with no family. Anyway, I always liked playing boy games and before long most of my friends were boys. Then, I went away to military school to learn all about weapons. Most of the cadets were boys. When I graduated, my friends and I served in the Space Corps for a few years, and then we hired out as mercenaries—paid soldiers." She shrugged. "What I'm trying to say is that I never played with girl things. I wouldn't know how to play with dolls or teach her how to fix her hair. I'm just not very good at girl things."

More at ease, You eased a little closer. "Boys get to do those things at an orphanage?"

"Well, sure."

A wistful look crossed his face. "I want to go to an orphanage."

Tears welled up in her eyes. She blinked them back. She would not cry in front of this brave child. "You wouldn't like an orphanage. What you need is a family."

"I have a father. He lives with his patron not far from here. I got to stay with him till I was five." He smiled. "It was wonderful, getting to see him every day."

Patron? "Ah, is his *patron* your mother?"

"Oh, no. If she were my mother, I would have more enjoyable duties." Realizing what he'd just said he rushed to assure Dev, "Not that I don't love serving you, ma'am."

"Hey, it's okay with me if you don't like being a servant. I wouldn't like it, either. Now tell me about your mother."

"She is a merchant. My father met her when he went to the market to buy food for the house." The

~109~

ghost of a smile tipped his lips. "My father said he loved my mother."

"That's a good thing. Babies should always have parents that love each other."

"Maybe, but the Patron was furious. My father was her concubine. She said no other woman was allowed to touch her property." His head fell forward. "As soon as I was born, the Patron had her executed. I never even saw her."

"Draco! I can't believe this place." Jumping up once again Dev paced back and forth. "This place is as bad as Pagoda." She looked around the room as if searching for an exit. "We've got to get out of here."

"Ma'am, please," You begged. "Don't do it. Don't try to leave." In desperation he flung his arms around her waist and hugged her. "I don't want them to hurt you."

Tim cried softly from his pallet.

Oh, hell. She held out one arm to the smaller boy. "Come her, Tim." He flew into her arms, and the three of them stood there, hugging and crying. Dev had never felt so helpless in her life. She was always in control. She could always fight herself out of any situation. But this—caring for young ones—was awful. She couldn't fight without worrying about her unborn child, and she couldn't escape without bringing the boys with her. She'd have to resort to thinking herself out of this predicament, something much better suited to Kevnor.

"Don't worry, boys, we'll get out of here somehow." Or many would die when she made the attempt. That she vowed.

***

"What is the meaning of this?" The strident screeching of her aunt, Nambia, awoke Dev from a hard won slumber. You and Tim sat up beside her, rubbing their eyes with closed fists. "I'll have you whipped," she threatened. "You are servants, not guests in the palace." She yanked the covers back. The look on her face was formidable.

"Halt!" Dev held her palm out to stop her aunt's rampage. "You will not touch these boys." Rolling to the floor she confronted the older woman. "They are my servants, not yours." Standing toe-to-toe with the harridan, Dev shouted, "I and only I will instruct them. Do I make myself clear?" She raised a brow imperiously. Nambia actually stepped back, but Dev was just warming up to her subject. "When I arrived, I was told I was the heir. Don't you think it's about time someone clued me in on how things run around here? I've been more a prisoner than a welcomed leader."

"Of course. I'll see to it immediately." Nambia turned to go.

"And I want a tour of this place, the entire palace as well as the grounds. I want to observe the warrior's training and meet with whoever maintains the palace records. I want an accounting of any and all expenditures for the last ten years." She looked regally down her nose. "I want a computer with access to the intergalactic web. I want an appointment with the family physician, the top political leaders and my mother. And I want Rumarian sour cabbage and Ickluk juice." She made a dismissive gesture with her hand. "Now."

Nambia spun on her heel and left the room. Dev glanced over at the two boys, and the three of them dissolved into laughter. After the night they'd had, they deserved a little levity.

Chapter Twelve

Zedne Gaaus bore a strong resemblance to his brother's son. The crew of the Freebird would have easily picked him out of the crowd. "He sure can't deny you," Mik commented as they waited at the bottom of the shuttle's ramp.

Zoë looked back and forth between the two men. "Nope. The nut didn't fall far from that tree."

"Let's just hope their characters are as similar as their faces." Callus cut to the heart of the matter.

Kevnor remained silent as he watched his uncle approach. The reunion was bittersweet. When Zedne was mere feet away, Kev touched a clinched fist to his chest and bowed his head in the traditional greeting.

Zedne repeated the gesture, then reached out to grab his nephew in a bear hug. "I thought I would never see you again." There was a catch in the man's voice. He was either genuinely touched, or a consummate actor.

"I wish it were under more pleasant circumstances," Kev replied. Turning, he indicated his friends. "Uncle, may I introduce Zoë Jarnus, Miklus Armstrong, and Callus Vukovik. Everyone, this is my uncle, Zedne."

Zedne stared at Zoë. "This little woman is a warrior?" he asked.

Mik groaned, Kev rolled his eyes, and Callus stepped back out of harm's way. "Excuse me." She smiled sweetly, stepping into the older man's personal space. "I don't think I heard you right."

Splaying his hands Zedne smiled his most condescending smile. "A beautiful little thing like you should be home, cherished by her husband and family, not out gallivanting through the stars with a bunch of ruffians."

"Can I hurt him, Kev, just a little?" she asked.

Before things got out of hand Mik stepped forward. "I know you didn't intend to insult, sir, but our society is quite different from yours. Among our crew, the women are equal. They can accomplish any and all tasks the men can. Besides, Zoë is Gaithran. We'd be lost without her, literally."

Zedne's brows rose almost to his hairline. "Gaithran? I've heard much about their navigational talents." Bending low toward Zoë he apologized, "I am sorry if in my ignorance I offended you. Here on Baux the women lead a much more secure life—their choice, I assure you."

Zoë shrugged. "Sounds like captivity to me, but whatever." She wouldn't push the issue now, but once Dev was rescued she planned to spend a little time with the women of Baux, explaining free will.

"I have arranged an audience for you with some of the most influential leaders." Zedne turned back to his nephew.

"Excellent. Will it require the presence of the entire crew, or can I handle it alone?"

"To tell the truth," Zedne admitted, "things will probably go better if only you attend. You know how clannish our people are."

"Good." Kev expelled a pent-up breath. "Mik and the others will be leaving as soon as they can refuel.

They have some related business to take care of before rejoining us in a few days."

Mik knew a cue when he heard one. He stepped forward, extending his arm in the way of warriors. Zedne clasped his forearm as he spoke, "We will maintain communication with Kevnor during our mission. Hopefully by the time we return you will have the logistics of the rescue planned. We offer our ship and our services in whatever capacity they are needed."

"Very well. I will arrange for your refueling immediately." As they walked, Zedne pointed out their surroundings. "This is the main terminal for official traffic. There is a passenger station just over that ridge. The large round building is our main legislative facility, and the mansion beside it is where our leader resides." Smiling he added, "The rest of us live much more modestly."

"Then you must all live a long way from town." Callus' droll comment brought quickly suppressed smiles to the faces of his friends. There wasn't one building in sight that didn't look like premium digs to them. Until they'd purchased the business on Bright's Planet none of them had a home other than their ship.

Zedne shrugged. "I suppose all things are relative. We are justifiably proud of our planet and our civilization.

Zoë smirked. She guessed that was just about the slickest way she'd ever been put in her place. But it didn't matter a bit. She was still set on having a little soiree with the local ladies.

Signaling over a young man, Zedne explained the need for haste in refueling the Freebird. Clad in a one-piece jumpsuit that made him look like an escapee from an interstellar dance troupe, the kid sashayed past the group, signaling that they should follow. Mik raised a brow at Callus, one side of his mouth curling into a half-smile. "I sure wish I had an ass like that," Zoë complained.

Callus huffed. "Your ass is just fine, little girl, and a sight more appealing."

"To you maybe. But I'll bet Charles wishes he'd come with us instead of staying on Rekjavik."

A slight blush tinted Callus' rough cheeks. "You may be right. Charles always did have an eye for the guys."

Zoë burst out laughing. "I think he had a bit more than an eye for them."

Clearly uncomfortable with the turn of conversation, Callus simply harrumphed and changed the subject. "I'm glad we got the Freebird back. I didn't relish leaving Doc and the rest without a ship. With all the on again, off again bounty stuff floating around, it made me nervous. Never know when you'll need to make a quick get away."

"Especially with Tessa," Zoë concurred.

"I miss her already," Callus said wistfully. Zoë was pretty sure he wasn't talking about the baby.

***

Zedne ushered Kevnor into the main conference room of the legislative building. "The others will be here within the hour. I thought we'd take a few minutes to go over our strategy before they arrive."

Kev raised a brow. "Strategy?"

"Of course. Politics is all about playing the game. You aren't that naïve, nephew."

"So, I need to know whose butt to kiss, is that it?" He really hated kowtowing.

Laughter rumbled from the older man's chest. "You wouldn't have been any better ruling than I would. Aren't we lucky succession fell in a different direction?"

Flopping down in a burgundy leather chair Kev agreed, "Yes. Now tell me what I need to know. Every minute we have to tippy toe is one minute longer my wife and child spend in captivity."

Joining Kev at the table, Zedne produced a folder, which he slid in front of his brother's son. "Here is information on each of the legislators we'll be meeting with. Look over the information just to give you an overview."

Kev peered down at the picture of the first man. "Alban, aggressively pushing for reform. He is the leader of a group that opposes the antiquated laws governing women. Father to six girls, he has refused to command any of them to wed outside their wishes." Kev looked up at his uncle. "This is a joke, right? Women here are sent into arranged marriages?" He stood and paced away from the table. "This place is barbaric. How could you deceive me into believing I could get backing for my quest?"

Zedne raised a hand to hold back Kev's tirade. "Keep reading. You need to know this stuff. I know it seems bad, but we aren't all that dreadful. And the feud with Iman has left many families with casualties. In the end, they will see it your way."

Kev began again. "Dugan, youngest of the leaders, keeps his own council. No one is sure of where he stands, but he always listens with an open mind.

Josept is the oldest of the group, a strict traditionalist who wants to maintain the status quo at any cost." Kev glanced up. "Great. That's encouraging."

Shaking his head, Kev continued, "Next up is Nemus. He votes conservatively but speaks out for reform." Kev mumbled, "So all we have to do is convince him to vote the way he thinks."

Zedne merely grunted so Kev continued, "Then there's Knust, a rabid liberal. He'll back pretty much anything that bucks the doctrines of the current regime." Kev grinned. "I like him already."

"Hurry," Zedne cautioned. "We have little time."

"Only one more. Reed. Now he's the guy to worry about. An eloquent spokesman, Reed is owned by the king one hundred percent." Kev frowned at his uncle. "So does that mean my cousin will be adamantly opposed to my mission? Couldn't I have an audience with him to try and resolve this from the top, so to speak?"

Zed sighed. "He has never forgiven you for being better when you were children. You were always faster, smarter, more adventurous. I'm afraid the old jealousies will make it nearly impossible to get his approval without the backing of the senate."

Closing the dossier with a snap, Kev stood and stretched. "Well, I'd better hit the head. This looks to be a long evening."

Long minutes after Kev exited the room, Zed continued to frown. "Hit the head?" His nephew had certainly lost the elegant manners his mother had spent most of her time trying to teach him.

Kev slipped into the room just ahead of the politicians, who arrived en masse. He didn't miss the unvoiced message. They might be opponents on the senate floor, but they were united as they faced the prodigal heir. Standing beside his uncle, Kev waited until everyone was in the room before offering the standard Baux salute. The salute was not returned. *Okay, so this was not going to be easy.*

Zedne drew breath to speak, but Kevnor forestalled him with a slight shake of his head. "Many of you knew my father," he began, "and respected him. As the last of his line I call on the loyalty you bore him. I claim the Bantuu."

A collective gasp filled in the silence following Kev's statement. Nervous glances were exchanged before Josept stepped forward to reply, "It is within your right, young Gaaus. And as a son of the realm you can expect the Bantuu to be honored. But what of your allegiance to Baux? You left us years ago and were raised up in the ways of outsiders. Would you bring their ways home to Baux?"

"Kevnor," Zedne whispered through gritted teeth, "do you think this wise?"

Ignoring his uncle, Kev answered Josept, "In truth, sir, I have no desire to return to Baux, but I will always be her son, and I will always return if asked, to serve in any capacity the senate requires of me. Raised in the outer worlds, my manners and lifestyle are not longer wholly Bauxite, yet my blood runs pure. Where else should I turn in my time of need but to the land of my birth, the people who share the blood bond?"

Shaken, the men scrambled to take a seat around the conference table. Young Dugan leaned over to whisper, "I have never heard of anyone invoking the Bantuu. Can he do that?"

Aloud, Nemus answered, "He can, indeed, invoke the ancient bond of blood. He can demand of his fellow Bauxites aide in this quest to retrieve his mate and unborn child." The man smiled slightly.

Zedne, too, sought a chair, flabbergasted by Kevnor's temerity. Kev raised the dossier he'd been provided over his head. "I was given these documents chronicling your political histories. As I reviewed the contents I realized that each of you is a patriot, though you might support different doctrines. You are all men who love Baux and strive in your own way to see to her prosperity and the preservation of her people. I must believe—" He slammed the folder down on the table. "—that any one of you, regardless of political intrigues, would do the same should your mate and children be threatened." One by one, Kev stared each man in the eyes.

Alban stood. "Son of the House of Gaaus, should anyone dare to take my wife or children I would not hesitate to use any means available to see to their safe return. You have my full support."

"What of the peace talks between Baux and Iman? This could throw us back into war," Reed complained.

Knust gained his feet. "The Imani have stolen the mate of one of our own. If we allow this, what is to prevent them from committing other atrocities at our expense?"

"I do not often agree with you, Knust," Josept said, "but in this I do. The mate of young Gaaus must be returned to her rightful place."

Dugan threw up his hands, letting them fall back to slap against his thighs. "I came to this meeting expecting fireworks. Surely this is the first time all of you have agreed on anything."

Zedne grinned. "Of a certainty." Perhaps his nephew had some of his grandfather's leadership abilities after all.

Chapter Thirteen

"What do you think?" Mik asked Callus as the engineer poured over the data he'd gathered on plasma domes.

Without looking up, he replied, "I think there's nothing built by man that I can't figure out...if left alone long enough."

"Come on, Mik." Zoë steered the captain away from Callus' workstation. "When the King of Tact is in one of those moods, it's best to leave him alone. Let's go see if we can reach anyone at the Nest."

That got Callus' attention. "Let me know if Marissa is well."

"Oh, no." Zoë held up her hand. "Don't bother trying to talk to us now. You've already hurt our feelings."

Callus just snorted and leaned back over his charts. "Tell her I love her."

Reaching over, Zoë closed Miklus' mouth with a finger under his chin. "We tried to tell you how it was between them."

Shaking his head, Mik laughed out loud. "Callus for a brother-in-law? Yeah, I guess I could live with that."

Mik slid into the seat at the communications station before Zoë could. "What time is it there now?" he asked. "Do you think they're asleep?"

Men could be so dense. "I think they'll want to talk to us no matter what time it is."

"Maybe Tessa will be up and I can talk to her, too." Mik's fingers flew over the panel. In no time Jim Darner's face appeared. "Doc. How's everyone?"

Jim squinted at the monitor with bloodshot eyes. "Asleep," he grumbled.

"Good to see you, too." Mik nudged Zoë with his shoulder. "Did you ever see a sorrier looking face in your life?"

"Not often," she agreed, leaning close so her face would appear on the screen.

"It's about time you lot checked in. The girls have all been worried sick." Jim failed to mention that he had, too.

"We're on schedule so far," Mik assured him. "Kev's on Baux, and the rest of us are on the way to pay an unexpected visit to an old friend."

"Be sure to give him my regards, too," Jim groused. "The son of a bitch."

"I don't suppose any of the girls are awake?" Mik asked.

"Hell no." Jim scratched his head. "But they'll have my hide if I don't wake them. Hold on..." His grizzled face disappeared.

In no time at all, two angelic faces, both sporting shocking green eyes and tousled black hair, replaced it. "Mik," Shesshie said at the same time Marissa said, "Where's Callus?"

"Don't mind me." Zoë laughed. "I'm certainly not important."

"Zoë," they chimed.

"Yeah, yeah, I know how it is," she teased. "I just don't have the appeal of tight abs and broad chests. Hang on, Marissa. I'll go get Callus."

"Thank you." Marissa blushed.

"How's Tessa?" Mik wanted to know.

"She misses her daddy." Shesshie's voice grew husky, "So does her mother."

Mik placed his palm against the screen. "I miss you, too." Shesshie put her hand on her monitor as if they were touching, palm to palm. "How are you feeling?"

"Fine. Not too much morning sickness." Her hand went to her belly. "I wish you were home."

"I want that, too, honey, but..."

Shesshie straightened up. "I know. I didn't mean I want you to ignore your obligations. I just wish it were over. Hurry up and kick ass."

Before Mik could reply Callus shoved him out of the way, his shorter but stockier frame taking up all the room. "Marissa? Are you there?"

Shesshie reached over and pulled her sister in close to her. "Here she is."

"I'm here, Callus," Marissa said unnecessarily. "Are you okay? Have you been eating properly?"

Mik and Zoë exchanged a glance grinning like fools.

"I'm fine. Don't you worry about me. I'll be home in no time. It's you I'm concerned about. Don't go walking at night without me. There's all kinds of strange animal life on Bright's Planet."

"I wouldn't want to walk without you, Callus..."

Zoë stuck a finger in her mouth as if she were trying to make herself vomit. Mik rolled his eyes in commiseration.

"...but when you return, I want to go back to that beautiful spot we visited just before you left."

Now Callus was blushing. It was a strange sight to see his craggy face tinted red. Then he smiled, transforming his face, and Shesshie and Zoë got a glimpse of what Marissa saw each time she looked at the stalwart engineer. He was a diamond in the rough.

"I know I'm just the captain here, but do you think I might get a few minutes to speak to my wife?" Mik couldn't keep from teasing his friend. It was about time the man found a woman who appreciated him.

Callus harrumphed. "You've already done your courting. You don't need to talk."

Everyone laughed. "Guess he told you," Zoë snickered.

"I've just about solved the mystery of the plasma dome," Callus confided to Marissa. "Don't worry, we'll be finished before you know it."

"News to me," Mik groused. "He won't tell me anything."

Shesshie laughed. "Just because you think you're a big shot doesn't mean the rest of us are impressed."

"Wait till I get home, wife. I'll show you big shot."

"Promises, promises." The images wavered. "Looks like we're breaking up. I love you, Mik. Hurry home to us."

"Me, too," he replied.

"I'll be waiting," Marissa told Callus. "Just make sure you keep yourself safe."

"Don't worry. You'll be seeing my ugly mug in no time."

Marissa looked scandalized. "You're not ugly," she insisted.

"Tell Doc and Eb I said to take good care of you all," Mik told them.

"We will."

"Don't use up all that Undaran milk bath you two," Zoë threatened, "or I might have to hurt you. I've been dreaming of a nice soak in a hot tub of that stuff."

The sisters laughed. "Don't worry, we'll save you some," Shesshie promised.

The connection ended leaving everyone homesick.

Shoulders hunched, Callus shuffled off toward his workstation. Zoë watched him go, aching for him. If she could have chosen a brother for herself, Callus would have been it. She prayed his relationship with Marissa wouldn't end up hurting him. He appeared tough, but inside he was just as fragile as the rest of them, seeking the love he'd never experienced when he was young. Glancing back at Miklus, she sighed. He was just as forlorn looking as Callus. A girl could only take so much depression. "I'm going to catch a few winks. If anything happens, call me."

"Sure thing." Mik didn't even glance her way.

***

Dev licked her lips, not wanting to waste a single drop of the Ickluk juice. How could she have gone for years without realizing how utterly divine the stuff was? You and Tim sat watched her, identical expressions on their faces. If the wrinkled noses and pursed lips were any indication, they hadn't yet developed a taste for the stuff. "Drink up, boys. It's good for you."

Leaning over to whisper to his older companion Tim whispered, "Do we have to?"

Bravely, You answered, "Dev likes it. Maybe we'll like it better if we drink more of it." Holding his nose he gulped down a swallow, his face turning an unbecoming shade of green.

Unable to hold in the laughter, Dev chuckled at their antics. "Never mind." She reached over and took their glasses. "I'll drink it for you. Perhaps you'd prefer something else to drink."

Their relief was palpable. Dev giggled. "I guess you have to be a little older to appreciate it."

"I don't think so." You's face was quite serious. "I heard Nambia say it was the nastiest stuff she'd ever tasted, and she's real old."

Dev nearly spewed her mouthful of juice across the table. The kids were a riot. She couldn't wait until hers was born. A change of topic was in order. "So, how'd it go at the practice session yesterday?"

You ducked his head. "Fine."

Frowning, Dev looked over at the younger boy. "What have you got to say about it, Tim?"

Looking to his buddy for direction he shrugged. "Okay."

Remembering their excitement about learning to fight, this was not the reaction she expected. "You don't sound very enthusiastic."

Jerking his head up You insisted, "Really. It was fine." Tim nodded.

Pushing her chair back from the table Dev motioned for them to follow. "Come on over to the mat and show me what you learned then."

Eyes round with apprehension, the boys glanced at one another. Slowly they rose and followed her to the mats she'd had installed in a corner of the massive room. For several minutes they stood there staring at each other. Finally You said, "We didn't learn anything, ma'am."

Hands on her hips and a scowl on her face Dev asked, "Why not?"

Inching closer to each other they stood silently, staring at the floor.

"Answer me," she snapped.

The boys jumped like she'd shot them. Dev was instantly contrite. "I'm not mad at you boys," she assured them. "I'm just pissed that my orders weren't followed. Now tell me what happened."

"None of the girls would talk to us," Tim blurted.

"They said we were only boys and they didn't have to talk to us if they didn't want to," You added. "Plus the teachers pretended we weren't there. We felt bad."

Closing the gap between them Dev sank down to her knees and put her arms around the boys. "Why didn't you tell me?" she asked quietly.

"We didn't want you to be disappointed in us."

"I could never be disappointed in you. Even if you don't want to fight I won't be disappointed. Everyone is different, and no one should be forced to be something they aren't."

"But we want to fight," Tim hurried to assure her. "They just won't fight us back."

Sitting back on her heels, Dev winked at the boys. "Okay, so here's what we're going to do. I'm going to train you, and when you go to the arena, you can spar with each other. I guarantee you when they see the moves I teach you, they'll be lined up to pair up against you on the mat."

Tim grinned. You shook his head. "No. They won't. We'll still be boys, and they still won't want anything to do with us."

Dev considered how the boys must feel, rejected since birth by everyone female they'd ever come into contact with. She had to turn that around, or they'd never fit into her world, and she was determined to take them with her when she left. "Okay, maybe we're taking this a little too fast. The first thing we'll do is help you to feel more confident. You, every time anyone talks to you, your name makes them think you aren't important, and you are. You're a wonderful boy. I propose we give you a new name, one close to your other name so it won't be too hard to get used to. How about the name Ewen? It's a great name, strong and beautiful. What do you think?"

"Ewen," Tim tried it out. "I like it." He nudged his friend, smiling.

The older boy frowned in concentration. "Ewen." Standing a little straighter he tried it out again, "Ewen. Yeah, I like it."

"Great." Dev ruffled his hair. "Next on the list is reading and writing. I'll have some books and paper and pens brought in right away. You're both bright boys. You'll be reading in no time. And we need to think about your clothes, too. What you're wearing brands you as servants. You two need some new clothes. I'll summon someone." Dev turned toward the door, but a tug on her arm stalled her.

"Ma'am, if you want something, we will get it for you. It's our job." Ewen's earnest face brought tears to her eyes.

What a horrible mess her life was. If anyone had told her even a month ago she'd want nothing more than to go home with two adopted little boys and her husband to await the birth of her child, she probably would have decked them. At the very least she'd have laughed. Now the scenario sounded like heaven. *Kevnor, where the hell are you?*

***

Kev paced the confines of the conference room. The panel of senators had withdrawn to discuss what form the aide they were willing to offer might take. Here was one problem he hadn't even considered. In his arrogance he'd assumed they'd just open up the royal fleet and he'd sweep down on Imani and take his woman back. Slamming a fist into the wall he split his knuckles and dented the plastifoam. "Draco!"

Councilman Dugan stepped into the room just as Kev was venting against the wall. "Have I come at a bad time?" The droll comment took Kev by surprise. Somehow he'd pegged the guy as one of those people without a sense of humor.

"Sorry," Kev mumbled. "I'll have it fixed."

Grinning, Dugan assured him, "Not on my account. I've punched a few walls in my day, too."

Kev eyed the other man skeptically.

"What? You don't think politicians have tempers?" Flipping a chair around to straddle it, Dugan continued, "I spent several years in the military before I was injured. Politics is my second choice in employment."

Finally, someone he could relate to. Or the man could be a plant trying to glean information. "Are you married?" Kev asked. That, at least, was safe territory.

"I was." Dugan frowned. "She took off with a merchant who came here to try and secure a contract with Baux for off world products."

What did you say to that? "Damn. I'm sorry, man."

Dugan shrugged. "I'm over it now. At least she left our son. If she'd taken him, I would never have rested till I got him back."

"Then you understand my determination." Kev began to pace again. "And my wife and I are very much in love. We've known each other since we were children. We attended the same military school. After that we went into the service together. When Miklus Armstrong came up with the idea of setting ourselves up in business, we jumped at the chance. We operated as mercenaries for several years. By the time we purchased the Freebird we were pretty well established and damn good at what we did. But Uldara changed all that."

"Uldara? Wasn't that the planet that was practically decimated by civil war?"

Kev's eyes clouded with memories of the bloody battles they'd encountered during that revolt. "Yes."

"I can imagine something like that would change a person." Dugan sounded sincere.

"It wasn't that, at least not the way you think." Kev grinned. "Our captain, Mik, found a newborn on the battlefield. All of us were orphans. We unanimously decided to get out of the business of war and do something less dangerous." Now he was chuckling. "Life's funny. We ended up leading a revolt on Pagoda instead of placidly shipping goods from place to place."

"You were in on that takeover at Pagoda?"

"We didn't plan to be, but the bastards kidnapped Tessa—she's Mik's baby." Kev met the other man's eyes. "No one takes what is ours. We still operate as a team."

Dugan glanced around the room. "You seem to be alone at the moment."

"By choice." The amiable Kevnor was gone, replaced by a dangerous warrior. "My friends are on a mission but will join me here in a few days." His black eyes had hardened to obsidian.

"And how will they play into your scheme? You called this fellow Miklus captain."

"This is my mission. My friends will follow my lead." The hair raised on the back of Kev's neck. "Why don't you just say what you mean, Dugan?"

Dugan held up a hand to forestall an onslaught. "Don't get your feathers ruffled. I need to know where everyone stands in this scenario. If I'm going to back your proposal, I need to be sure it's tactically sound."

Kev took a deep breath and expelled it slowly. He had to keep a cool head. This man could be just what he needed to tip the scales in his direction. He needed more than the blessings of the senate. He needed funds and troops. "My first intention is to negotiate. My wife is very—how do I put this? She's a trained warrior, and she won't take being held against her will very well. By the time we arrive they may be anxious to be rid of her. At the very least negotiations will give me a chance to scope out the planet and look for weaknesses.

"Assuming they aren't inclined to talk to us," Kev continued, "my team and I will attempt to take her with us when we leave. If none of those things work, I plan to wage full war against the Imani."

"It's been done," Dugan pointed out, "and not very successfully."

"In my opinion," Kev told him, "the feud has been going on for so long there is no passion in the troops of either side any more. Believe me when I say I have plenty of passion concerning this matter."

Pushing up out of the chair Dugan nodded at the larger man. "That's all I needed to hear. Commitment. You have my support." He turned to leave but swung back with another question. "How do you plan to get you and your team to negotiate? You have no political clout."

"We plan to be *aides* to some official representative." Kev raised a brow. "You wouldn't happen to know anyone who would volunteer for the job, would you?"

Shaking his head and smiling, Dugan walked toward the door. "You don't lack balls, I'll say that for you." The door clicked softly behind him.

***

The boys soaked up knowledge like little sponges. Dev couldn't believe how quickly they'd learned to read. A few days' time and they could read the primmer she was working with completely unaided. And Ewen had a talent for numbers. In no time at all she'd have him doing basic algebra. "Excellent," she encouraged Tim as he read to her, "in no time at all you'll be ready for the next book."

"But I don't know my times tables." His bottom lip stuck out in an endearing way.

She flicked it with her finger. "Don't pout. You'll get them eventually. You just have to keep practicing."

"Math's easy," Ewen bragged.

Dev gave him a stern look. "We all have different strengths and weaknesses."

"I know," he assured her. "Tim is much better at remembering the fighting routines you teach us."

She should have known he wouldn't belittle the younger boy. They were as close as brothers. "True. So why don't you go over to the mat and practice your weakness while Tim and I spend a little while longer on his."

Sighing heavily, Ewen shuffled over to the practice mat and began to run through his katas.

Dev picked up a stack of handmade flash cards. "Tim, let's work on the four's tables, shall we?"

"Those are hard ones," he whined.

She ruffled his hair affectionately. "Exactly why we need to work on them." Holding up the first one she waited patiently for him to count on his fingers.

"Twelve," he announced proudly.

"Great. Now how about this one?"

"Forty-four."

"Excellent." She shuffled the cards and pulled one at random.

"You are doing them a disservice." Nambia entered the room without warning.

"Ever hear of knocking?" Dev asked.

Nambia's brows rose. "I am assigned to your security. I don't have to ask permission to enter your presence." Glaring down at Tim, she signaled for him to leave the table.

He sat defiantly for about three seconds before he scampered over to join Ewen on the mats.

"You are interrupting instruction time," Dev said coldly.

Not waiting for an invitation, Nambia sat down in the chair Tim had vacated. "You are complicating their lives with all this." She waved her hand to indicate the lessons spread out on the table. "They will never be content with their lives if they are too educated." Frowning at the boys as they sparred, she added, "And teaching them to fight is nothing short of signing their death warrants."

A soft fluttering in her abdomen distracted Dev for a moment. Unable to resist the urge, she placed her palm over the slight bulge. She so did not want to share such a poignant moment with her aunt. Hurriedly she said, "No one suffers from education. And within a month those boys will be able to challenge any girl their age, I promise you."

Scoffing, Nambia assured her, "No female would humiliate herself by facing a thrall in combat."

Dev's voice took on a dangerous tone. "Thralls? Those boys are no longer servants. They are mine, and when I leave this cursed place, they will be with me." She took a deep breath and continued in a hoarse whisper, "It is my fervent hope that one day they return and take over this entire fucking planet. So take good care of yourself, *Auntie*, because I would love to see you serve them for a change." Shaking with anger, Devona crushed the stack of cards in her hand. "Now state your business and leave us alone."

Face flushed, Nambia glared at the younger woman. "The queen wishes to see you. Now."

"Very well." Dev stood and adjusted her clothing. "Draco, I hate this thing." She'd never get used to the loincloth. "It's the most uncomfortable thing I've ever worn. Give me a pair of pants and a t-shirt any day."

"You will grow accustomed to them." Nambia's comment grated on Dev's nerves. One of these days she was going to deck the woman, pregnant or not.

"Boys, continue to practice. I'll be right back."

Ewen ran over to stand beside her, Tim close behind. "Ma'am, it is our duty to accompany you."

"At least the children know their place," Nambia mumbled under her breath.

Chapter Fourteen

"Wake up the pip squeak," Callus said as he strolled onto the bridge, eyes twinkling. "I've figured it out."

Mik leaned over and keyed the intercom. "Zoë, get your tiny hiney out here. Callus has good news for us."

Within minutes, Zoë was back on the bridge wearing tight pants and a cropped top. "And for your information, Captain, there's nothing tiny about my hiney." Glancing over her shoulder toward her rear she informed, "Lush. That's the word for my ass."

Grinning, Mik told her, "I knew that would get you out here in a hurry."

"I must have pissed off somebody pretty powerful in the cosmos to end up with a bunch of crusty old soldiers who think they're comedians," she groused. "So what you got, Callus?"

"I have figured out how to monitor Maltoran's ports, so I can replicate the genetic code they attach to the ships to allow them to enter the dome." Shaking his head he added, "The bad news is, we can't get in until someone else enters, so I can download the information."

"How long will it take you to get us in after someone else enters the dome?" Mik asked.

Callus shrugged a shoulder. "I'm guessing about two hours."

Stepping over to the navigational station Zoë pulled up a holovid of the solar system they were entering and indicated a large asteroid. "We can set down here and monitor the area. If we get any closer, we could be spotted. There don't appear to be any moons orbiting Maltoran, and the nearest planet is even further away than this asteroid."

"Good," Mik approved. "We certainly don't want to alert anyone to our presence." A mischievous smile broke over his face. "We want this to be a big ol' surprise party."

Two days later they were still waiting for some traffic into or out of the system. "Draco, I hate waiting." Mik flopped down in a chair at the table. "Do we have any more of that juice?"

Zoë sniggered. "Getting in touch with your feminine side, Captain?"

"Watch your mouth, Little Bit, or I might have to challenge you to a sparring session." Tossing back a glass of the vile stuff he confided, "After about a hundred glasses of the stuff, you begin to develop a taste for it."

"Kev loaded enough of the stuff for an entire fleet of ships." She laughed. "Oh, and any time, Captain. Without Shesshie here to take care of it, I volunteer to take your butt down a peg or two. She'll thank me for it when we get home."

Zoë's last comment struck them both, and for a moment they just sat there. Funny how much home meant to them now, after years and years without one. "Yeah, she probably will." Mik rubbed his fingers through his hair. "I sure miss her."

Reaching over to pat his forearm Zoë assured him, "We all do."

"Hot damn, we've got 'em!" Callus' voice boomed over the intercom. "Get your asses up here pronto."

Grinning, Mik hoisted himself out of the chair. "Showtime." Before he could get to the door he heard the click, click, click of Zoë's heels as she rushed down the hallway.

Callus was pounding away at the keyboard when Mik got to the bridge. "Get the Bird ready for liftoff. I'll have this set up in just a minute."

Mik slid into the pilot's seat and fired her up after a quick systems check. "Say the word."

"Now." Callus punched the final code in with a flourish. "I've preset the coordinates."

"Trying to take over my job?" Zoë asked sweetly. "Because if you are, I'll take a seat in Dev's spot. I've always wanted to fire the pulse cannon."

"Nah." Callus leaned over to kiss her on the forehead. "I don't want your job, little girl. And you won't need to fire the cannon. I've discovered a flaw in the system that supports the plasma dome. We're gonna have fun this time."

"I like the sound of that." Mik spun around to ask, "Are you going to tell us or not?"

""Well." Callus paused for effect. "I don't know..."

Zoë reached over to pinch him. "Don't make me hurt you," she threatened.

"Ouch. That hurt." He rubbed his arm.

"You big baby."

"Out with it," Mik ordered.

"This is beautiful. You're gonna love it." Pulling up a schematic drawing of the dome, Callus pointed to the control center. "All we have to do is have about thirty minutes in there. I'm going to reprogram the bio-exchange system."

"Damn it, Callus." Mik took a threatening step toward him.

Callus was undaunted. "Don't you see, Captain? The next ship that enters or exits the dome will cause a virus that will spread like wildfire. It'll eat itself up in a matter of hours and everything on that rock will be absorbed by the very unfriendly atmosphere...even Umland."

"Hours?" Zoë asked. "That slimeworm will slip out in his fancy ship before the destruction is complete."

"Oh, I forgot to mention that part."

"Here it comes," Mik groaned.

"While I'm doing my thing, you and Zoë will need to disable Umland's fleet."

Mik roared with laughter. "Just one small omission, huh?"

"Well," Zoë quipped, "I said I wanted to try out Dev's job. I guess I get my wish. Lucky me."

Slipping into the plasma dome was remarkably easy. No one even suspected such a feat was possible. No one knew Callus Vukovik. If integrity weren't an integral part of his personality, he could have been one of the richest men in the universe. As it was, he was totally devoted to his friends. No enticement was great enough to dislodge his honor.

"Check her out." Callus whistled when Zoë pranced into the room decked out in every weapon her tiny body could hold. Walking around her in a circle he asked, "How do you walk with all that stuff on?"

Huffing, she countered, "Marissa is going to be very upset with you when I tell her how you picked on me."

"Okay, okay. You got me. I'm sorry."

"Too little, too late." She winked at Miklus.

Mik rested his arm over his engineer's shoulders and confided, "Never take on a woman, my friend. You'll never win."

"Damn straight," Zoë nodded. "Now are we going, or not?"

"Absolutely." Mik set the security system and opened the maintenance hatch on the belly of the ship. Silently the three of them dropped to the ground and made their way to the control center. Using hand signals well-known by his compatriots, Mik led them in and eliminated the guards.

Moving straight to the control panel, Callus went to work. "I'm all set here," he told them. "You two go do your thing."

"Is it just me, Captain, or does he seem to be in an all fired rush?" Zoë winked at Miklus. "You'd think he had a woman waiting for him or something."

Callus pretended to ignore her, but he was grinning like a Noththarian possum. "You just tend to your job, little girl, and I'll tend to mine."

Shaking his head, Mik mumbled, "Callus in love. What's the world coming to?"

***

Miklus and Zoë kept to the shadows as they moved. Umland's private ship was their first target, with only two other small transports in the landing field. One oversized hangar would have to be checked also, but even if it contained another vessel, their work would be relatively easy...as long as they didn't get caught.

Having worked together for many years, they functioned with complete accord. Having been briefed by their engineer, Mik easily disabled the alarm system and boosted Zoë up into the sleek cruiser. When he'd hoisted himself up after her, she whistled softly. "Would you look at this, Captain? Just think of the fun we could have in this baby."

"Yeah. Too bad we're about to reduce her to microscopic bits. I could get used to this kind of luxury." Peering into a well-appointed stateroom he added, "Shesshie and Tessa would appreciate this place, too." Mik moved purposefully as he talked, making his way unerringly to the bridge.

While he slid beneath the control panel, Zoë took a seat at the communications station. "Why don't I just change the password on this baby while we're here?"

The hollow sound of laughter emerged from beneath the molded plastic. "You have an evil streak in you Zoë."

"Damn straight. That's why you love me."

Checking their watches, they left Umland's toy and slipped aboard a bulky transport. "Well, well, well, isn't this interesting?" Mik mused, looking around.

"Didn't take him long to get back in business, did it?" The rows of shackles made her skin crawl. She still had nightmares about the conditions they'd encountered on Pagoda. "You go do your thing, Mik. I'm spending my time on the computer. Maybe I can come up with some information on just who's been working with our old pal."

"Great idea. But make it quick. We've got a schedule to keep."

"Aye, Capt'n." Zoë disappeared down the hall. In moments she was back, hands held over her head. "Ah, Captain. We have a little problem."

Mik banged his head as he crawled out from under the control panel. "Draco, that hurt like a—"

"Just keep your hands where I can see them." A short, orange clad man prodded Zoë in the back with a blaster. "Or the bitch gets it."

Mik rolled to his feet, careful not to antagonize the man. A quick glance told him his navigator had been stripped of her arsenal. This was not good. "Let's not be hasty," Mik told him. "I'm sure we can straighten this mess out."

"We don't need to parley. What we need is for you to toss your weapons over there." He pointed with his other hand. "And sit in that chair so I can tie you up. Then we'll contact the boss and see what he wants me to do with you."

Zoë pulled her raised hands back and clasped them behind her head. Mik frowned slightly. She was up to something, but he'd be damned if he could figure it out. Moving as slowly as possible, he complied. "So tell me, how many slaves can this baby haul?"

Puffing his chest out the man bragged, "Last run we delivered five hundred head."

His terminology pissed Mik off. "Oh? Adults or children?" He had a rotten feeling about this.

"Mostly kids, but we did have a few women and two comely young men." He winked at Mik. "If you catch my meaning."

The entire time the men were talking, Zoë had been inching away from their captor. Mik needed to provide a diversion. "And who the hell would buy that many slaves since Pagoda was closed down?" Pretending to stumble he angled away from the man.

As a matter of instinct, the blaster swerved to follow Mik, who seemed to be the greater threat. Big mistake. Zoë whipped a garrote out of her hairdo, flipped it over the man's head and crossed the ends, pulling with all her might. The pressure on his larynx cut off the man's scream. Without breaking pressure Mik took over. "Nice move. Remind me not to piss you off."

"You going to tease me about my do again?"

"Not in this life." Mik chuckled. Pulling the wire a little tighter before loosening it slightly, Mik asked, "Are you going to play nice and tell us what we want to know, or are you going to die for Umland?"

The man's eyes bugged out as he tried to draw breath. Unable to speak, he nodded.

Dragging him over to sit in the chair, he found himself bound securely in moments. Mik stood looking down at him, revulsion on his face. "Who did you make the delivery to, scumbag?"

"Umland will kill me," he whined.

"I'll kill you." Mik's predatory stare apparently convinced him.

"Gorgon. We dropped them on Gorgon." He wiggled against his bindings. "I done what you wanted, now let me go."

"Gorgon, huh? Who accepted the delivery?" Mik casually played with the thin wire.

"The boss' brother. Seems he's the new king or something. Now really, that's all I know."

Zoë sauntered over, slipping weapons here and there into pockets in her clothing. "I have one question myself. Just where did you acquire the five hundred people you delivered to Gorgon?" A thin stiletto was the last item she held, and she placed the tip against the man's carotid.

"Iman. We picked up the livestock on Iman." He craned his neck, trying to get away from the sharp blade.

"Who was your contact?" She purred.

"I don't know. I'm just a crewmember. I don't know the important stuff."

Applying pressure Zoë watched as the thick red liquid eased around the tip to drip down the man's neck. "Wrong answer." Her voice was sultry.

"It was all legal. The queen's sister sold them to us. Now get this crazy bitch away from me," he shrieked.

With economy of motion, Mik grasped the man's head and snapped his neck. "You don't deserve to live even a few hours more."

"My sentiments exactly." Zoë wiped her blade on the dead man's clothing and silently slid it into its sheath.

They met with no further resistance and rendezvoused with Callus just as he was finishing up. "How'd it go?" he asked.

"Swell." Zoë was still fuming.

Callus knew that tone of voice. "What happened?"

"Our friend Draxor is at it again already," Mik told him. "Apparently, his family is back in power on Gorgon. His brother just took a shipment of five hundred slaves."

"Shit."

"Oh, it gets better," Zoë assured him. "The slaves came from Iman. And the queen's sister was the flesh peddler."

Jaws clinched, Callus turned toward the door, his powerful compact body making short work of the distance. "Let's get the fuck out of this foul place."

***

They had barely cleared Maltoran's orbit when the dome began to disintegrate. Readings showed several breaks in the exoplasma allowing an influx of noxious gases. Callus grinned maniacally, watching the results of his handiwork. "I love my work," he admitted to his comrades.

"You're a sick bastard." Mik clapped him on the shoulder. "That's one of the things I like most about you."

Disdaining the readouts, Zoë peered out a porthole. "Look, you can see the difference even from this distance."

Mik moved to her side. "You sure can. Draco, I didn't think it would happen this fast."

"What can I say? I'm good," Callus assured them. "Besides." He shrugged. "I knew if I gave that worthless slimeworm any time at all he'd figure a way off planet." His brows drew together in a scowl. "I just don't trust him to die, you know what I mean?"

"I know exactly what you mean." Zoë nodded.

"Yeah, well he won't be flying out of this." Mik pointed toward the planet displayed in the window. "Look, there's already a magnetic storm encroaching on the city."

Sure enough, a massive whirling maelstrom was eating away at the buildings that sat along the southern most edge of the settlement. As they watched, the dome shivered and collapsed in on itself, leaving the buildings and all life forms at the mercy of a very hostile environment. Within thirty minutes not a speck remained of what had once been a technological tribute to the ingenuity of man.

"Shall I lay in a course?" Zoë asked.

"Sounds like a plan," Mik answered. "I, for one, am anxious to get back to Baux. I didn't like leaving Kev there alone to face the sharks."

"Not to mention the delay to rescuing Dev," Zoë reminded him.

"And getting back home." Callus glanced at his friends who had burst out laughing. "What?" he asked.

Waving him toward the hallway, Mik wiped tears of mirth from his eyes. "Nothing. Nothing at all, Callus. Just go catch some shut-eye. You've been awake for hours working on that little surprise party."

"I don't know what's so funny about me wanting to get home," he mumbled as he shuffled toward his cabin.

Chapter Fifteen

Queen Lila looked somewhat better this time than she had before. Sitting up in a chaise lounge, the brightly colored pillows that surrounded her seemed to give her color. "Come closer," she said imperiously. "Sit close to me. I want to ask you a few questions."

Signaling the boys to wait by the door, Dev walked over to stand beside her mother. Raising one brow in question, she waited.

"Sit," the queen repeated.

"I'll stand," Dev replied.

"Suit yourself. We need to discuss the matter of your behavior. You are embarrassing my line."

"Oh? Can't have that now can we?" Dev grinned.

"This is a serious matter. Complaints have been made about the way you treat those two boys as though they were your children."

Dev glanced at Ewen and Tim where they stood near the entryway. They could hear every word that was being said, and she didn't want their feelings hurt. "They are my children," she announced in a firm voice.

Allowing her head to sink back into the pillow, Lila closed her eyes for a moment. "Very well. I'll see to it that they are dowered if it pleases you that much." She sat up straighter to make eye contact with Dev. "But you have absolutely got to stop teaching them as though they were female. It simply isn't done."

Leaning over her mother Dev whispered, "I will not. I don't care for you, your society or your rules in the least. As long as I am kept prisoner on this wretched planet, I will continue to do as I see fit. And I will not rest until I gain my freedom."

"You are the heir," Lila snapped.

"I am not," Dev ground out between clinched teeth. "I am a free woman. I have a home, a husband, and friends elsewhere." Nostrils flaring Dev snarled, "My husband and friends will come for me. You can save your planet the grief of facing them if you let me go now."

Lila scoffed, "My warriors will not be intimidated by a handful of mercenaries. They will capture and execute each and every one of them if you do not submit yourself to the role you were born to, Persis."

Refusing to rise to the bait, Dev just smiled. "You don't know my friends," she said. "They will have me out of here one way or the other. The amount of destruction will be entirely up to you, *mother*." She made the term sound like a curse. Hitching the infernal loincloth back into place she turned on her heel and strode toward the door. "Come on, boys, grandmother isn't feeling well today."

Lila gasped. "I am not grandmother to those boys," she shouted.

"If you claim me, you claim them because from this day forward they are mine." Looking back over her shoulder she added, "You get all of us or none." Herding the boys before her, Devona left the queen's presence.

When she passed Nambia in the hall, she told her, "You can go in now. And don't bother to follow me around any more. I'm more than capable of guarding myself."

Eyes narrowed, her aunt watched her go then slipped into Lila's quarters. "I see it didn't go well," she said.

A slight smile quivered on the queen's mouth. "She's very strong willed. Too bad we weren't able to raise her here on Iman. I think she would have been a formidable ruler."

"You speak in the past tense."

"Indeed. That young woman will never lead anything on this planet other than perhaps a revolt." Pushing aside her lap blanket she held her hand out to her sister. "Please, take me back to my bed. I feel weak."

Ignoring Lila's hand Nambia propped her hands on her hips. "We have drained the royal coffers to bring Persis home, and now you say she is unfit to rule? I fear your mind has become as weak as your body, sister."

Hand drifting back to lie beside her, Lila's eyes snapped with the fire of her indomitable will. "I might be trapped in a useless shell, but I assure you my mind is as sharp as ever. That woman will cause us more grief than you can imagine if you persist in trying to force her into the mold of heir. She is strong willed, intelligent, and determined. Mark my words, if she remains on Iman, she will bring this regime to its knees."

Spinning to pace to the window, Nambia took a cleansing breath to lessen the pounding in her head. "I don't understand you, Lila. You have spent several fortunes and years of your life searching for your heir, and now that you have her, you want her gone again? If that isn't madness, what is?" Perching on the foot of the chaise, she looked into her sister's eyes. "I have served you all these years because I believed you were the best woman to rule Iman. Don't make me rethink my loyalties."

Lila's indrawn breath was her only reaction. "Take me to my bed," she ordered coldly. "Then send Aldora to me."

"Aldora," Nambia said contemptuously, "now there's a snake if I ever saw one." Despite her anger, she was gentle as she lifted her sister and carried her to the bed.

"Aldora is in charge of my military. She has earned that post through her bravery and veracity."

"If you believe that, you are a fool." Nambia left her pronouncement hanging in the air when she withdrew from the queen's chambers. *Ah, sister, you are too easy.* There was a bounce to Nambia's steps as she departed.

***

"Do we have to?" Ewen fiddled with the edge of his tunic.

"Yes. You do." Dev remained firm in her resolve to see the boys treated equally in the arena. "We will observe the girls as they train. It will help you prepare to spar. We will discuss the weakness of each pupil."

Tim was quiet, but his eyes followed the swift sure movements of the girls as they fought on the mats. "That one—" He pointed at a child with long brown braids. "—leaves her left side open every time she makes an aggressive move."

Nodding, Dev praised, "Good. I saw that, too. And what about her opponent?"

"If she has a weakness, it is her reluctance to use her feet. She is small and would be much more effective if she used some powerful kicks."

Ruffling the lad's hair Dev nodded. "Good."

"I will never be good at this, just as Tim will never be good at numbers. Why do I have to stay here and be humiliated?" The question was asked without whining or pleading. It was simply a question.

Dev's heart clinched. Suddenly she feared she was committing the same mistake her mother was, expecting him to be something he could never be. "Ewen, I don't expect you to be a great fighter." She knelt to face him eye-to-eye. "I just want you to learn to defend yourself. I will be proud of you whatever you choose to do in life, but you cannot be a victim. The world is full of those who prey on the weak, and you must not be one of them." Pushing the soft blond hair back from his face Dev told him, "While it's nice to win, people will respect your courage and determination for doing your best. And you are certainly capable of defeating quite a few of these girls. I have been in the business of fighting all of my life, and trust me when I tell you that you aren't the worst fighter here."

Brown eyes trusting he asked, "Do you really think so?"

"I know so." She rolled gracefully to her feet.

Sliding closer Tim whispered, "See that one with the black hair and the yellow loin cloth?" Ewen nodded. "She's bigger than you, but you are faster to block a punch, and your footwork is more sure."

Grinning Dev put a hand on the shoulder of each boy. "He's right. You can take her."

Ewen smiled and looked more closely at the class as they trained.

"Get those males out of my arena." Dorina, the head instructor, stalked toward them as they stood on the sidelines.

"I don't think so," Dev replied.

"I have dominion over this facility."

"You don't have dominion over me," was Dev's clipped reply.

Though her hair was beginning to grow back, it stood up in spikes, and her scalp was still somewhat visible. The royal tattoo was easy to spot. Dorina came to an abrupt halt. "Persis, I didn't recognize you."

"Call me Dev."

Frowning, the woman asked, "Why would I call you Dev?"

"Because that's my name. Now what would you say to a little sparring between my boys and a couple of the girls?"

Clearly outraged, she replied, "Males want to compete with my girls?"

"Sure. Why not? It'll be good for all of them to practice with different partners."

"Males are not allowed to learn the arts of war on Iman. Surely as the heir you are aware of this?"

"Oh, I've been told." Dev grinned. "I just don't take orders very well. Come on, what could it hurt?"

"It could cost me my job."

"What if I ordered you? As the heir."

"You are not yet invested and therefore have no real power." Dorina was clearly trying to keep from offending the woman who would one day be her queen.

Dev sized the other woman up. "How about if you and I had a little contest?"

"To what purpose?"

"Winner takes all." Dev was smiling. Those who knew her knew to be wary when she wore that particular smile.

"I am a simple warrior. Speak plainly."

"If I win, the boys get to train here from time to time. If you win, we leave and never come back."

Though her stomach was barely rounded Dorina obviously realized Dev was pregnant. "I can't fight you."

"No. But we could still have a contest." Raising her brows Dev asked, "Don't you train with any other weapons?"

"Of course. But blades would be even more dangerous than hand-to-hand combat."

"How about firearms? Anything from laser crossbows to blasters would be okay with me."

Now Dorina was smiling. "I think that could be arranged." She signaled her second in command and within minutes targets had been set up and an array of weapons assembled. "Challenger may choose first. Shall we say two out of three?"

"Excellent," Dev replied, sizing up the choices. "Phazers first, I think." She palmed a small handheld pistol.

Selecting a similar weapon, Dorina stepped to the firing line. After taking careful aim, she fired repeatedly until the weapon was drained of its fifteen shots. She had scored three bull's-eyes, and had hit the surrounding ring eight times. Four shots were on the outer rim of the target.

Dev stepped up to the line, and without hesitation she fired all fifteen rounds. Fourteen hit the center, one on top of the other. The fifteenth was slightly off center, but still within the bull's-eye. Dorina was not amused.

As her first choice, Dorina selected a pulse riffle. It held three charges, and the targets were three-dimensional holograms of a human image. She made a head shot, clipped the right shoulder and scored a direct hit to the chest. Smugly she turned to her opponent. "I am battalion champion with the pulse riffle."

"Peachy." Dev shouldered the familiar weapon and ripped off her three consecutive shots, all to the head. "I, on the other hand," she told her opponent, "haven't been in a competition since leaving the academy." Grinning, she added, "But I have been undefeated on the battlefield."

Tim and Ewen clapped and hooted their support.

"Shall we call it now, or do you want to go the last round just for fun?" Dev inquired sweetly.

"You have clearly won," Dorina conceded. "But I would love to see you throw knives."

Shrugging, Dev hefted a small throwing knife to test the balance. Whirling, she hurled it at the first target Dorina had used. The handle quivered as it settled into the red center. "Will that be all?" she asked.

"When would you like to schedule the first matches?" Dorina snarled.

"Oh, the end of the week I think. How about ten in the morning?"

"Fine." Pivoting smartly, Dorina yelled to the students, "The show's over. Get back to your training."

Heads held proudly, the boys followed Devona out of the arena. "That was pretty cool," Ewen told her. "Only now we have to fight those girls. We're not ready."

"I am," Tim bragged.

"No, you're not. But you will be. We're going back to our rooms and train." Once they rounded the corner so they couldn't be seen Dev stopped and faced her young charges. "I know the technique they teach. I can teach you how to counter that, no problem. If you listen and do what I tell you to, you'll do fine." Making eye contact with Ewen she said calmly, "Even if you don't win, your opponent will know she's been in a fight. In all honesty, sweetie, I think you'll win."

"Me, too," Tim insisted.

"You, too," she concurred. "Now come on, we've got lots of work to do in only a few days."

Chapter Sixteen

Jacton hadn't changed much as far as Kev could tell. He was still a pudgy little prick. Only now he was the King of Baux. Zedne had grilled him on protocol, but he wasn't sure anything other than Dev's safety could make him kneel to another man. He mimicked his uncle in what amounted to genuflecting. "Your Highness," he grated.

"Cousin," Jacton replied. "The years have been good to you." He waved imperiously toward two chairs that had been brought for their use. "Please, be seated." It could have been oversight that he failed to offer a seat to their uncle, but Kev doubted it.

"I'll stand with Zedne, if you don't mind," Kevnor replied.

One imperious brow rose at his audacity. "I intended that you both sit."

Kev stepped back so his uncle could be seated first. Zedne managed to keep his mirth under control, but no amount of suppression could keep the twinkle from his eyes. "Thank you," he said simply, taking his seat.

As Zedne had explained it, Kev was required to wait until the monarch broached the subject. He chafed at the delay, but kept reminding himself of the stakes. "I understand your reign has been profitable for Baux," Kev said. He wasn't above a little flattery to get what he wanted. "I know your father would have been proud."

"As would yours," Jacton replied. "I have heard that you are an accomplished...mercenary." Somehow he made the compliment sound like a slur.

Refusing to rise to the bait, Kev continued, "Thank you. My friends and I found the job quite lucrative, though recently we retired from that profession. We now own a small shipping business."

"Indeed. Who would have thought?" Jacton mused.

"It's not nearly as exciting," Kev lied, thinking of their recent escapades on Pagoda, "but I've recently taken a mate, so it seemed prudent." He hoped to segue into the topic of Iman.

Naturally his cousin refused to follow his lead. "Zedne mentioned that you arrived with an entourage."

"Just a few friends. They will return shortly to aid me in my quest." Kev wondered absently just how much more obvious he could be without putting the royal nose out of joint.

"Your fellow mercenaries, I believe." Damn the man.

"Three of them anyway. The others are at home, on Bright's Planet, minding the store so-to-speak."

"Interesting. What sort of things do you haul?"

Zedne's eyes narrowed watching the interaction between the cousins. He'd thought Jacton would have recovered from the inadequate feelings Kev had engendered when the boys were young. No one had said so specifically, but he'd always believed Jacton's father had ordered Kev's enrollment in the off world military academy. Jacton had always been eclipsed when Kevnor was in the room. Sighing, he reconciled himself to the fact that he served the wrong nephew.

"Anything that's legal." Kev's jaw kept flexing with irritation.

"Anything?" Jacton brushed at imaginary lint on his trousers. "Even slaves?"

Kev jumped to his feet. "Enough," he roared. "I refuse to continue with this bullshit. Either you will aid me in rescuing my wife, or you won't. If you refuse, tell me now so I can make alternate plans." The veins stood out in his neck, and his hands were clinched into tight fists at his sides.

Jacton smiled. "Well, cousin, you do have limits like the rest of us after all." He waved Kev back into his chair. "Sit down and let's hear what you have in mind."

Taken aback, Kev searched Jacton's face. Was the man sincere or was he playing a royal game? "The plan is simple. Dugan has agreed to travel to Iman as a diplomatic liaison. My team and I will attend him. If we are able, we'll sneak her out with us and avoid any warfare." Kev shrugged. "If not, I'll blow that place apart to get to her."

"Will you now? And catapult Baux back into war? We've just arranged the first truce in twelve hundred years. Have you given any consideration to that, cousin?" His tone was mild, but Jacton's words brought Kev up short. No. He hadn't given any thought to the people of his home world.

"The truth? No. I hadn't." Kev found himself rethinking his plan. "You're right. I can't ask the people of Baux to take on my problem." He stood again. "Thank you for your time, Jacton." He bowed slightly from the waist. "Zedne, I'll see you back at the house."

"Hold on a minute." Jacton was clearly not done. "Will you quit popping up and down out of that chair? You're giving me a headache. I never said I wasn't going to help. I just asked if you had considered all angles." Jacton slid his chair over to the computer terminal that sat on a nearby desk. "If I can get this damn thing to work properly," he groused, "I'll show you what I had in mind."

Kev stepped closer. "Allow me," he offered. "I have an affinity for these babies."

Within minutes, he pulled up the plans Jacton had outlined in his personal log. Scanning the entries, Kev began to smile. "You have a wicked streak in you, Jacton."

"So I've been told." The king smiled. "The beauty of it is if you pull this off, your wife will become the sovereign. At that point, we will be able to negotiate a truce that will benefit both planets and hopefully put an end to the bloodshed."

"Brilliant," Kev complimented.

"May an old man make a suggestion?" Zedne asked.

The two younger men turned to hear what he had to say. "Tell no one of this except Kevnor and his friends."

"We'll have to tell Dugan." Kev couldn't see any way out of it.

"What do you suspect, Zedne?" Jacton asked. Kev had been gone since he was a child, but Jacton knew their uncle to be canny and very knowledgeable.

"Nothing concrete," Zedne admitted. "But something's afoot. Since I can't pin down who's involved, I recommend we don't allow anyone else in on the change in plans. It will be easy enough to appear to be following Kevnor's original plans until the last possible minute."

Kev nodded. "Fair enough. My team and I can take care of things."

"There will only be four of you."

"We've faced worse odds. Besides, there will be five. You forget Devona's already there."

"She is a woman, and pregnant at that." Jacton reproached.

Kev smiled. "Her belly won't affect her trigger finger." As long as she had a weapon, Kev was confident of his wife's abilities.

***

"How much longer till we reach orbit around Baux?" Mik asked.

"Another three hours," Zoë told him. "I've already contacted planetary defense at Kev's suggestion. They're expecting us."

"Efficient as ever," Mik complimented. "I'll go wake Callus. We need to eat and clean up before we arrive. I don't want any delays once we land."

Zoë slid from her seat. "Good idea. You guys eat. I'll hit the shower."

Mik laughed. "How do you women do that?" he asked. "No matter how I work it, you always get the shower first."

"We're just smarter than you men," she teased.

"So Shesshie keeps telling me."

"You should listen to your wife." She scampered by him, in a hurry to reach the head.

Callus was already awake when Mik knocked on his door. "Come on in," he called. "I've been up thinking about that plasma dome."

"Only you would do that." Mik laughed. "What's got your brain turning?"

"Now that I fully understand the technology, we could utilize it on Bright's."

That sounded interesting. "How?"

"We could use the same technology to secure the planet, so we wouldn't have to worry about the Nest when we're gone."

"We already have a suitable climate. And couldn't the same trick be used on us that you used back there?"

"In all modesty, Captain, not everyone could do what I did. I have some plans for a constantly evolving dome that would be impossible to infect the way we did on Maltoran. And, if by some miracle, the dome were breached, the atmosphere of the planet wouldn't cause such destruction because it's not a hostile planet. An added benefit would be our ability to control the environment if we wanted to, increasing the growing season and even converting desert lands to fertile."

Mik whistled. "Whoa. That's quite a project. What would something like that cost anyway?"

Callus blushed. "Well, it would be costly."

"That's what I was afraid of." He laughed. "But the idea has merit. I would love to be able to leave knowing my family was not in danger." Twisting around to pop his back Mik said, "Work up some figures. If we can't do it right now, we can work toward it."

"Fair enough." Folding up his desk, Callus said, "I think I'll take a quick shower."

Mik shook his head.

"No?" Callus looked confused.

"Zoë beat you to it," Mik confirmed his worst fears.

"Damn. Neither of us will get hot water now."

"Don't I know it." Mik sighed. "At least we can get something to eat. Come on." The two men raided the cupboard, preparing one of those cholesterol-enriched meals men love.

***

Kev met them at the terminal. "Draco, I'm glad to see you," he said, pounding Mik on the shoulder. "The delay has been chafing my ass."

"I'll bet." Mik grinned. "And you missed one hell of a good time on Maltoran. Seeing that place revert to its original state with Umland on the surface was—"

"Beautiful," Zoë finished for him. Raising up on her tiptoes, she hugged Kevnor. "It brought tears to my eyes."

He hugged her back enthusiastically. "Wish I could have been there. But I've been making progress here. We should be able to set the plan in motion within two days."

"Speaking of plans, what have you come up with?" Mik wanted to know.

Peering around his friend's body, Kev asked, "Where's Callus?"

"He'll be along." Mik snorted. "He was talking to Marissa."

"How is everyone back home?"

"They're all fine. No sign of trouble, at least not yet. I don't want to push our luck though." Mik jogged back up the ramp and yelled, "Come on, Callus, you're holding us up." Turning back to Kev he added, "I don't like being away."

"Keep your drawers on," Callus mumbled as he strode out of the Freebird. "I'm coming."

"I hear you pulled one of your brilliant stunts." Kev held his arm up for the other man to shake.

Callus grasped it. "Naturally."

"Modest as ever," Zoë quipped. "But hey, he's got grand plans for building one of those plasma domes over Bright's. What do you think about that idea?"

Kev frowned. "I think it sounds expensive."

Callus shrugged. "But worth it. If we had a dome like that, we'd never have to worry about whoever was left behind."

"Sounds promising. Maybe when we get Dev back we can sit down with my cousin and toss some figures around. He might want to hire you to upgrade the defenses on Baux."

"What's this?" Mik chided, "A hint of warmth in your voice when speaking of the dreaded emperor?"

A lopsided grin gave them a glimpse of the boy Kev had been when they first met. "Yeah, well maybe I misjudged him. He seems okay. In fact, he has a pretty sound plan for the mission."

Brows drawing together Mik eyed his friend skeptically. "Correct me if I'm wrong, but I thought this mission was your baby."

"It is, Mik, but I haven't been on Baux in a long time. The politics here are convoluted."

"And that's a surprise?" Zoë asked.

"No, of course not, but in this instance it can be used to all our benefit." Dropping his voice Kev reported, "Jacton knows there is a traitor working with the Imani. If we plan this thing right, we can flush him out when we go to retrieve Dev." Holding his arms out he shrugged. "It's a win-win scenario. I get the backing of the Baux government, and they get their villain."

"Just what kind of support is the government offering?" Mik wanted to know.

"That all depends on whether or not phase one goes smoothly. If we don't get Dev back right away, Jacton has pledged his entire armada."

Callus whistled. "It's been a while since we tried working with a uniformed force that size."

"Hey." Zoë stepped close so she could bump him with her hip. "Not to worry. It'll all come back to you."

Ignoring the banter, Mik cut to the meat. "Do you trust your cousin, Kev?"

Not taking the question lightly, Kev thought for several minutes before replying, "Yes, I do."

"That's it then. Do you need to brief us with the others, or are they already up to speed?"

Kev scratched his head and glanced down at the pavement. "Well, we're sort of it."

Callus groaned. "I might have known," he groused. "The only person liable to get us into a bigger clusterfuck than Mik is you."

"Thanks for the vote of confidence."

"Are you going to fill us in or not?" Zoë badgered them.

"Zedne and I are the only people outside Jacton who know the plan so far. You three are the only others who will know unless we deem it necessary to inform others during the mission."

"Whoa. Let me get this straight." Mik halted abruptly. "We're going to Iman with all but the four of us flying blind? What kind of fucking plan is that?"

Scowling at the unfavorable summary, Kev ground out, "We are posing as aides to one of the senators, Dugan, and will attempt to slip Dev out without causing a major bloodbath."

"And if it doesn't work?" Zoë demanded.

"Then we cause a major bloodbath," Kev said quietly.

"How does this guy Dugan fit in?" Mik wanted to know. "Is he trustworthy?"

"Damned if I know," Kev admitted. "I like the guy. I didn't get any of the bad vibes I generally do when someone is lying to me. He's former military, has a son and an ex-wife who ran off with some merchant. The few times we've spoken, he's seemed sympathetic and supportive. Yet Jacton cautioned me against trusting anyone. He said he's sure information is leaking out but doesn't have a clue where the breach is."

"How do we get ourselves into things like this?" Mik wondered.

"Just lucky, Captain." Zoë batted her eyelashes at him.

"Fuck you." Mik laughed.

"Where does your uncle fit into this?" Mik was back to running fingers through his hair again.

"I'd like to say here on Baux, but the old fool refuses to let us go off without him." Affection was apparent in Kev's voice. "He said we youngsters were too hotheaded."

"Does he know what this particular group of youngsters does for a living?" Callus lifted his shaggy brows.

"He knows, but I suspect he hasn't considered all that being a mercenary entails."

"Do you think we can keep him safe?"

Kev shook his head. "I don't know, Zoë. It worries me, but he's plenty old enough to make up his own mind. Besides, at his age, I'll probably be looking for a little excitement, too."

Mik snorted. "Married to Dev? I don't think so."

"Good point."

"I wonder how she is?" Zoë's quiet question sobered them all.

"I don't know." Kev cleared his throat. "But she'd better be just fine, or there'll be hell to pay. I promise you that." His dark eyes smoldered with the promise of retribution on anyone who harmed his mate.

Chapter Seventeen

Dev felt as though she'd swallowed one of those Prima Lizards the boys were always talking about. Her stomach fluttered and rolled, and it wasn't the baby causing the upheaval. She was a nervous wreck as she watched Tim and Ewen bow to their opponents. "Come on, boys, you can do it," she whispered to herself as the bell sounded to begin competition. Though she didn't give a flip if either of them ever won a combat competition, she knew it was important to them. And they were important to her.

As expected, Tim went on the offensive immediately, striking hard with his feet and blocking blows with his arms. He had a gift for reading his opponent and didn't hesitate to take advantage of it. Dev smiled with approval when he pinned the taller girl in a matter of moments. Smirking, he reached down to help the fallen girl up. She not only refused the gesture but spat on the mat before turning away. The smirk grew into a full-blown grin as he turned to wink at Devona. Cheeky lad. She grinned back.

Ewen took the opposite approach. He allowed his adversary to strike first. Blocking her blows, he continued to study her patterns, merely defending himself. Then he struck, sweeping her feet out from under her and kneeling on one knee with the other pressed against her throat effectively disabling her. He didn't budge until the girl conceded the match. Without asking, he grabbed her by the hand, pulled her to her feet, turned on his heel and stalked away. She glowered at his back, but his actions had nipped in the bud any idea she had of belittling him. Dev's breast swelled with pride.

"We expect to be welcomed when we join you for training tomorrow," Dev announced as she followed her protégée's from the room. As soon as the door closed behind her she jumped into the air. "Yes," she hissed, raising a fist triumphantly.

"My lady," Ewen looked shocked. "You'll harm the baby."

"With a little jump like that? I don't think so." She rubbed her tummy. "He's as excited as we are."

"Do you think so?" Tim's eyes were as round as saucers, watching her.

"Yeah, I do. He's rolling all around. Here." She took the boy's hand and pressed it to her stomach. "Can you feel him?" A wave of sadness rushed through her as she realized how much Kev was missing.

Steering the small hand to the right spot, Dev watched the awe spread over the youngster's face. "Ewen, you gotta feel this," he encouraged. "Here. Touch her here." Tim pointed to the spot he'd just vacated.

Ewen gingerly laid his own hand over the undulating bulge. "It's alive."

Dev ruffled his hair. "Of course he's alive, silly. And one day he'll need his big brothers to teach him how to fight. You guys were awesome."

"I knew I could take her," Tim bragged. "I watched her fight before. She's slow on the right side, and she always glances at where she's going to hit."

"Excellent observation," Dev approved as they resumed their walk. "How about you, Ewen? What did you think of your opponent?"

Frowning, he considered. "She was very good," he admitted. "At first I thought she might get the better of me, but once I let her hit me a few times, I realized I was stronger than she was. The rest was easy. And that seems strange, because she's one of their best trainees."

Her thoughtful little Ewen had hit on the very real advantage all males brought into a fight: superior body strength. "You're exactly right, Ewen," she praised, "and that is exactly why I set myself up as a weapons expert. It is a simple biological fact that men carry more muscle mass. Females can't hope to defeat them through strength alone. They have to outsmart the male, or outgun him." She grinned conspiratorially. "Not having occasion to engage in hand-to-hand combat with men, I was banking on that little fact to be unknown here on Iman."

"Well they know it now." Tim looked a little worried.

"Maybe," Dev conceded, "but maybe not. I think it'll take them a while to be able to admit that males are superior in any way to females." Throwing an arm around her boys, she hugged them close. "Meanwhile, I predict you two will be very much in demand as sparring partners. It'll drive them crazy that a couple of mere boys can whip their little butts."

Tim took a stab at the air. "I'll whip them all," he declared.

"Don't go getting too cocky. You still have to whip those multiplication tables, young man."

"Aw," he pouted.

"I'll help you, Tim," Ewen promised.

Nambia was waiting in their chambers when they returned. "Send the slaves away," she demanded.

"My children can stay if they wish. You are the interloper, Nambia. If you want privacy, take your old ass out of my suite."

Lip curled, Nambia sneered, "These urchins are not your children. And I require a private conference with you."

"You might try asking." Dev's cheeks were flushed with anger. "And as far as I'm concerned, they are my boys."

"Suit yourself. You can engage in whatever fantasies you wish. Neither you nor those brats will ever leave Iman."

Dev shrugged. "Believe what you wish. Kevnor will rescue me." Crossing to the glass doors she looked back at the older woman. "Step out on the porch with me if you want to talk."

When the door snickered closed behind them, Nambia came right to the point. "An envoy from Baux is due to arrive tomorrow. You will remain in your quarters while the dignitaries are on the planet."

"By the teats of the whore who bore you, I will not."

Displaying some of the speed for which she was famous in her youth, Nambia whirled around, pushing Dev against a pillar with a palm to her throat. "You will." She glanced over her shoulder suggestively. "Or you'll be sorry."

Anger welled up in Dev. In two moves she'd freed herself and twisted her aunt's arm up behind her. "Don't ever threaten what's mine, bitch, or I'll deal with you personally. Now, you people kidnapped and brought me hear, claiming I was your long lost princess. I will not be treated as a prisoner."

"You are subject to royal commands, the same as the rest of us," Nambia ground out.

"We'll see." Dev shoved her aunt away and reentered her chambers.

Ewen and Tim hurriedly grabbed up the flash cards, trying to look as though they hadn't heard every word spoken on the balcony. "I know you heard us," she said, walking up beside them. "It's okay."

"Why is she always so mean to you?" Tim asked. "Isn't she your aunt?"

"So they say," she replied. "But I refuse to claim her."

Ewen grinned. "Can you do that? Just not claim her?"

Dev shrugged. "Sure. Why not? I claimed you two as my kids. Why can't I un-claim her as my aunt?"

The topic of their conversation stormed through to the hallway. "Don't try to leave your quarters," she gritted out as she passed.

"I won't try. I'll do it," Dev promised.

The door slammed shut. An unnatural quiet followed the dramatic exit. "What now?" Ewen's young face was lined with worry.

"Let's see." She crossed to the door and opened it. Armed guards snapped to attention on either side of the portal. When she attempted to step outside, the guards placed a hand on their weapons and shook their heads. "So, I am a prisoner?" she asked.

"Princess, this is for your own good," one replied.

"By whose authority?"

"The queen's, ma'am."

"And she gave you these orders directly?" Dev sounded skeptical.

"Of course not. She's not herself. The Lady Nambia made her wishes known."

Frowning, Dev returned to her apartment and closed the door behind her. "Just as I thought," she mumbled. "My freaking aunt is behind all this." Turning to the boys she motioned them over to sit beside her on the settee. "Boys, I need your help."

"Anything, lady." Young Tim's earnest little face looked up at her.

"In a few minutes I'm going to send you on an errand. I need to see if you two have access to the rest of the palace, or if you are also prisoners."

"We're slaves," Ewen insisted. "No one will stop us."

"We'll see. Since I've made it clear you are no longer my slaves, but my children, the orders may have been extended to include you."

"If we can get through, what will we do?" Tim wanted to know.

"First of all, you'll get us something to eat. Later you'll go to inquire about practice tomorrow. Then, I think I'll have a craving for something exotic."

Ewen smiled. He was catching on. "You want to get them used to seeing us come and go again, right?"

"You are a very cleaver boy." She tapped him on the nose with her index finger. "After a day or so, I'll be able to send you on some much more important missions, and no one will question you." She held their hands and looked at each one. "This could turn out to be dangerous. If there was another way, I wouldn't risk it." Glancing at the balcony she sighed.

"Not too long ago, I would have simply climbed out the window and down the side of the building, but junior here—" She patted her belly. "—is getting too big for me to climb about like a monkey."

"What's a monkey?"

"It's a furry little animal with a long prehensile tail that can climb just about anything. It even swings by its tail from the branches of trees."

"Oh." Tim's eyes were round with interest. "I'd like to see one of those."

"Perhaps you will. When we get out of here, I'll ask Kevnor to take us to one of the zoo planets. We'll have a lovely vacation and see all sorts of exotic creatures. Would you like that?"

Both insisted they would. But they didn't seem convinced that Kev would ever come to rescue them, or that he'd be successful if he did show up. Dev smiled. They didn't know her Kev.

***

Zedne's home was just off a busy main street of the city, yet the high privacy fences made it seem isolated, once you were inside. Even the gardens seemed secluded, the hustle and bustle blocked by the impermeable material. She hadn't realized just how much the sound was blocked till Zoë was startled by a knock at the street side entrance to the garden. She hadn't heard anyone approach. Looking around to see if anyone would answer, she decided to answer it herself rather than disturb the servants. Lifting the latch, she stepped back to let the ten-foot gate swing inward.

Leaning over to dust off his trousers, Dugan explained, "The front of the house is crawling with

~174~

participants in the First Day parade. They're kicking up quite a lot of dust out there." Rising from his task he continued, "Thanks for your trouble…"

"No problem," Zoë assured him. "I was already out here enjoying the plants." She felt her heart rate pick up when their eyes met. He was one of the most attractive men she'd ever seen, and she'd seen a lot of them.

Dugan froze mid-sentence, his eyes raking the tiny woman from head to foot.

Stifling her laughter, Zoë stepped back, motioning the stranger inside. "Well, are you going to come in, or just stand there staring?"

Jerked back to reality, Dugan stood with military stiffness before bowing slightly from the waist. "Your pardon. I was expecting one of the staff."

"Yeah, well, you got me. You got a problem with that?" One pert brow rose in question.

"Certainly not. I'm just surprised. Zedne's guests don't usually open the gate for late arrivals."

"Well don't get your panties in a wad, I'm not exactly a guest. Are you here for the briefing?" Leading the way, Zoë headed back toward the main house. "We were hoping to be ready to leave first thing tomorrow."

Reaching out to stop Zoë with a hand on her arm, Dugan asked, "Are you part of Kevnor's team?" He didn't even try to hide the incredulity in his voice.

Bristling with indignation, Zoë jerked free from the hold he had on her. "Yes, I am. I hope that's not a problem for you. I know how women are treated here on Baux, but I assure you the rest of the universe acknowledges that we are equal to men in both intelligence and ability."

Shaking his head in denial he rushed to reply, "No, I don't think that at all."

"You don't think we are intelligent and capable?" Gorgeous or not, she might have to hurt him.

"No. No, that's not what I meant," he rushed to explain. "I meant I know women are worthy allies and adversaries." He couldn't believe he was bungling the conversation so badly.

"Damn straight. Don't forget it." Turning on her heel, Zoë hustled into the house, her nicely rounded rear twitching with each step. Dugan watched her for a moment, an appreciative smile on his face. This mission might not be so bad after all.

Stopping on a dime, the little termagant barely missed slamming into Kevnor when she rounded the corner. The big man reached out to steady her. "Easy, Zoë. What's got your tail in a twist?"

Turning to point at the man trailing her she sputtered, "Him."

Kev smiled when he saw Dugan. "You're here. Good. Now we can begin. I see you've already met Zoë."

"You could say that."

"This is Dugan?" Zoë asked. "This is the man who's going to take us into Iman?"

"Why yes, he is." His inscrutable brown eyes glanced back and forth between the two. "And I expect you to both behave with professionalism when dealing with one another."

"Understood," Dugan acknowledged.

Nodding, Zoë continued on to the study where the rest of the crew awaited.

Eyes sparkling with interest, Dugan observed, "She's something isn't she?"

"Oh, she's something all right. Just keep in mind that she is as a sister to me." On Baux, that was tantamount to a warning.

"I would never harm a woman, particularly one under your protection."

Kev burst out laughing. "Don't misunderstand me. My teammates and I would certainly exact revenge if anyone harmed her, but Zoë doesn't need my protection. My comment was intended to remind you that Zoë was raised and trained with the rest of us. Don't think for a minute that her diminutive stature makes her one whit less of a fighter. She could take you down in a heartbeat, and her body count is as high as any of the rest of the crew's." Kev smiled. "That little woman is probably more than you can handle."

Bristling with righteous indignation, Dugan sputtered, "What's that supposed to mean?"

"Relax. I wasn't questioning your manhood. I was simply pointing out that you were raised in vastly different ways. Zoë is a very independent woman, my friend. She doesn't need a keeper or a protector. She needs a companion, and she won't settle for less."

"What makes you think I couldn't be that companion," he asked softly.

Narrowing his eyes thoughtfully, Kevnor replied, "The way you were raised." He waved a hand about to encompass his surroundings. "Try to imagine yourself in the role of a woman here on Baux."

"Don't be ridiculous."

Slapping his new friend on the shoulder, Kev steered him toward the scheduled meeting. "My point exactly. Zoë would find life as a woman here just about as appealing as you would."

Dugan mulled that over as they made their way along the hall.

Chapter Eighteen

Aldora stood at attention before the queen's sister. "You requested my presence?"

"Sit down. You'll give me a stiff neck looking up at you."

"I prefer to stand," the younger woman replied.

Nambia slammed her fist down on the arm of the chair she sat in. "I didn't ask what you wanted. I said sit down."

Gingerly, Aldora sank into the opposing chair. "Yes, mother." The muscles in her cheeks flexed as she clinched her teeth.

"I heard what happened in the arena today."

"The brats took us by surprise," Aldora fumed. "It won't happen again."

"What if it does?" An imperious brow rose.

"I said it won't." Aldora eased even closer to the edge of her seat. "My girls have doubled their training schedule."

Nambia waved her to silence with a flick of the wrist. "That isn't important. What's important is that your cousin has the grudging respect of the students as well as the other instructors." Her face grew mottled with rage. "That is not what we planned."

Aldora surged to her feet. "*She* is not what we planned. Her skills are such that she might have been raised on Iman. How can we discredit her?"

"I'm not sure, but with the delegates from Baux due to arrive in a few days, something's bound to come up."

Now there was an interesting tidbit. "Delegates from Baux are coming here? Whatever for?"

"Oh, that fool Jacton thinks he can negotiate for the return of our princess." Nambia's fingers gouged into the arms of her chair.

"I don't get it, mother. If we don't want her and they do, why in the name of the goddess did we spend a fortune to bring her back?"

Muscle ticking in her cheek, Nambia gritted, "I never expected Umland to find her. I thought I was just going through the motions so that when my sister died there would be no impediment to my ascension."

Aldora's eyes narrowed speculatively. "I thought I was to rule."

"You are. But the natural progression is from my sister to me. Once the throne was offered to me, I would claim that in the best interest of Iman, leadership should pass to a younger and more vigorous woman." Nambia snorted, "Goddess knows we could use an aggressive monarch for a change."

Aldora's brows rose. "No one is more aggressive than you, mother."

Waving away the comment she continued, "As a young woman, we could expect you to reign for many years. And at your age, you're well able to provide several heirs. Iman doesn't need to be in a situation like this again. Persis would not have been worth the search, let alone the credits, if she'd had several sisters." Leaning over she smoothed the hair back off Aldora's brow. "With you here, I can't imagine why they bothered anyway."

"Thank you mother, but we are the branch, not the trunk, of the royal tree."

"Just because she was born thirty minutes before me, she's gotten everything. Everything." A sardonic smile twisted her lips. "But that will all be over soon."

"Why have you drawn this out so long?" Aldora leaned closer to whisper, "She should have been dead months ago."

"Patience. A hurried illness would have provoked suspicion. Besides, I wanted to establish myself as the doting sister. Public opinion is so important at times like these."

"Persis is so sanctimonious. I want to cut that brat out of her."

Nambia nodded. "In time. All things in good time."

Aldora's spirits lifted. "So I can have her?"

"You will be the queen." The statement hung in the air between them.

"I will, won't I?" A sly smile blossomed across Aldora's face. "And there'll be no one to gainsay me."

"I believe that's how autonomy works, precious."

***

Kevnor was antsy in the captain's chair. He much preferred his seat at the communications station, but this was his gig. When he reclaimed his wife, he wanted her to know it had been he who had rescued her. His Alpha nature wouldn't allow it to be any other way.

"Course plotted," Zoë reported.

"Let's get the hell out of here, Callus," he told the engineer.

No response was necessary as the subtle shift in the Bird let them all know she was no longer standing still. "Estimated arrival time?"

"Exactly twenty-nine—" Zoë said just as Dugan contradicted her.

"Thirty-two point seven, Captain," the Bauxite assured him.

Rising slowly to her feet, Zoë turned to face the man who stood directly behind her. "I am the navigator," she ground out between clinched teeth. "When the captain addresses navigation, he is speaking to me."

Dugan winked at her. "Even when you give him faulty information?"

"I am Gaithran. I do not make mistakes in points of navigation."

Stepping closer and leaning down till he almost touched her nose with his, Dugan assured her, "You are wrong this time."

"I have never been wrong before." Her complexion became mottled as her anger grew.

"Well mark this on your calendar, little woman, because this time you are dead wrong. I've made this trip dozens of times, and I tell you it is exactly thirty-two point seven hours."

"Miklus," she called out, "please note the time of departure. I want to know precisely how long it takes us to make orbit around Iman."

Sharing a knowing look with Kev, Mik assured her, "Will do, *little woman.*"

Turning slowly to face her crewmate, Zoë promised, "I will kick your ass if you ever call me that again."

Unable to contain his mirth any longer, Mik burst out laughing, crossing his index fingers in front of him as if to ward her off. "Okay, okay. I get the message."

Dugan harrumphed.

Zoë turned on him. "You would do well to take my warning to heart. I might be a *little woman*, but I am capable of backing up my threats."

"Don't get your nose out of joint just because I'm a better navigator than you." Dugan didn't know it, but he was treading on very thin ice. "I was only joking with you. After all, you are a woman, and you are little."

That did it. Zoë spun around, aiming for his nose with the heel of her right hand. Dugan caught her hand in his, holding it between them. She arched toward his face with her left fist. That too became his captive, so she slammed a knee toward his groin. Angling his body, Dugan slipped his leg behind the one bearing her weight and pressed on the back of her knee, buckling it and sending her toward the floor. She never made contact, however, because he held her up by her hands, still gripped by his. Off balance, he pulled her body into his, wrapping both arms around her to keep her secure. His lips grazing her ear he whispered, "The next time you take a swing at me I'm going to paddle your bare bottom till it stings. Then I'll see what I can do about quenching the sexual fire my hand ignites." He ended with a slight nip to the lobe before turning and striding from the bridge.

Mouth agape, Zoë watched him depart. She couldn't decide whether she was furious or turned on, but she had no problem deciding he had a mighty fine ass. Without a word she sat back down and checked the readouts. With supreme effort she managed not to squirm in her seat. All that talk of spankings had her more than a little uncomfortable.

Not daring to look at his buddy, Kev kept his eyes studiously on the view screen. Dev was only a few hours away. He concentrated on that and the plan they'd developed. With a little luck, he'd have his wife and his life back in only a few days.

Not quite so circumspect, Callus said drolly, "So, that was interesting."

Screw decorum. Kevnor burst out laughing. Callus and Mik joined him until tears streamed from their eyes. "You guys are dead meat," Zoë warned. "When I tell Dev, Shesshie, and Marissa about this, you will all be sorry."

Even that dire threat couldn't suppress their mirth. Rolling her eyes with disgust, Zoë headed for the galley. "I'm going to get something to eat. Call me if you need me." As the door swooshed behind her she could still hear their guffaws.

Dugan was leaning against the counter when she entered the room. "Great. Just what I need." Brushing by him she headed for the cooler.

Snagging her by the arm Dugan assured her, "Yes, I am just what you need." Without preamble, his mouth swooped down on hers, claiming the attention of every cell in her body. Draco, the man could kiss.

By the time he pulled back, his taste was forever imprinted on her. She swiped the back of her hand across her lips. "I didn't give you permission to do that."

"I think that's your problem, Zoë." His softly accented voice sent jolts to her womb. "You've always been in control with men, and it's against your nature."

"Bullshit. Just because the men on Baux subjugate their women doesn't mean I like it."

"I'm not talking about lifestyle, and you know it." Filling his hand with her hair he tilted her head back. "I'm talking about sex." He tugged on her just enough so she could feel the slightest discomfort. "I'm talking about submission and dominance. I'm talking about finding a partner who can show you that fine line between pleasure and pain. I'm talking about you screaming my name, begging me to stop...and begging me not to."

No man had ever talked to her like that. No man had ever been so forceful. No man had ever had her panting with need. "I'll never beg any man for anything." Her voice was husky with desire.

Dugan leaned down to nip her bottom lip, soothing it immediately with his warm wet tongue. "Oh, you'll beg," he vowed, "and you'll love every minute of it."

Desire shimmered through her body, causing her breasts to swell and her pulse to throb between her legs. Before she could frame a reply, he spun on his heel and left the room. She sagged against the countertop. If his delivery was even half as good as his promise, she was a goner. A half smile curled the left side of her lips as she reached for a container of juice.

***

"What'd you make of that?" Mik asked, wiping tears from his eyes.

"Pretty obvious he has the hots for her," Kev replied.

"Ya think?" Callus couldn't seem to wipe the grin from his face. "I always knew it would happen one day. I'm just glad I was here to see it. After all the hell she gave me about Marissa, paybacks are gonna be a bitch." Whistling, he leaned back over the equation he was working on.

"Now Callus—"

"Don't even go there, Mik." Holding his palm out facing his friend, Callus shook his head. "That little gal has picked on me from the day she laid eyes on me, and never once have I gotten the better of her. I refuse to let my little sis get away scott-free."

"Your funeral," Mik mumbled.

"Message incoming," Kev announced as he keyed the com.

Jacton's image filled the screen. "Report, cousin."

"Not much to report yet." Kev's droll response didn't sit well with the monarch. "We only left a short while ago."

"You left long enough ago for a coded transmission to be broadcast from your vessel."

Kev surged to his feet. "Draco! That's impossible. The Bird—"

"I know you did not just doubt my word." Softly spoken, Jacton still managed to convey his displeasure.

Hands flying over the panel in front of him, Mik interceded, "I'm sure Captain Kevnor didn't intend to impugn your integrity, Your Highness. Aboard the Freebird we pride ourselves in maintaining a tight ship. That includes security." Sitting back in his seat, he crossed his arms over his chest. "There it is," he stated. "Exactly twelve minutes ago. The recipient is somewhere in the capital city of Iman. What's it called, Callus?"

"Bedoa, I believe, Captain...uh, I mean Miklus."

Kev slapped his palms against his thighs. "That's it," he announced. "If I'd been at my usual post, the transmission wouldn't have escaped." He rose and headed for the communications station. "Up," he ordered.

Stumbling to his feet, Mik vacated the chair, shrugging. "So, what do I do? Clean the head?"

"Don't be an ass." Kev made a few adjustments to the instruments in front of him. "Go sit in the pilot's chair. You do what you're best at. I'll do what I'm best at." He frowned toward his cousin's smiling countenance. "That doesn't mean I'm not it charge. I'm just a much better communications officer than I am a captain."

Jacton held both hands up in surrender. "I didn't say a word." The image winked out as the transmission ended.

"Sorry about the slip-up, Kev." Callus' craggy features pulled into a worried frown.

Kev waved his apology away. "No harm done." He grinned. "Actually, it's a relief."

"Any chance you can pinpoint the point of origin?" Mik asked.

"Not at this late date. But you can bet your left nut I'll nail the sucker if he sends another." Kev keyed in the command to track all transmissions as he spoke. "And I have managed to retrieve the message." The forward screen filled with letters and symbols. "What do you make of this?"

Callus and Miklus moved closer, eyeing the jumble. "Not much." Mik shook his head.

Callus frowned, concentrating. "This almost looks like a mathematical equation." Stepping closer he pointed to the first line. "See?"

"Damn." Kev sat up straighter in his chair. "You're right." His fingers flew over the keyboard.

"Usually am," Callus bragged.

Kev took time to salute him with his middle finger.

Gradually a sentence appeared, followed by another. "This almost looks like a love letter," Kev grumbled.

"It's more than that. Someone is setting up an assignation." Mik ran his fingers through his thick hair. "At the freaking palace, no less. This is going to be more complicated than I thought."

"With Dev, it usually is." Kev sighed.

Chapter Nineteen

Dev laughed at the plethora of food adorning their table. "You boys must have made a hundred trips around the castle. If I ate even a small portion of this stuff, I'd be as big as a house."

"A palace." Tim giggled.

"A planet." Ewen joined the game.

"A planet is it?" Dev lunged at Ewen, tickling him on the ribs. "Are you calling your mother fat?"

"No, no," he gasped, laughing until he sank weak-kneed to the floor. "You're not fat. Just pregnant. I swear."

Kneeling beside him, Dev tickled him a couple of more times just for good measure. "Well, that's more like it." She sank back on her heels. "Now what shall we do with all this food?"

Tim was already piling a plate with the delicacies. "Eat it," he advised around a mouthful of Framada fruit fluff.

"I'll remind you that you said that when your belly's aching," she promised.

"Why don't we share it with the other slaves?" Ewen asked quietly.

Dev's heart swelled in her chest at his earnest compassion. "A lovely idea," she declared. "How do we go about sneaking them in?"

"All you have to do is make some more demands, Princess." Ewen's eyes twinkled. He was a very bright boy.

Getting ungracefully to her feet, Dev crossed to the sofa. "Let's see, I need a hot bath, a massage, my nails done, my hair cut, some new clothes, the entire suite cleaned...any more suggestions?"

Standing at attention, Ewen bowed formally from the waist. "I'll get right on it, my lady." He ruined the effect by blowing her a kiss before exiting the room.

Tim stood looking back and forth from the table to the door, full plate in hand. "He can take care of it by himself," Dev assured him. "Finish your food."

"What if the guards don't let him pass?" the little one worried.

"Then they wouldn't let you pass either and I'd have two of you to rescue instead of one. Besides, they haven't said anything so far."

Nodding, Tim agreed. "They've gotta be getting used to seeing us come and go, that's for sure."

"Have you encountered any problems?" Dev took the opportunity to question Tim without Ewen present. She feared the older boy kept things from her in an attempt to shield her.

"Well, except for that Aldora woman, everybody's been okay," he said around a mouthful of glazed Tortuga nuts. "Not counting Nambia, of course."

Of course. Her aunt was the mother of all bitches. "What did Aldora do?" Carefully modulating her voice to nonchalance, Dev pumped the kid for information.

"She hit Ewen." An indrawn gasp sucked crumbs down the wrong way, and Tim choked and coughed. Dev crossed to pat him on the back and placed his plate on the table until he could regain his equilibrium. He dashed tears from his eyes. "I wasn't supposed to tell you that."

"Don't worry. I won't tell Ewen. But it's wrong to keep things like that from me, Tim. I need to know all

I can about my enemies. It could be important at some point."

"But I promised."

"And promises are important. On the other hand, it's important to know when to make a promise and when not to. Now tell me everything that happened."

"Me and Ewen were just walking down the hall, going to the kitchen for some more food, when she stepped out of a door into our path. We tried to stop, but I bumped into her. She took a swipe at me, but Ewen stepped between us, and she hit him instead."

"Where was this? What room did she come out of?"

"Nambia's room. She seemed mad, too. I don't know why she'd be so mad about a kid bumping into her. I mean, she's a warrior. It couldn't have hurt that much."

Dev frowned. Interesting. What business could the captain of the guard have with the queen's sister? Nambia didn't have anything to do with the military did she? Gleaning information from this place was harder than finding a virgin on Pagoda. The door opened and Ewen appeared with several of the staff. Dev smiled her welcome. The answer to her problem had just entered her suite. "Welcome. Please, fix a plate and enjoy yourselves."

The men just stood there, lined up against the wall, eyes downcast. *Okay. This might take some finessing.* Dev squared her shoulders and moved closer. When she stood opposite the oldest guy, who was perhaps forty-five, she stopped. "You," she said, "come with me." Not looking back she crossed to the burgeoning table. "Prepare a plate for me. Only the most delicious and costly food." When he had complied and held the plate out before her she commanded, "Now eat it."

Forgetting years of training, the man raised his gaze to hers for a moment, shock evident. "Beg pardon, ma'am? I don't think I understand your wishes."

"I wish for you to eat the damn food. Is that too difficult for you?" She tried to sound harsh, but her twinkling eyes gave away her amusement, if anyone cared to look. Of course they didn't.

Glancing at the other servants, he balanced the plate on one hand and reached for a slice of Prima Lizard tongue in Ickluk sauce. His eyes closed in ecstasy as the meat dissolved on his tongue. He did not need to be prodded again. In no time the plate was empty. He stood on shaking knees awaiting the punishment he was sure to come.

"Was that so bad?" Dev teased.

Voice breaking, he mumbled, "It was delicious, ma'am." After a fortifying breath he inquired, "What service will be required to pay for this pleasure?"

"I can only think of one thing that will atone for your temerity. I order you to eat another plate full." When the man stood rooted to the spot for several seconds, she reached out and pushed him gently on the arm. "Don't dawdle. You heard my order." Turning, she addressed her dumbfounded audience. "Each and every one of you is commanded to eat this food until it is all gone." When no one moved, she snapped, "Do you not understand my wishes?"

That got them moving, though they more closely resembled a group headed to the gallows than men about to be fed delicacies they'd only dreamed about. She glanced between the boys and shrugged. "You two have any suggestions?" she asked them. "Maybe you should show them by example."

"Don't look at me," Tim groaned. "I can't eat another bite."

"Well I can," Ewen assured her and elbowed his way up to the banquet. "I have always wanted to try these," he said popping a Coregon grape in his mouth. "And just smelling this stuff drove me crazy when I was serving Lady Nambia." He heaped a mound of Narituk potatoes on his plate.

A couple of the younger men followed his lead, placing often seen but never tasted dishes on their plates. One or two even licked their fingers after biting a particularly divine culinary concoction. Eventually each man had food in his hand, but many still refused to eat.

Dev decided to pull out all the stops. Taking a deep breath she placed her hands on her hips and addressed the group. "You are the sorriest excuse for men I've ever seen. Even the slaves on Pagoda had more spirit than you. When my friends and I led their revolt, they were right there beside us, fighting for their freedom." She snorted. "You bunch of pussies won't even eat." Turning to Ewen, she asked, "Did you only bring the eunuchs to eat with us?"

Aghast, Ewen assured her, "None of the men on Iman are castrated unless they break the law."

"Well, you certainly can't tell they have any balls." Dev injected all the derision she could into the statement.

A tall red haired man stepped forward, made eye contact, and shoveled an entire mini loaf of Muskvin Pâté into his mouth defiantly. The corner of Dev's mouth curled up. You could always count on testosterone in any corner of the universe.

"Well, that's more like it." Grabbing her own plate she ladled on the goodies and sat down on the floor to eat. "Any of you guys feel like taking a load off, feel free to sit anywhere." With that, she ignored them and ate.

The boys settled on either side of her. "Tell me again about Kevnor," Ewen prompted.

Dev winked at him approvingly. "My husband is tall and strong, a formidable warrior. Soon, he will be here to rescue me."

"Impossible." Tim followed the dialogue they had planned. "No one escapes Iman."

Dev shrugged. "I will escape. And I will take you two with me. You are my sons now, and I want you raised in a place where men and women are equal, where you can choose your own destiny and learn to love without restriction."

"Where is there such a wonderful place?" Somewhat stilted, their rehearsed conversation had the desired effect. The distance between where they sat and the others stood was growing smaller.

"Most of the galaxy is like that." Dev assured him, then injected heartfelt venom in her next statement, "Iman is the sewer of the known world." That got her a few grins. "Haven't any of you ever wanted to change things around here? Do you really like living like you do?"

"What good does it do us to make ourselves more miserable by longing for the unattainable?" a voice asked from the group. Shuffling feet and muted grumbles backed him up.

With athletic grace Dev rose to her feet. "I cannot believe you buy that drayhorn drivel. By sheer numbers and superior physical strength, you men could overcome the women on this planet."

"We are untrained."

"We have no skills, no leader."

"We are not stronger than the warriors."

In his high-pitched young voice Ewen told them, "Yes, you are stronger. I have proven this, and so has Tim."

"Yeah," Tim backed him up. "We whipped all the girls at practice." Blushing over his blatant lie he hurried to add, "Well, all the best ones anyway."

Dev ruffled his hair. "You certainly did, and after only a couple of weeks of training."

"You have had warrior training?" one of the braver of the servants asked.

"Yep. And I can read and do math, too," he bragged. "My mom taught me." Puffing out his chest he smiled up at Devona.

"Who is your mother that she would break the law?"

"I am his mother," Dev insisted. "From now on, Ewen and Tim are my boys, and when I leave this dung heap, they will be with me. Now you can continue the way you are, or you can put an end to this degrading lifestyle. I really don't care. But a chance to be trained in some basic martial arts might never come along again, so be sure what you want before you leave this room."

A youth of about sixteen stepped out of the group. "Are you saying you will train us? Will you lead us with your big belly and your royal pedigree?" he scoffed.

Three steps, a well placed foot and a twist of her wrist had the boy on the floor. "Don't ever," Dev ground out between gritted teeth, "use that tone with me. Not because these lunatics think I'm their long lost princess, but because I am the first officer of the Freebird, and a damn good one." She turned her back to walk away, and the humiliated boy swept a foot out to trip her. Anticipating the move, Dev jumped, spun, and delivered a roundhouse kick to the kid's chin. He didn't know it, but her excellent use of force gave him a bruise rather than a broken jaw. She knelt beside him. "I despise a liar and a backstabber. If you ever display dishonorable behavior around me again, I'll kick your ass myself." She glanced down at her little rounded belly. "Stomach or no stomach. Do I make myself clear?"

"Yes, ma'am," he whispered.

"Now get up and come over here." Dev strode to the small table where she ate her meals with the boys. "Sit down." She indicated the seat across from her. "I'm going to give you another demonstration," she told him, slamming her right elbow down, hand held up in the air. "Now put your elbow down and grasp my hand," she instructed. After grasping his hand in hers Dev demonstrated. "You try to push my hand backward and I'll try to push yours backward. Do you understand?"

A few moments later the lad pressed her knuckles against the polished wood. A look of shocked awe suffused his face. "I beat you," he announced unnecessarily.

"Indeed you did. The question now is how? You have no training. I easily overcame you a few minutes ago."

He shrugged. "It is a mystery to me, lady."

She leaned forward capturing his eyes with hers. "You beat me because you are stronger than I am. It is a simple fact that males have greater musculature. I can outmaneuver you because I am trained to do so, but if you ever got your hands on me, you would win." She could practically see the wheels turning in his head as he thought over what she'd said. "I grew up training with men. I would never allow you to get close enough. The women of Iman don't seem to be aware of that. It is an advantage you could use to your benefit."

Chapter Twenty

"We have to go under the assumption that our names are known among the Imani," Mik suggested. "Assumed names would be prudent."

"I concur," Zoë opined.

Dugan whistled. "Whoa. I didn't know you were capable of agreeing."

Raising a superior brow, Zoë quipped, "You're still pissed because I was right on the arrival time."

"I still can't understand that. I have made this trip many times and travel time has never varied."

"You have never made this trip aboard the Bird," she bragged. "Callus made some modifications to the engines. We are always faster than other ships."

Callus was chagrined. For the last full solar day he'd given her hell about Dugan, and she still praised his work. Maybe he should let up on her.

"His social skills might suck, but his engineering skills are legendary," she added.

On second thought, maybe he wouldn't. Callus narrowed his brown eyes menacingly.

"Back to the issue at hand," Kev steered them. "We need names, preferably close to our own so we won't fuck up at a crucial moment."

"I'll use Mark," Mik decided.

"Callus...Dallas...sounds good to me," the engineer announced.

"I think Ksor will do for me," Kev told them.

"I think I'll be Eula," Zoë insisted. "I've always loved that name."

"Eula! That's nothing like Zoë." Callus voiced what they all felt.

Her shoulders squared stubbornly. "I want Eula," she insisted.

Support came from an unexpected corner. "I think Eula is a perfect choice," Duggan agreed. "Exotic and unique, just like Zoë."

"So, you don't think the name Zoë is exotic and unique?" she snapped.

"I didn't say that. I said for a temporary name Eula suited you."

"For crying out loud, Zoë," Mik groused. "Give the guy a break. You can't even agree with him when you agree with him."

"I would love nothing better than to break him," she insisted.

"I welcome the attempt at the first opportunity," Dugan smiled.

"Ew," Callus cut in. "I don't want to hear this."

Zoë was the image of innocence. "What?"

Kev shook his head. *Mik never loses control like this.* "People, get serious. We have already docked, Zedne will be here momentarily, and we need to be prepared." He didn't have time for Zoë's obstinate streak. "I don't care if you call yourself goddess, just pick something, let us know, and stick to it."

"I have. Eula."

"Eula it is. Everyone remember that." Kev turned to speak to his uncle. "Ah, Zedne, your timing is impeccable. We were just choosing aliases for this venture. Our real names are too well-known in certain circles."

Nodding, Zedne agreed. "So, what have your come up with?"

"Mik will be Mark, Callus will be Dallas, I have chosen Ksor, and Zoë will be known as Eula."

Zedne smiled. "Eula. A perfect choice. On Baux it means *of stubborn nature.*"

Brown eyes flashing, she spun to glare at Dugan. "You bastard. You set me up."

"On the contrary, my lineage can be traced for thousands of years." Straightening his impeccable jacket he winked at her. "Don't forget, it was you who chose the name. I was just being agreeable."

"The shuttle is ready to board," Mik announced. "Let's get this show on the road."

Zedne briefed them again during descent, "Remember, you are all to act as aides. That means you don't contradict me in front of anyone, not even the servants. It is imperative that we keep up appearances at all times. And Zoë, if you have no objection, I think you should pose as Dugan's wife. On Iman a woman of consequence would have a lot of freedom to move about. A woman who allowed herself to be subservient would be looked down on."

"Couldn't I pose as your wife? That would give me even more clout." She did not want to share quarters with Dugan. Okay, she did...just not like this.

"True, but less mobility. My spouse would be more closely watched." Zedne flicked his wrist dismissively. "Besides, who'd believe a beautiful young woman like you would be married to an old man like myself? No, no, my dear, Dugan is the most likely candidate for your make-believe groom."

Dugan said nothing, just stood there burning her alive with his eyes and the promises they conveyed.

***

The red carpet might have been rolled out, but the atmosphere in the palace was anything but warm and welcoming. The hallways they passed through were lined with warriors whose looks alone should have reduced them to burning embers. Kev and Mik exchanged a surreptitious glance, each aware that the other was on high alert. Zedne led the way with shoulders squared. Each member of the Bird's crew gave him high marks for intestinal fortitude.

"The queen is indisposed at the moment," an attractive middle aged woman addressed them, "but she has bid me extend her welcome and promises to meet with you at her earliest convenience." She signaled two of the warriors. "Follow Ketina and Tresha. They have been assigned to you and will be available just outside your quarters should you require anything." Couched in diplomacy the threat was understood by all. They would be under constant military supervision.

"We appreciate your hospitality." Zedne smiled. "Senator Dugan and his wife will naturally require their own suite." He leaned in to speak candidly, "And of course our aides must be housed separately."

"Is that what you call servants on Baux? Aides?" Her tone expressed her distaste. "How interesting." She tapped Zedne lightly on the arm. "Never fear, we are well versed in the treatment of thralls on Iman. They will be housed in the servant's quarters."

Excellent. Zedne has arranged for me and Mik and Callus to be less severely monitored. Kev smiled inwardly, taking mental notes of the palace's floor plan as they went. They passed more than fifty warriors between the front door and the wing where the diplomats would be housed. Either they were big on ostentatious displays or they were very nervous.

Tresha, a curvaceous brunette, stopped before a door at the head of the massive staircase. "Sir, I believe you will be comfortable here." With a flourish she opened the door to reveal an opulent sitting room. "Your sleeping quarters are to the left and the bath chambers adjoin it." Stepping back, she waited for Zedne to precede her into the room.

Like a gaggle of geese, they all filed in behind him. "This is most generous," Zedne complimented. "I'm sure I will be most comfortable here." Turning to Kev he indicated a large armoire. "You may place my baggage there."

About fucking time. Kev lowered the matched leather bags to the floor. Careful to keep his eyes downcast he asked, "Shall I unpack, sir?"

"No, you can wait until you're shown to your quarters, then return to help me."

"As you wish."

Displaying abs that had all five men sucking their collective stomachs in, Ketina stood like an Amazon goddess, waiting her turn. Right on cue, Zoë commented, "I sure hope our rooms are as lovely."

Dugan slipped a proprietary arm around her waist and pulled her up against his side. "I'm sure they will." Bending down he planted a kiss on her forehead. "Only the best for my girl."

Tresha cringed visibly. Mik bit the inside of his mouth severely to keep from laughing. Dugan was damn good at baiting the women.

Zoë casually placed the heel of her boot on the top of Dugan's arch and stepped down. "You spoil me," she cooed.

Without so much as a twitch, Dugan lifted his foot, throwing her off balance. Gallantly he steadied her. "Careful, dear." You could practically see the steam rising from his *wife's* ears.

Ketina cleared her throat, clearly uncomfortable with the by-play. "If you please." She indicated a doorway across the hall. Again they filed out like obedient children.

Once the diplomats were settled a servant was called to escort Kev, Mik and Callus to their temporary chambers. As it turned out they were afforded one small room with three pallets on the floor. A communal bathroom served the servants on the entire wing. The men silently cursed their hosts for the shabby accommodations.

A thin lad of about fifteen entered the room they'd been assigned carrying a load of bedding. Since Callus and Mik were already stretched out on their pallets, arms crossed under their heads and eyes closed, Kev instructed the boy to drop the load on his pallet. Sensing an opportunity to glean a little information, Kev squatted to divvy up the blankets and spoke over his shoulder to the young servant. "Is she as beautiful as they say?" he asked casually.

"Who?"

"The princess. The word on Baux is that she's a real looker."

"I haven't actually seen her. She's housed on the east wing, and I serve here on the south." He leaned down and lowered his voice conspiratorially. "But I have a cousin who's seen her. He didn't mention her looks, but he said she sure is a strange one."

Kev stood slowly, not wanting to intimidate the boy. "How so?"

"She spent an entire day demanding one outrageous delicacy after another, then called in a bunch of the staff and made them eat it. Not that they minded," he snorted. "Who wouldn't want a taste of braised Gevian tongue?"

"Who indeed?" Kev worked to keep the scowl off his face. His wife was up to something, and he'd bet his interest in the company that it was neither safe nor something he'd approve. "Hasn't she been here for weeks? And you haven't even caught a glimpse of her? What, does she stay in her apartment all the time?"

"She goes places—at least she did until a few days ago—but I just don't get out of the kitchen very often." His bony chest stuck out with pride. "I'm training to be a cook you know."

"No. I didn't. Congratulations." Kev strained to look suitably impressed. "Uh, why doesn't the princess go places any more? She isn't sick is she?"

"Not that I know of. Rumor is that her aunt doesn't want her near the Bauxite delegation."

Kev's brow rose. "Why not?" The bitch had her under house arrest.

"I have no idea. Politics are beyond my understanding."

I have to get to Dev, the quicker the better. "Well, thanks for stopping by to welcome us." Kev held out his hand for the lad to shake, but the boy just stared at him. Leaning forward, Kev grasped his hand and pumped it up and down. "It's called a handshake," he explained. "Most civilized worlds do some similar form of greeting."

"Oh." The kid returned the gesture. "Handshake. I like that." He smiled, revealing a missing tooth.

"What's your name?" Kev asked.

"Lysander. What's yours?"

"Ke—"

A bout of coughing erupted from the pallet where Mik had been feigning sleep. He sat up, thumping himself on the chest.

Damn. He'd almost given his real name. "Ksor," he told Lysander, crossing to thwack Mik on the back. "And this is my friend Mark. The guy who's still sleeping is Dallas."

"Pleased to meet you all." Lysander showed off his newfound knowledge holding out his hand for Mik to shake.

Mik solemnly shook the boy's hand, recognizing in him the same sort of crushed spirit their young friend Eb had exhibited not so long ago. "Don't hesitate to call on us if you need anything," Mik offered.

Lysander laughed. "You're new here. What help could you possibly be?"

Eyes twinkling, Mik shrugged. "You never know."

The door had barely closed behind Lysander when Kev turned to his friends. "Did you hear all that?"

Callus, who now sat tailor fashion on his bedding replied, "Sure did. And I'd be willing to bet Dev's not taking house arrest well."

"That's pretty much a given," Kev concurred. "It's what she's doing about it that scares the hell out of me. I've got to get to her."

"It's not even dark yet," Mik cautioned.

"They'll expect us to wait till nightfall to attempt something. A bold move will catch them unawares. What I need is some of those pants like the other servants are wearing. I'll bet no one will even question me if I'm wearing those."

Callus harrumphed. "You go walking around without a shirt and they'll notice all right. None of these guys has a single tatt." Back in their mercenary days the crew of the Freebird had all gotten matching tattoos on the back of their left shoulders. Kev had added several more since then.

"Good point. Surely they don't all go shirtless."

"All the ones I've seen do." They room they'd been assigned was on a sublevel. Callus glanced up at the only window, nestled just below the ceiling. "Give me a boost up and I'll see what's outside."

Kev crouched under the window, boosting Callus up to stand on his shoulders. "Hurry up. You weigh a ton."

"Quit whining."

Mik crowded closer. "Can you see anything?"

"A bunch of knees."

"Very funny."

"There's an inner courtyard full of guys, all standing around talking."

"Ouch. Get your toe out of my collarbone," Kev groused. "What are they wearing?"

"Pretty much the same stuff. But there are a couple of guys with shirts on. They look fit enough. I can't figure out why they have shirts on."

Mik snapped, "We need details, Callus."

"There are exactly five shirts that I can see. One guy is bald, two have blond hair and one has brown mixed with gray. The last fellow is red headed." Leaning down he grasped Mik's hands and jumped from Kev's shoulders.

"About fuckin' time." Kevnor massaged his aching shoulders.

"Pussy," Callus teased, jumping back to avoid the half-hearted swing Kev took at his head.

"Come on, Callus, what do you think? Can Kev pass for one of the guys in shirts?" Mik wanted to know.

"Probably. The ones in shirts seemed to be better built and better fed than the others. My guess would be that they are special in some way."

"What way?" Kev frowned.

"I don't know. Special. Who knows? Maybe they're just the meanest and win all the food fights."

"Well I need one of those shirts." Kev headed toward the door.

"Wait." Mik held up his hand. "I'll go with you."

"Me, too," Callus offered.

"Nah, I can manage. Besides, one of us is a lot less likely to attract attention than all of us together."

Chapter Twenty-one

They wouldn't even let her go to practice with the boys. That really pissed her off. "How'd it go?" she asked them as soon as they returned to their quarters.

"It wasn't too bad," Ewen told her.

Tim rolled his eyes. "They wouldn't let us spar at all." Ewen elbowed him in the side. "Ouch. Why'd you do that?"

"You were supposed to keep that between us," the older boy whispered.

Dev ruffled his hair. "Never mind, Ewen. Sometimes you have to tell your mother so she can handle it when others don't act right. It's a parent's job to stand up for her children."

"It is?" Tim asked, wide eyed. "No one ever told me that before."

"Somehow that doesn't surprise me," Dev quipped. Eyeing the boys she observed, "You got your share of dirt somewhere. If it wasn't on the sparring mat, how did you get so dirty?"

"They wouldn't fight us, but they sure didn't mind pushing us around." Crossing to the table Tim checked it out for any remaining food. "Those pigs ate it all."

"Don't worry, we'll get some more. In the meantime you two are getting a bath." Twin groans expressed their feelings on that idea. "Go on now, both of you. Wash up and I'll get you some clean clothes."

Dragging their feet, the boys dutifully made their way into the bathing chamber. Rubbing a bulge that appeared in her belly she commented, "Yes, your brothers are a couple of little heathens. Your dad's going to love them." Humming a little tune she sorted through the laundry for undergarments and pants. A furtive noise caught her attention and she froze, cocking her head toward the balcony. On silent feet she crossed to the glass doors, picking up one of the wooden practice swords on the way.

When the door eased open, Dev drew back the cudgel and swung it with all her might at the encroaching figure. Just as she was about to make contact she recognized who she was aiming at and dropped the stave and squealed—a very un-warrior like sound.

"Damn it, woman, you almost took my arm off." Kevnor rubbed at his forearm that met her weapon on its downward swing.

"Kev!" She burst into tears and threw herself into her husband's arms.

Injury forgotten, Kev closed his arms around her, assailing her with lips and hands. He couldn't get enough of her. Backing her against the wall, he pressed into her body, drinking in the taste and feel of her. "Honey, are you okay?" Not giving her a chance to answer, he kissed her again, staking his claim in the most primitive manner. One hand eased her thigh up to rest at his waist while the other dipped beneath her brief top, filling his palm with her aroused breast. His grinding hips kept time with his plunging tongue. She met him with equal fervor, sucking at his mouth and clawing at his shoulders. When his engorged penis rubbed against her, desperate whimpers escaped. Kev redoubled his efforts.

"Get away from my mother!" The angry declaration barely penetrated his foggy brain before the abandoned stick thwacked him in the back of the knee.

"What the fu—?"

A small body wedged itself between the straining adults, pushing furiously against Kev's stomach, barely missing the very eager proof of his affections. "You're hurting her."

"Ewen, Tim, no." Dev tugged her clothing back into place. "Don't hurt him. This is your father."

That pronouncement brought all three males to an immediate halt.

Realizing that heaven had been stripped from his grasp, Kev's disappointed flesh sagged. Kev knew just how it felt. With a quick crotch adjustment, he glanced at the boys and back at his woman. "Would you care to explain to me what's going on?"

Dev stepped away from the wall, drawing the boys to her, an arm around each one. "These fierce young warriors are Ewen and Tim. I have adopted them."

It didn't take a genius to see the hope and fear in the eyes that silently observed him. Kev frowned as he took a minute to size up his new family. "Warriors, you say?"

"Yes, sir." The smaller lad stepped forward. "Mom has been teaching us, and we beat the best girls at the training camp."

"Well I should hope so." Kev nodded wisely. "They're only girls after all." To his wife he said, "Care to fill me in?"

Before she could answer, Ewen interrupted, "We were her servants. She said she'd train us and teach us to read and write. Then she said she'd take us with her when you came for her." His face was a mask of indifference. "But if you don't want us, it's okay."

Emotion clutched at Kevnor's chest. "Not want you? A couple of fine boys like you? Of course I want you. Besides, our baby will need two big brothers to guard him when your mother and I are busy."

"Mom says the baby is a girl," Tim confessed.

"All the more reason to have two big brothers." In a stage whisper Kev confided, "Girls can be a lot of trouble."

Dev bristled. "This one's going to be in about a minute."

"See what I mean?" Kev laughed. "Now why don't you two go finish drying off and get dressed and let me and your mother talk. We have a lot to plan if I'm going to get you out of here."

"Yes, sir," they said in unison, dashing off to do his bidding.

When they were out of earshot, Dev whispered, "You don't mind do you?"

Gently he reeled her into his embrace. "No. I don't mind." He kissed the top of her head. "Though I wouldn't have minded a few more minutes alone with you." Sighing he steered her to the sofa. "Now fill me in, but quickly. I only have a few minutes on this visit."

"When can we leave? I'm sick to death of this place."

"I can well believe that," Kev agreed whole-heartedly.

"As you can see, I'm a prisoner here. Nambia, my aunt, seems to be running things. From what I have been able to glean from the servants, my mother has been on the edge of death for a long time. Her sister has graciously stepped in to run things." Bitterness tinged her voice.

"Do you suspect foul play?"

Dev shrugged. "Who knows? Nambia appears to be a devoted sister." Thinking of the disparity in her behavior in the queen's presence and other times she added, "Though something's not quite right there. My gut tells me there's a lot more going on than meets the eye."

Kev digested what she'd told him. "Any idea who might be sending coded messages to Baux?"

Synapses popping like firecrackers, the pieces of the puzzle began to fall into place. "As a matter of fact, yes. Before they were assigned to me, the boys sometimes served Nambia. They swear a man who slept with her mistreated them. And only a couple of weeks ago, I witnessed the arrival of a ship in the middle of the night. A hooded figure entered the palace in her wing." Eyes alight, she jumped up to pace the room. "The bitch is plotting to take over the throne."

Clad in the skimpy attire of the planet his wife caused a rather uncomfortable physical reaction as he watched her, breasts jiggling and somewhat broader rear enticing. "Are you sure it's Nambia, or is that your personal dislike insinuating itself into the scenario?"

Trust Kev to zero in on the very thing that disturbed her. "Good question," she admitted.

The naked boys scampered to the pile of clothing laid out on the bed and hurriedly dressed. "Are we leaving now?" Tim asked. "Do we have time to eat first?"

Dev and Kev burst out laughing. "I'm afraid you'll have time for several meals before we manage to get you all out of here," Kev told him. "But don't worry. I'm here now and I'm not leaving without you...all of you." Winking at Dev he asked, "Do you think we can afford to feed him?"

The smiles faded from the boy's faces. "He can have my share," Ewen offered.

"I don't have to eat that much," Tim assured him at the same time.

Dev started to speak, but Kev interrupted her. "Come here boys," he told them. On shaking legs the lads inched closer. "In this family we like to tease and joke, so you'll need to get used to that." He pulled the boys in until he had an arm around each one. "But never forget that we always take care of each other, so no matter how much we tease, or argue, or even get mad enough to fight, we never let each other down. That means that even if we only have one loaf of bread, we all share it." He waited for each boy to nod then continued, "No matter how much you eat, or if you get in trouble and have to be punished, your mother and I will still love you and take care of you. Do you understand?"

Instead of answering his question Ewen pointed out, "You've made mom cry."

Kev looked up in shock. Dev almost never cried, certainly not twice in one day.

"Don't worry," she assured her men as she dashed tears from her eyes. "They're happy tears."

"There are different kinds?" Kev asked stupidly.

Laughing and crying at the same time she confided, "Apparently there are." Rubbing her stomach she added, "Pregnancy is teaching me a lot."

Through the years of fighting, both in the military and as mercenaries, the crew of the Freebird had faced some difficult situations. Nothing, Kev realized, compared to the difficulty of leaving the boys and his woman ten minutes later.

***

"You know this is dangerous," Nambia gasped as her lover plunged again and again into her wet depths. "We could be discovered."

Moving a hand from her hip to her shoulder he pushed her head farther down as she leaned over the edge of the bathroom counter. "I couldn't wait," he panted. "I had to have you."

The lip of the sink gouged into her stomach. She relished the pain as she arched her back to take him deeper. "Harder," she insisted.

Knowing what she liked he smiled at their reflection in the mirror, watching as she shuddered when he reached beneath to pinch her nipple. Moaning, Nambia fumbled to reach her other breast pinching and tugging at her own turgid nipple. Spasms shook her as she came.

The man behind her smiled and pulled out. "You know what I want." She fell to her knees before him, lapping and sucking at him until his cock disappeared into her mouth. "Take it all," he commanded, and she complied, opening her throat to accommodate his engorged length. When he came in hot, salty bursts, she massaged his balls until he was completely drained, licking the last drops as they spilled from her lips.

Fingers entwined in her hair, he tilted her head back to look at her. "Make certain you are alone tonight." Stepping into his hastily discarded trousers, he left the room.

Chapter Twenty-two

Mik and Callus sprang to their feet when Kevnor entered the room.

"What happened?" Mik asked.

"Did you see her?" Callus wanted to know.

"Patience." Kev smiled, stripping out of his purloined garments.

"Patience, my ass." Mik slugged him in the arm.

Tackling him from the other side, Callus wrestled Kev down to the floor. "Tell us," he demanded.

"Okay, okay." Kev laughed, shoving them aside. "I saw her. She's fine and the baby is fine and I now have two sons."

"What?"

"You heard me. Dev and I have two boys." He shook his head, smiling like a simpleton. "That woman never ceases to amaze me. She took in the two boys they assigned to be her servants and the next thing you know she adopted them."

Nodding sagely Mik agreed, "That's our Dev. Always the unexpected."

"I always thought she was about the most *unmotherly* woman I ever knew," Callus grunted. "Guess I thought wrong."

"Did you come up with a plan?" Mik wanted to know.

"Loosely."

"Are you going to *loosely* fill us in?" Mik groused.

"I'm going back tonight. We'll plan more then."

"Impossible," Mik declared. "They'll be expecting it. You'll get your ass caught. Then we'll have to get you both out of here."

Kev smirked. "You have so much faith in me."

"It's not about faith. It's about you making stupid decisions," his friend insisted.

"Not to worry. I've got it covered. I'm not going to sneak in the window. I'm going to walk right in her front door." When the other two looked skeptical he explained, "At precisely eleven tonight Dev is going to get a mad craving. When the boys go down to the kitchen, I'm going to help them carry the stuff back up. The guards will only see some poor schmuck carrying stuff."

"I suppose you plan to wear the same clothes you did today?" Callus inquired.

"Why not?"

Callus and Mik exchanged a knowing glance.

"Okay, what do you two know that I don't?" Kev asked.

"It seems the shirts mark a man as someone's concubine," Mik smirked.

"What?" Kev shouted.

"I may be mistaken, but I don't think concubines would be toting stuff up from the kitchen," Callus just had to add.

"Draco!"

"Yeah. My thoughts exactly," Mik agreed.

"Okay, okay." Kev paced the small space. "I'll send her a note explaining things. We'll just regroup and go at it from a different angle."

"Maybe something will occur to us when we meet with your uncle later. We've been summonsed to attend him in half an hour."

Stepping into his own pants Kev nodded. "Yeah, Zedne might have some ideas."

"I say let's leave now and reconnoiter," Callus suggested. "This place is huge. We need to familiarize ourselves with the layout."

"Good idea." Kev nodded. "But I have a rudimentary understanding already. When I was able to get a better look at the place, I realized that it's built like a huge X, each wing facing a global position."

"Interesting." Mik ran his fingers through his hair. "How many levels?"

"Three. All the living suites are on the second and third floors. The first floor serves as reception, entertainment, and recreational facilities. The kitchen and slaves' quarters are all on the sublevel, as you've already surmised."

Callus grunted. "Makes it damn hard to sneak out with those tiny windows."

"And I find it interesting that our window looks out on the inner courtyard," Mik observed. "Even if we climbed out, it would be into a secured area."

"You don't know the half of it," Kev agreed. "This place is crawling with warriors, all armed to the teeth."

"But they're all women," Callus stated the obvious.

Kev raised a brow and just stared at his friend for a moment. "Women. You mean like Dev and Zoë?"

Callus grunted. "I get your point."

"Let me just point out that these women are all warriors. It's their culture. They fight as fiercely and with as much determination to win as any man. If—when—we engage them in combat, do not hold back."

Callus looked chagrined. "It's a lot easier to fight women who are wearing some kind of uniform instead of those skimpy outfits."

"Agreed." Mik chuckled. "They make it blatantly obvious they're female."

***

"Come in, come in." Zedne waved them into the suite, glanced up and down the hall, and closed the door behind them. "Where have you three been? We're due to meet with the queen in a few minutes."

Kev glanced at his wrist. "We're right on time," he observed.

"Didn't you get my message? I sent a house boy to tell you the schedule had been changed."

"We never got any message."

"Never mind now. I have to leave." Zedne donned his brocaded jacket, flicking imagined dust from the sleeve. "Stay here until I return."

Kev barred his exit. "Wait just a damn minute. We're supposed to go with you."

Agitated, Zedne tried to step around his nephew. Kev once again placed his body between the door and his uncle. "You're not leaving this room until you fill us in."

Frowning, the older man sighed. "The queen is currently awake and has requested to see me. It would not be in the best interest of our cause to keep her waiting."

"Why. Are. We. Not. Included." Kev's dark eyes glared intensely.

Zedne laughed. "You're not essential personnel as far as these women are concerned. They don't negotiate with underlings."

Kev was not amused. "We assumed this guise so we could take the time to come up with a plan that would cause the least damage to the inhabitants of Iman. I am beginning to rethink my caution on their behalf. I will blow this entire planet sky high if I have to. Keep that in mind, uncle. I'll be waiting here for your return. Don't keep me waiting."

So, the lad has some of his old man in him after all. Authority sits well on his shoulders. Too bad we have differing political views. "I assure you I will hasten back as soon as I am able." Zedne left the room.

"Well, that was diplomatic." Mik flopped into a nearby chair.

"Screw diplomacy. I want my wife and my kids out of here. Now." Kev rarely lost his temper. When he did, no one with any intelligence got in his way. Callus stepped aside as he strode to the window.

"Tonight, I will send a message to Devona. Tomorrow, I will go to her and damn the consequences." Gripping the windowsill with white knuckled intensity, Kev concentrated on regulating his breathing and with it his out of control temper.

Turning he paced his uncle's quarters, checking the bathroom, sleeping chamber, and even the closets. As he closed the door on a massive armoire something caught, preventing it from closing. When he bent to remove the garment, his hand encountered something wet. "Shit."

"What is it?" Mik asked.

Gingerly, Kev raised the pants his uncle had worn earlier in the day. "I'm not sure, but I think Zedne pissed his pants...and I put my hand in it."

"That's nice," Callus replied drolly.

"Isn't it?" Kev tossed them back on the floor and headed for the bathroom. "I hope he has antibacterial soap." As he reached for the sink Kev felt a hair stuck to his fingers. Looking down he realized it was quite long and much lighter than his uncle's hair. A frown knitted his brow. With his other hand he extracted the hair from his damp fingers. "Son of a bitch."

"What now?" Mik called from the other room.

Striding back to the abandoned trousers, Kev picked them up again and held them up to the light. "Come here," he called to his friends. "Tell me what you make of this."

Mik and Callus examined the damp spot on Zedne's trousers. "If I didn't know better I'd say your uncle employed an age old method of reliving tension," Mik replied.

Kev held up the long strand of hair between his thumb and forefinger, waving it back and forth. "I don't think he took care of business alone."

"That's crazy." Callus frowned. "He doesn't know anybody..."

"Or does he?" Kev's voice was quiet. Deadly quiet.

***

The queen's chambers were dimmed. Zedne could barely make out her features as she lay on the divan, her pale complexion fading into the beige bolsters that surrounded her for support. "Come close," she commanded her voice nearly as washed out as her countenance. "I want to see the face of my enemy."

Zedne turned on the charm for which he was famous. "Truly, I am not your enemy, lady. I seek peace for both our people."

Lila gave a surprisingly hardy bark of laughter. "Yes, you are my enemy. You seek to dominate the women of Iman and change forever the traditions to which we have clung for centuries."

Face carefully devoid of expression, Zedne held his hand over his heart and bowed slightly from the waist. "I only want lasting peace and the return of Devona Dimetri. What could be less threatening?"

Collapsing back against the plethora of pillows Lila smiled faintly. "You know the human body is truly amazing," she whispered.

Zedne wondered if she'd finally slipped into insanity.

"All these months—years really—that I've lain in my sickbed wasting away, my body has tried to heal itself. Oftentimes, it compensates for the loss of one function by allowing another to take over its purpose."

"That's very interesting, your majesty, but..."

She continued as though he hadn't interrupted. "Take eyesight for instance. There are days when I can see fine, while at other times my vision is so blurred as to render me practically blind. But on those occasions, my sense of smell seems to be increased greatly." She turned her face toward Zedne. "Don't you find that fascinating, ambassador?"

Struggling to follow her train of thought Zedne shrugged. "I suppose so, highness."

"Today for instance I can detect the Hynnea blossoms in the garden, the rather disagreeable fragrance of the herbal concoction the healer has mixed for me to drink, and the distinctively pungent smell of my sister's custom ground bathing crystals mixed liberally with the smell of semen." A slight frown marred her delicate brow. "Now what do you suppose that means, Zedne of Baux?"

Zedne's hands gestured wildly. "You are mistaken, Your Highness. In your weakened state you have mistaken the fragrance of..."

Slapping a palm flat on the cushion she sat straight up. "Don't you dare patronize me! I have ruled this planet since I was a girl, and I have learned a thing or two about dealing with subterfuge." Her strength tapped she slowly wilted back so her head could rest. Closing her eyes she shielded the tears that gathered there. "Though I admit my sister had me fooled for a while. I couldn't figure out how she managed to outsmart the Baux fleet time after time. She was never that good a tactician. Now it all makes sense. You were feeding her the information all along."

Banking on the queen's failing eyesight, Zedne surreptitiously palmed a dagger and held it pressed to his side, ready for any eventuality. "You malign me, majesty. Your sister and I are doing everything we can to—"

"Please. I'm a dying woman. Don't waste my time." Her nostrils flared. "You might as well come in, sister. You're as much a part of this as either of us."

"More," Nambia bragged. "It was I who conceived of the entire plan."

Tired beyond belief, Lila sighed. "And what is your plan, Nambia? What reason could you possibly have for poisoning your sister and queen?"

"Mere minutes separated our births, yet you got everything. For years I have stood in the wings while you took center stage. No more. Now I will rule Iman, and Aldora after me."

Lila smiled. "Persis will rule, Nambia. She is the heir. You have committed cold-blooded murder for nothing."

"You have always underestimated me. I have my infrastructure set up already. The transition will go quite smoothly."

"But Persis..."

"Persis is an outsider. No one wants her here but you, and half the time you don't want her here. We will deal with her and her brat once I have assumed the crown."

"My cabinet—"

"Has been in my pocket for years."

"Persis has royal blood."

"As do my daughter and I. And once it is learned that the father of Persis' child is Bauxite, even the staunchest conservatives will turn against her."

"I can't believe I shared the womb with a viper."

Nambia preened as though she'd been given high praise. "Thank you, sister. I don't believe you've ever given me such a compliment."

"It was not praise but criticism I offered." Lila's breath was choppy and shallow.

"I believe you have both forgotten the threat of those who accompanied me here," Zedne injected.

Nambia waved away his warning. "They are under constant supervision. If they try anything untoward, my warriors will cut them down where they stand."

Zedne raised a brow. "Your warriors will try," he said dryly.

"My troops have trained since birth. They are adept and lethal not to mention how greatly they outnumber the few people you arrived with."

Zedne turned the full impact of his gaze on Nambia. "Kevnor and his friends have trained all their lives, too, and they have actual combat experience. The only fights your women have engaged in have been aerial in nature. There's a big difference when you face your opponent hand-to-hand."

"I am not concerned," she assured him.

"Perhaps you should be."

"I tell you, everything is under control." Her cheeks were flushed with anger. Zedne had no power on Iman, no right to question her.

Zedne smiled reassuringly. "You know your troops." Glancing at the queen he asked, "Why don't you finish her off?"

"If my sister died at my hands and the people found out about it, they would see the crown stripped from me." Narrowing her gaze at her lover she commanded, "You do it."

"Not me." Zedne held his hands up in surrender. "I'm not going to do your dirty work. What if you decided to use me as a scapegoat and turned me over to the executioners?"

Smart man. She stepped closer, running her hand from his shoulder to his elbow and back. "I wouldn't do that. You're my lover. One day you'll share the throne with me."

Lila laughed. "Surely you don't believe that drivel."

"Whether or not I believe her isn't the point." Zedne made eye contact with Queen Lila. "The point is, I won't leave myself vulnerable."

"And you can never rule with Nambia," Lila continued. "On Iman it is forbidden for a man to have any position of government, even at the lowest levels."

Nambia cast her sister a superior glance. "It is time for change on Iman. I plan to establish quite a lot of changes. Perhaps I'll change legislation to allow for a consort."

"Yes, and perhaps I'll get up from this bed and walk out the door," Lila quipped. "But it's not likely."

Chapter Twenty-three

The door opened and three servants stepped in, closing the door quietly behind them. Dev and the boys looked up from the table where they were working on the reading lesson for the day. "Yes?" she asked, a frown marring her brow. She hadn't requested anything.

The men exchanged glances before one answered, "It's true then. You are teaching the young ones to read."

Smiling, she replied, "Yes. My sons are learning to read, write, and do math."

"And fight," Tim reminded.

Dev ruffled his hair. "Yes, and to fight."

"You would acknowledge male children?"

"Of course." Dev rose and stepped closer to the three men. Taller than she by several inches, they were slim but well muscled and appeared to be triplets. It was hard to tell for sure due to disfiguring scars that marred their otherwise handsome faces. One bore a scar that ran horizontally across his left cheek, one had a vertical scar on his right cheek and the other had an X carved in each cheek. The scars were raised and puckered. "Can I offer you refreshment?" she asked, indicating the fruit and cheese she had set out on the table for an afternoon snack.

"But we are servants."

Dev lobbed pieces of fruit at the men, who caught them handily. "Yeah, and I'm supposed to be some kind of princess, but I'm treated like a prisoner.

Lovely planet you've got here." Sarcasm dripped from her words.

"We're leaving here," Ewen told them proudly. "Our mother and father are taking us with them when they leave."

"No one escapes Iman."

Dev raised her brows. "So I've heard." She sounded unconcerned. "Did you guys want something, other than food?"

"We didn't come for food," said the one with the X's, around a mouthful of Zanatu orange.

Dev straightened at his tone. She was tired of pussyfooting around. "Then why did you come?"

As one they moved closer. Dev noticed the athletic grace they displayed. These guys were more than scullery slaves.

"We came..."

"To meet..."

"Our sister."

Her jaw dropped. "Your sister?" They couldn't possibly mean what she thought they meant.

"You are our sister."

She sat abruptly back down on her chair. "I am an orphan."

"You are our sister," Mr. X said. "It is well documented, if you check the Hall of Records."

"How can that be? No one ever told me I had brothers." Though she denied it, Devona knew it was true. She felt the connection. Tears filled her eyes. "I have brothers," she whispered, looking from one to the other. "I have three brothers." Ewen and Tim moved to stand beside her, putting their thin little arms around her in a gesture of support and solidarity.

"I am Arek, the eldest," said the man with the horizontal scar.

"Born second, I am Aron." His cheek bore the vertical scar.

"And my name is Aden." The X's carved into the third man's face restricted much of the movement, but he managed the approximation of a smile.

"Why have they kept this from me?"

"We're males, of no consequence to the Imani," Arek said bitterly.

"Except to make sure they don't inbreed," Aron continued. "That's the only reason we're listed in the Hall of Records at all."

"The only thing worse to *them* than a boy is a defective girl," Aden sneered. "At least they allow us to live."

Dev was horrified. "You don't mean they—"

"Kill the defective girls? Yes," Aden interrupted.

"That's horrible."

"Isn't it though?" Arek agreed. "That's why we didn't come to you at first. As the heir, we assumed you'd be like they were."

"Then we began to hear stories," Aron continued. "That you were different."

"That you had adopted two boys."

"That you planned to leave here."

Returning the boy's affection, she squeezed them before sitting forward to speak to her brothers. "All of those things are true. My husband and his friends came with the Bauxite ambassador. When they leave, we will be with them."

"You will just walk away from Iman?" Aden's voice was cool.

"What would you have me do?" Dev answered, defensively. "I have a life away from this hell. I have a husband, friends, and a child on the way." Sighing, she admitted, "I have been trying to get the slaves I come into contact with to fight back, but they seem uninterested. I can't fight the entire planet alone." She laughed. "I'm good, but not that good."

Arek placed a hand on his brother's shoulder. "She's right, Aden. You know she's right. We have tried all our lives to get the men to rise up to no avail. What makes you think the men would follow a woman when they won't follow us?"

"Hey now," Dev bristled.

Aron was quick to soothe her. "No offense, but women have been the cause of the men's suffering. Why would they trust one of you?"

"I see what you mean." Dev sighed. "I just can't imagine totally giving up, living a life of slavery without rebelling. It's just not in my nature."

Aron's mouth kicked up in a smile. "It must be a family trait. We, too, are unable to remain in slavery without at least trying to change our lifestyle."

Interesting. "How so?" Dev asked.

"Since we were small," Aron told her, "every chance we got we hid and watched the warriors train. At night, whichever one of us had learned something new taught the others. We sparred with one another until we became quite good."

"Or so we thought," Aden continued. "When we were thirteen, we stormed the castle."

Dev was impressed. "Didn't think small, did you? What happened?"

Arek shrugged. "We didn't get past the guards at the door. The palace guards are the elite of the warriors. Twenty women had us pinned down and in chains within five minutes."

"Ouch. That must have hurt your egos as much as your bodies at that age," Dev reasoned.

"Yep," Aron agreed. "We went in convinced we were the toughest things going. It was quite a blow to our manhood."

"Not as much of a blow as Nambia had in mind," Arek reminded.

"What?" Dev asked. "What did that bitch do?"

"You've just risen even further in our esteem," Arek told her, "with your opinion of our dear aunt."

"Are you going to finish the story?" Ewen broke in.

The men seemed startled that the boy had dared to speak. Ewen blushed. "Well, I want to hear what happened," he insisted.

"Me, too," Tim echoed.

"Well," Aden took up the tale, "we were dragged before Queen Lila."

"Your mother," Dev reminded them.

"Yes, our *mother*." Aden's tone was not complimentary. "But *Aunt* Nambia was there as well. She insisted we be castrated on the spot for such audacity."

"Oooh." Dev crossed her legs.

"Yeah," Aron agreed. "But for once Lila stood up to her. She said if the women in charge of security for the training facility had been doing their job, nothing

~231~

would have happened, and they should be grateful it wasn't a contingent of Baux who had been infiltrating the compound, stealing training information. She said the women should be stripped of rank and we should be marked so everyone would know we were trouble." He fingered the scar on his cheek.

Dev leaped to her feet. "Your mother—*our* mother—put those disfiguring marks on your faces?"

"With her very own knife," Arek assured her. "Then she gave the order that sand should be rubbed into the wounds so the scars wouldn't heal smoothly."

"After that we were only assigned the most physically demanding tasks." Aden shrugged. "But that pleased us just fine. It kept us in top physical condition and out of the city."

Aron smiled conspiratorially. "When you're not in the city, you aren't monitored very well. We had lots of chances to reconnoiter. Our scarred faces did nothing to deter our determination to overthrow the government."

A thought suddenly struck Dev. "How the hell did you get in my apartment?" she asked.

"We just walked in," Aron bragged.

"Right past the guards?" Dev raised a brow inquisitively.

"Not exactly," Arek stammered.

"We gave them a little break," Aden confessed.

"Why are the hairs suddenly standing up on the back of my neck?" Dev rubbed her neck as she spoke.

"Don't worry, we didn't kill them," Aron assured her. "They're just bound and stored in the hall closet."

"Draco! I hope you haven't ruined everything." Dev paced the room, rubbing her belly. "Your father's going to kill them," she mumbled.

"Don't worry about him. We can handle him."

Dev turned to glare at her brothers. "Don't bet on it. You three might be accomplished, but Kevnor and the rest of us were part of a crack team of special operatives, trained from early childhood to go into the most dangerous situations. When we left the military, we hired out as mercenaries for a time. And guys, we were the best."

Arek nodded. "Understood."

Dev resumed her pacing.

Tim stepped boldly up to the three men. "Don't worry." He indicated his mother. "When she's walking like that, she's thinking. She always thinks of something."

"Thanks for the vote of confidence," she told him, "but I'm afraid it'll take more than thinking to get us out of this one." She stopped beside Ewen. "Boys, I need you to run some errands for me."

Nodding, his young face solemn, Ewen assured her, "Anything."

Dev knelt to be near eye level. "Do you think you can find the rooms assigned to Dugan and Zoë? I need to talk to Zoë. Make sure she understands the severity, but try not to say too much in front of Dugan. I'm not sure if we can trust him."

"I can do it, mother." Grabbing his brother by the arm, Ewen steered him toward the door. "Come on, Tim, we've got an assignment."

***

Dugan lounged on the bed as Zoë scurried around the room, checking for detection devices and storing her clothing in the bureau drawers. He couldn't help admiring the view when she bent to reach the bottom drawer. She had the finest ass he'd ever encountered. Round and firm, sticking out just enough to entice him. He couldn't wait to get the chance to release her unfettered desires. She didn't know it yet, but he was the man who would define sexual fulfillment for her. He could just imagine her passionate screams as he brought her to orgasm over and over.

Cocking a hip and placing her fisted hand on it Zoë told him, "Don't even think it."

"What?"

"Don't give me that innocent look." Zoë waved a hand toward the bed. "You didn't get that thing thinking pure thoughts."

Glancing down Dugan admired his rather impressive boner. "We both appreciate you." Stroking himself he patted the bed beside him. "Sit down and we'll be glad to demonstrate just how much."

Zoë blew a raspberry at him. "In your dreams."

"There, too."

A knock on the door interrupted what was sure to be an interesting argument. "I'll get it." Zoë hurried to the door, grateful for the distraction. "Yes?" She whipped the door open as she spoke.

Two small boys stood on the other side, holding baskets of fruit and wine. "Here are the refreshments you requested." The older boy stepped through the door, the younger lad right on his heels.

"I didn't order any—"

Dugan's arm snaked around her to close the door behind the boys. "Thank you." He took the basket of wine from the smaller of the two. "I think it's a ploy," he whispered into Zoë's ear sending shivers down her arms.

Stepping from one foot to the other the youngsters motioned them away from the door. Large brown eyes pleaded with Zoë to believe him. "Our mother sent us. She said she had to see you."

Her brows furrowed. "Who is your mother?"

"The princess."

"Dev? Dev is your mother? Since when?" she scoffed.

"She 'dopted us." The smaller kid's chest stuck out. "She's gonna take us home with her."

Shaking her head Zoë snorted. "The entire crew has lost their collective minds."

Dugan placed a restraining hand on her arm. "Did Dev say why she wanted to see Zoë?"

"Who are you?" Zoë snapped.

"I'm Ewen. He's Tim." Ewen stepped between his brother and the small angry woman, crouching in a fighter's stance. "Don't you hurt him." Tim shoved at the larger boy to no avail.

Zoë stepped back as though he had hit her. "I wouldn't harm a child."

Dugan chuckled. "You looked pretty scary to me."

She elbowed him. "Can you tell us why she wants to see me?" This time she was careful to modulate her voice.

"She *said* you would help us."

Zoë made eye contact with Ewen. "I would die for her as she would for me."

"See?" This time Tim was successful in wiggling his way past his brother.

"Is she in danger?"

Ewen raised a brow but said nothing.

Zoë burst out laughing. "You're Dev's kid all right." She ruffled his crop of coarse blond hair. "Why don't you boys sit down and tell us all you can."

Ewen glared at Dugan. "Not him. Only you."

Shrugging, Dugan headed for the bathroom. "I need a shower anyway."

When they were alone, Ewen lowered his voice, "Mom said she needs you because she can't leave our apartment."

"Plus our uncles tied up the guards, and she's afraid the shit's about to hit the fan." One of Dev's favorite expressions coming from the mouth of an angelic six-year-old was too much.

Zoë burst out laughing. "I guess we'd better go investigate. And what's this about uncles? Dev is an orphan."

"Nope. She has three big brothers, only she didn't know it till today." Tim was a fountain of information. "And they all have really ugly scars on their faces. And they're big and they tied up the guards." He looked her up and down. "They could beat you up."

"Don't let my size fool you. A lot of men have underestimated me."

Tim nodded. "Yep. Me, too."

"Cocky little brat." Zoë grinned. "Now I know what Dev sees in you. How many guards are posted in this hall? Can you give me directions to her apartment? Will I be stopped if I'm just walking down the hall?"

Tim's eyes glazed at all the questions she was firing at him. Ewen clicked off answers. "There are only two guards on this hall. We can take you to her, or I can draw you a map. We don't get many visitors from off world, but I imagine the guards will question you if they see you."

"How far away is she?"

"We are on the south wing. She is housed in the east."

"Which floor?" Zoë crossed to the balcony doors and looked out. A long veranda extended the length of the wing. The adjacent wing had a similar balcony, but the curved wall of the interior structure separated them by about twenty feet. Too far to jump. She looked up toward the roof. That was a possibility if she could find some rope.

"What are you doing?" She jumped at the sound of Dugan's deep voice directly behind her. The man moved like a cat.

"Sizing the place up. I need to get to Dev."

"Is she on the roof?"

"No, smart ass, she's in the east wing."

"Why don't you try the hallway?"

"There are some complications. I don't want to be seen."

"Surely as official representatives of Baux we can expect a tour of the palace."

"Your point?"

"Just get a guard to escort us."

Zoë displayed her teeth in a faux smile. "And how do you propose we get to Dev? I doubt her private quarters are on the tour." She swished her ass back toward the kids. "Besides, the guards on Dev's hall have been disposed of. That just might set off alarms in our escort's brain, don't you think?"

"Disposed of? Disposed of how? When did this happen? It could jeopardize the entire mission. I knew those guys were a bunch of hotheads."

"Excuse me? My friends are not hotheads, and they are not responsible for the disappearing guards."

"Who did such an idiotic thing?" He waved toward the boys. "Them?"

"Of course not. It appears Dev's previously unknown brothers showed up at her place."

"Did they have to kill the guards? Why didn't they just knock?"

"They didn't kill the guards," Ewen offered. "They just tied them up and stashed them in a closet."

"Fabulous." Dugan dug through his bags till he came up with a compact little device that looked suspiciously like a weapon.

"What's that?" Zoë moved in for a closer look.

"A miniature pulse pistol. I'm not taking you out of this room unarmed. I'll bet there's an entire garrison housed in this palace." He shook his head. "I'm good, but not that good."

Zoë flung his clothes aside as she rifled through his suitcase. "Got any more in here?"

"No, I don't."

"That's pretty selfish of you."

Bent over as she was he couldn't resist slapping her on the butt. "Stick with me. I'll protect you."

"That'll be the day. I take care of myself."

Chapter Twenty-four

"Do I look okay?" Kev smoothed his hand down the front of his shirt.

"You don't do anything for me, but you look okay." Callus grinned. "For a prostitute."

"Fuck you."

"Like I said, you're not my type."

"Would you cut the comedy routine?" Mik ran the fingers of both hands through his hair. "Let's go over the plan again. I have a bad feeling about this."

"Bad feeling or not, I'm going to Dev's room. Now."

"I still think you should let me go." Mik scowled. "I only have the one tattoo. I could probably get by as a regular servant. I could smear some soot or dirt or something over the tatt."

"Forget it." Kev closed his eyes for a few seconds, and they were less turbulent when he reopened them. "Look, I appreciate the gesture, but if it were Shesshie in this mess..."

Holding up a hand in surrender, Mik nodded. "Just be careful."

"Always." The grin he flashed before easing out the door was pure Kev, and it scared the hell out of Mik.

Callus opened the door after him a few minutes later, glancing down the now empty corridor. "I still say we should have waited in Zedne's room. I wanted a few words with that bastard before we made a move."

Rolling his head to release tension, Mik agreed, "Yeah, that made good sense, but Kev's in charge of this one."

"I just hope we live through his first command."

Reaching beneath his bedding, Mik tossed a pair of slave's pants to Callus. "Put these on," he said as he donned an identical pair. "I'll be damned if I'm going to sit here like a cruiser in space dock while he gets his ass killed. You coming?"

Peering around to see the back of his shoulder, Callus grunted. "That damned hair growing on my back finally came in handy. You can barely see my tattoo."

"What are you talking about? With that ugly mug they'll be too stupefied to see anything else." Mik scooped mud from his shoes and smeared it liberally across his shoulders and arms as he spoke.

Callus patted his cheek gently. "This isn't ugly. It's manly. I have it on good authority."

Mik chuckled. "Don't go getting cocky. My sister-in-law is love blind."

"Love blind, huh? I like the sound of that." He slugged Mik in the arm. "And you're just jealous because I don't have to get dirty and you do."

As they rounded the corner all banter stopped. Kev couldn't be far ahead of them and they didn't want him to know they were following him. The man could get down right testy.

***

Kev passed several guards as he wended his way through the central lobby, but none of them challenged his presence. Climbing the stairway to the eastern wing he began to think he just might pull this off when a hand grabbed him on the rear. "Nice ass."

Grasping the wrist of the offending hand, he pulled it away from his body. "Sorry. I'm taken."

Hardy laughter echoed down the otherwise empty corridor. "Who owns you? I'll buy you from her."

He did not want to have to put this woman down. It was bound to attract attention. "She won't sell, at least not now. She just purchased me a few days ago."

"We are all sisters. If she won't sell you, I'm sure I can convince her to share you for a time." This time she grabbed his pec. "Ummm, I wonder if *all* your muscles are this firm. Perhaps I should check." When she slid her hand down toward his crotch, Kev knocked it away with his forearm.

Like lightning she palmed the blade she wore at her waist and held the tip beneath his chin. "You dare touch a member of the guard? Who is your owner? I'll see you flogged for this."

"I don't fucking think so." In two moves Kev disarmed and overpowered her, fully expecting her cries to summon a hoard of her warrior friends. She didn't make a peep. "I doubt the princess will have me flogged. She isn't into S&M."

"The princess." The warrior spat on the floor. "That is what I think of the princess. She is not Imani."

"She couldn't agree more. My question is, why did you bring her here in the first place if she doesn't want to be here and you don't want her?"

"The queen has grown weak from her prolonged illness. She should have abdicated rather that bring Persis back."

"Who the hell is Persis?"

The woman's eyes narrowed. When she opened her mouth to yell for help, Kev clipped her on the jaw, successfully silencing her. "Who the hell is Persis?" he repeated.

Hoisting the unconscious woman to his shoulder, Kev grunted. "I don't know what I'm going to do with you, but I know I'm not carrying you very far. You weigh like a ton of Darneuvian marble."

"Want a little help with that?"

Spinning, Kev nearly hit Callus in the head with the woman's feet. "Draco! What the hell are you doing here?"

"You're welcome for guarding your back." Considerably shorter but powerfully built, Callus eased the dead weight from his friend onto his own shoulder. "You weren't kidding," he grunted. "She's no lightweight."

Kev massaged his shoulder, trying to restore circulation. "No shit. Now what are you doing following me?"

"You attended the same classes I did. Always guard the leader's back, remember?"

"Yeah, I remember." Glancing around Kev wondered, "So, where's Mik?"

"Mopping up more of your sloppiness."

"Sloppiness my ass. I haven't encountered a single problem till this bitch grabbed my ass and wouldn't take no for an answer."

Callus looked his friend up and down. "There's no understanding women."

"What's that supposed to mean?"

"Apparently you're more appealing to the fairer sex than I thought. Several warriors stopped us when we entered the central reception area to ask about you. It's my guess that Mik is still fielding questions."

"Great. Give me back the behemoth and return to Mik."

Ignoring him Callus asked, "Do you intend to just carry her around all over the palace?"

"What I thought was that I'd find an empty room and stash her."

"Well, look for a room will ya? I wouldn't mind putting this dainty little bundle down, know what I mean?"

Grinning, Kev stepped from door to door trying the knobs. At last he found one that was open. Much to his surprise, the utility closet already contained two bound warriors, spitting mad and glaring at him with evil intent. "Well, well, well. Looks like we might have allies we don't know about."

"What?" Callus peered into the small room and whistled. "Looks like the place to store this one. Here, take her."

Kev eased the woman down to the floor and reached for the bag of cleaning cloths to gag her as the other two were gagged. "I don't know who tied the others up, but why reinvent the wheel?" Taking a roll of multiplex cord from the shelf he wrapped it around the woman's neck once then bound her hands crossed over her chest. If she pulled on her wrists to try to get loose, she would choke herself. *Pretty ingenious.* Her legs were tied at the knees and ankles. Just for good measure, he pulled off her boots and tied her big toes together. That was a little trick he'd learned on Delphi XII. Some people had very dexterous feet.

"Hurry," Callus cautioned. "I hear footsteps."

The first occupants of the room began to wiggle and strain. With no time to worry about them, Kev applied the same silencing method to them that he'd used on the other warrior. They sagged back to the floor and Kev shook his hand. Without a sound, the two men eased the door closed and sprinted down the hallway.

Mik was making as much noise as he could without being too obvious. "You ladies don't need him. Why don't you just raise my status and I'll show you all kinds of gratitude." Flexing his arm and holding it out he bragged, "I could take on three at once."

Kev and Callus understood the warning and waited just around the bend until the others drew abreast. Within seconds they were stashing three more women in the closet. "This place is getting down right crowded."

***

"Where is that man?" Lila was so weak she could barely speak.

"I sent him back to his room. I wanted to have a little sisterly talk." Pulling up a chair Nambia sat down and took her sister's hand. "Just like we used to."

Unable to pull her hand free Lila submitted, reserving her energy for conversation. "Why?"

Nambia shrugged. "I suppose even I have my limits. I don't want your last moments to be spent alone."

"How...?"

"How did I kill you? Easy. Zedne helped me find a lab off world that would extract the venom from the Toinn spider. I've been injecting it into your food for several years now in increasingly larger doses."

"Brilliant."

"Thank you. I knew it would be difficult to trace, but if somehow traces of the venom were found..." She shrugged. "Well, it is an indigenous species after all."

"What now?"

"Oh, I will graciously accept the throne as is my right. In a few years I'll turn things over to Aldora. She'll make a great queen."

"And you?"

"Zedne and I have plans. Plans you wouldn't understand."

"T-try me."

"I have needs, sister dear. Physical needs. None of the emasculated specimens of manhood on Iman can excite me. Zedne understands my needs." A fine tremor shook her body as she spoke.

"When...?"

"Did I meet him? Oh, quite a few years ago, when you sent me off world to negotiate weapons with the Famadaa. Zedne was there on behalf of the Baux. We were instantly attracted to one another."

Lila felt her throat begin to close. "Aldora..." she rasped.

Nambia nodded. "I see you finally understand. Zedne is Aldora's father. We have dedicated our lives to seeing our daughter on the throne. Both Zedne and I were denied our right to rule by a simple accident of birth. We would not let the same thing happen to our child."

Lila squeezed her sister's hand as a paroxysm shook her body. Gasping for breath she vocalized her last word, "Doctor."

"Oh, don't worry, Lila, the doctor's in the next room. Who do you think has been preparing the doses I've been feeding you all along?" Tucking her sister's hand beneath the comforter, Nambia kissed the pallid forehead. "I'll be sending her in shortly to pronounce your death."

Shallow breaths gave way to gurgling that pushed foaming sputum from between Lila's blue lips. Closing the lids over her sister's clouded eyes, Nambia smiled. "The queen is dead. Long live the queen."

***

There were no guards posted at Devona's door. "If that woman has done something stupid, I'm going to whip her ass." Kev sprinted down the hall and threw the door open, terrified his wife's quarters would be empty. Only his well developed instincts and years of training saved him from a serious headache when he blocked and sidestepped a powerful kick aiming for his head. "What the fuck?" Sweeping the feet from his opponent, Kev caught him with a punch to the kidney.

When the other two men stepped up to join the fray, Dev took the only action she could. "Aron, no." She flipped the brother nearest her, straddling his chest and holding the tip of a well-honed blade to his carotid. "Don't move. That is my husband." The odds were as even as she could make them. The rest was up to Kev. "They're my brothers!" She hoped her warning penetrated his blood lust.

"Brothers?" Bounding through the open door, Mik signaled Callus to take out one of Kev's opponents. "Draco! Where'd you get brothers?" Stepping between his friend and the remaining triplet, he made short work of separating the two. He caught a clip to the jaw from one and a painful wrist for blocking a kick from the other before reason ensued. "Didn't you hear Dev? We're on the same team here." Glaring at Kev, he wiggled his jaw to make sure it wasn't broken. "Will somebody please tell me what the hell's going on?"

No longer fighting but far from allies, Kev and the scarred man glared at one another. "Who is this man, Dev?"

Ignoring Kev, she looked down at Aron. "If I let you up, do you promise to behave?"

A little nervous about nodding with the blade at his neck, Aron grunted and hoped she'd take it for an affirmative answer. Easing back, she lowered her blade and slid it into the sheath strapped to her thigh. With only slightly less than her usual grace Dev stood up to face her spouse. "Kevnor, meet Arek, Aden and Aron, my brothers. Guys, this is my husband Kevnor and our crewmates Mik and Callus."

Giving one last jerk to the arm of the man he had pinned to the floor, Callus rolled to his feet. "Geesh, you don't do anything halfway, do you Dev? Wasn't one enough for you?"

Taking command as usual, Mik relaxed his stance. "Did you take out Dev's guards?"

"We did." The man with the scarred left cheek eased back as well. "I am Arek, the eldest."

"For all of three minutes. I am Aron." Fingering his right cheek the man added, "the one with the vertical scar, if you're looking to tell us apart."

"And I'm Aden." Rotating his shoulder Callus' opponent frowned at him. "Are you the husband?"

"Nope. I'm Callus, engineer aboard the Freebird. Loverboy's the one receiving your sister's tender affections." Sure enough Dev had crossed to Kevnor and wrapped herself around him.

"If anyone cares, I'm Miklus. I captain the Freebird." Closing and locking the door, he took in Dev's brothers. "Can we count on your help or do we need to tie you up in the closet, too?"

All four blonds broke out laughing. "I take it you found my guards?" Dev's shoulders still shook.

"Yeah. And we added to the collection by four." Kev checked the chronometer on the wall. "What time is a change of guard scheduled?"

Arek, Aron, and Aden shrugged. "We never thought to check," Arek admitted.

"Great." Mik ran his fingers through his hair. "Amateurs."

"We have about half an hour," Dev informed them.

"We need to get Zoë and Dugan." Kev extracted himself from his woman. "Unless I miss my bet, the shit's about to hit the fan."

"I've already sent for her." Dev glanced back at the timepiece. "The boys went to get her quite a while ago. I'm beginning to get worried."

Just then the doorknob rattled. "Mom. Mom, let us in," a frightened voice penetrated the wood.

Kev crossed to open the door while Mik and Callus took up positions on either side of the portal. Flinging it open, he hurried the kids inside, followed closely by Zoë and Dugan.

"What the hell happened to the guards?" Dugan asked as the door was secured behind him. "The change is scheduled for less than a quarter of an hour from now. Didn't you people think something like missing guards would be noticed? I thought you were trained professionals."

"We are. They aren't." Mik hitched a thumb at the three blond men clustered around Devona.

"Who are they?"

"We are capable of answering for ourselves." Aden scowled.

Exasperated, Dugan sighed. "Okay, who are you?"

"Her brothers."

"Whose brothers?"

"Dev's," Kev supplied. "Dugan, this is Devona, my wife and the heir to the throne of Iman."

Dugan bowed from the waist. "Majesty."

"Please. I get enough of that crap from the locals." Motioning her wide-eyed sons closer, Dev put an arm around each of them. "You did well." Pivoting so they faced the three men behind her, she made the introductions. "Ewen, Tim, I'd like you to meet your uncles." One by one she pointed out the men. "This is Arek, Aron, and that one is Aden."

"This is all very nice," Zoë pointed out, "but we have a crisis situation here. Could we put off the reunion until after the battle?"

Stepping up to take command, Kev rattled off orders. "Mik, you and Callus need to locate and appropriate arms for us." Narrowing his gaze he turned to his newfound brothers-in-law. "Any of you know where the armory is located?"

"We all do." Arek stepped forward. "I'll be glad to go with them and show the way."

"Good. And make it quick. We need to get to the ship with as little loss of life as possible. We came here to get Dev, not engage in battle."

"What about Zedne?" Zoë asked.

"What about him?" Callus grumbled. "The bastard's been feeding information to his enemies for who knows how long."

Dev glanced at her husband. "Your uncle?"

"Apparently so. We found—" He glanced at the boys and curbed what he'd been about to say. "—*evidence* that he's been fraternizing."

Curiosity was eating her up after that, but Dev wisely decided to wait until later to question him further. "Okay. What's our role?"

"You and the boys need to stay here and appear totally shocked that your guards aren't in place." When Dev started to protest, Kev continued over her objections, "Until you have weapons I don't want you in this." He glanced at her belly. "Not in your condition."

She made a rude noise. "I can still handle myself."

Black eyes spitting fire he heated her with his gaze. "I am in charge of this operation. You will take orders the same as everyone else." Softening a little he added. "Guarding our three children is your primary function this time."

How did you argue with that? "Understood." Tight-lipped she kept her thoughts to herself.

"Zoë, you and Dugan and I will return to my uncle's quarters. I really want to hear what he has to say."

"What about us?"

Kev looked at Aden and Aron. "I was kind of hoping you might stick around here and look busy. You know, as backup for Dev and the boys."

Aron fingered his right cheek. "Any warrior who sees us will know we're exiles. We aren't even supposed to be inside the city, let alone the palace."

"Great." Frustration rushed through his body like a drug. He glanced at his friend and captain. "Any bright ideas, Mik?"

"Afraid I'm fresh out."

"Am I allowed to speak at least?" Dev raised a brow at her husband that promised retribution for his earlier comments.

Kev sighed. "Of course. You're part of this team aren't you?"

"I wasn't sure there for awhile." Turning to her brothers, Dev asked, "How about I take you two prisoner?"

"What?"

Ignoring her overbearing spouse, Dev continued, "I can pretend to have captured these two trying to get into my apartment. When the new guards arrive, I can insist that they help me try to get to the bottom of the missing guards. The warriors are arrogant enough to believe they can solve the problem without calling for assistance." She glanced over at her brothers, grinning. "After all, they're *only* men."

"We can store those two in the closet with the others."

"That will buy us a full four hours," Dev concluded.

Kev paced for a few minutes. "That just might work. Do you think you can get to the armory and meet us in say two hours?"

"No problem." Arek turned to leave.

"Hold up," Mik said. "Where are we supposed to rendezvous?"

Ewen took Dev's hand for courage enough to address the dangerous looking man. "How about the practice building? It's out of the palace and on the way to the terminal."

"Isn't that place crawling with warriors and trainees?"

Dev ruffled the boy's hair and smiled at Kev. "Not two hours from now. It'll be mealtime by then. They all meet in the mess hall to eat."

"Well okay." Kev smiled at his son. "Good thinking, Ewen." The boy's thin chest expanded at the unexpected praise. "Does everyone know where the training building is?"

"I don't." Zoë glanced around. "Well I don't. The only place Dugan and I have seen is the inside of our apartment and the cursory tour we were given upon arrival."

"Come with me." Dev took her friend to the balcony. Indicating a nearby building she said, "That's it. The white one with the red tiled roof."

"Got it." Leaning closer Zoë squeezed her friend's arm. "We'll be home in no time, sweetie."

Dev's eyes teared up. "I know." She glanced over at the corner of the queen's wing, barely visible from the balcony. "And I can't wait to leave this place. But I can't help but wonder…"

"Don't," Zoë interrupted. "'What ifs' and 'could have beens' will drive you crazy."

Swiping at her nose with the back of her hand, Dev squared her shoulders. "You're right."

Zoë winked. "Usually am."

Chapter Twenty-five

Zedne strode down the hallway, nodded to the guards and slipped into his chambers. The place was in total darkness, and he fumbled for a light. "Fucking incompetent servants," he mumbled. The flare of light blinded him for a moment. What he saw when he could focus almost stopped his heart. His nephew sat casually on the end of his bed, dangling the trousers he'd stashed in the closet by one finger.

"Care to explain this, uncle?"

"Explain what? That those are my pants?" He wasn't an accomplished statesman for nothing. Though his pulse pounded, his face gave nothing away.

Kev shook his head. "It's not going to work. You're busted."

Stepping from the shadowed recess of the adjoining bathroom Dugan scowled at the older man. "Yes, Zedne, I'd like to hear your explanation, too."

Smiling and shrugging, Zedne spread his hands. "Dugan, you've worked side-by-side with me for years. This man—" He glanced at Kev. "—is a virtual stranger to you. Don't tell me you're buying into some story he's made up."

"Why would he make up a story about you, Zedne? You're his uncle. You helped get him passage to Iman. You negotiated a meeting with the queen so he could bargain for his wife's return."

"How do I know? Maybe the stress has affected his reasoning."

Rising from an upholstered chair where she'd previously gone unnoticed, Zoë entered the conversation. "There's just one thing wrong with that scenario, Zedne. Kev doesn't get stressed. He's the coolest head under fire I've ever seen." She shook her head. "Fact is, someone with long blond hair has been giving you head in this very room. The women around here don't seem the type to fraternize with the enemy, so, in my book, that makes you the prime suspect as the traitor the Baux have been looking for."

Panic etched his face when he realized they knew. Spinning toward the door he opened his mouth to call out "Guard—" His words were cut off, blood spurting from the wound in his neck. Groping, he found the hilt of the knife imbedded there. His knees crumbled and he sank to the floor.

Dugan braced him with a foot on his shoulder and pulled the blade free, wiping it on Zedne's shirt. "On behalf of the people of Baux, I sentence you to death for treason."

"Draco, Dugan." Zoë stood dumbfounded, staring at this new aspect of the man who made the blood run thick in her veins. "I didn't know you could throw a knife like that."

Eyes burning with heat, he swept her from head to toe. "There's a lot about me you don't know. Yet."

"You threatening me, Dugan?" Her dusky brown eyes sparkled with humor and something else. Interest.

"Not threatening. Promising." Tracing the line of her cheek with his knuckle, Dugan admired the contrasts of color and texture. She was as smooth and dark as a Xyderan chocolate. "When this is behind us, we'll spend a month at my family estate in the Lymond Province." Leaning close, his breath brushed her ear when he whispered, "Nestled between the ocean and the mountains, there's not another living sole for miles."

"Give it a rest, will you? I feel like a fucking voyeur." Kev dragged his uncle's body into the bathroom. "Besides, we need to meet up with the others in less than an hour. I thought Zedne would never get here."

"It does make you wonder what he was up to." Zoë crossed to the balcony and looked out. The guest quarters were on the second floor, an easy route considering their training and experience. "We going down from here or out through the building?"

"Why make trouble for ourselves?" Kev shrugged. "Let's go down the side."

Dugan peered over the rail. "You got a rope?"

"Yeah, right up my ass." Anxiety warped Kev's sense of humor.

"Very funny." Dugan was having none of it. "How do you plan to get down two stories, jump?"

"We won't need to. The outside surface isn't smooth. We'll just climb."

Dugan stared at Zoë. "You people are crazy. We could break our necks."

"I thought you were into thrills, Bauxite." Zoë's eyes offered a challenge he couldn't refuse. Gazes still locked he stepped over the rail. "Don't worry," she whispered. "If you bruise something, I'll kiss it better."

A thud and a muffled curse were his only reply.

***

The palace was behind them. Arek couldn't believe the efficiency with which the other two operated. He doubted his brothers would believe him when he recounted this story. They'd tease him about stretching the truth, but the truth didn't need to be embellished. He'd sacrifice the smooth surface of his right cheek for that kind of ability. Then he'd never bow to another human, man or woman.

Mik signaled that someone approached, and the three flattened themselves into a shadowed doorway. Inches away, the guard on patrol passed by, totally unaware of their presence. Arek actually thought about making a noise so he could observe the swift and efficient takedown of the warrior. How could he learn if he couldn't observe? Then again, he didn't want to lose face with Mik and Callus. Their respect was something worth keeping.

As soon as the woman was out of earshot, they sprinted the final stretch of open ground between them and the armory. Callus had the lock picked in seconds, and they eased the door closed behind them after they slipped inside. Mik whistled softly. Arek was inclined to agree. The amount and variety of weapons was impressive. The question was, why the fuck didn't they use them? He'd never once seen an Imani warrior carry anything other than a knife, short sword or the occasional bow.

Mik lifted a brow.

"Don't ask me." Arek kept his voice low.

"Either the Imani have a tradition they're reluctant to break, or someone's caching weapons for nefarious purposes."

"My vote's on the second scenario, Captain." Callus ran a hand lovingly over a rack of pulse riffles. "Cause these babies could do some major damage. One of those lovelies in loincloths has her eyes on the throne."

Nodding tersely, Mik cut him off. "Not our problem. Just choose the lightest and most efficient weapons. We need accuracy and speed. This is a rescue mission. Only a rescue mission."

"Understood."

"We are not getting involved in local politics."

"Understood."

"I mean it. Shesshie and Miranda are waiting for us. We will not delay so much as a day."

"Understood." Callus' grin completely overshadowed the plainness of his features. "The question is," he mumbled, "do you understand?"

"Shesshie would nail my balls to the wall if I got involved in what was going on here. I promised her we'd be back ASAP, and I mean to keep my word."

"Am I missing something?" Arek's quiet question put an end to the banter.

"Nah. Not really." Callus began to toss weapons at the other two. "These look good." A dozen hand phazers were tossed in rapid succession. Mik snagged a canvas ammunition bag, emptied the contents, and began to fill it with the pistols. "Oh, yeah." He clipped a belt that already held a supply of disrupter grenades around his trim waist.

"Got one of those for me?"

"Nope. There's only one." Still grinning Callus tossed a small plastic box at Miklus. "You'll just have to make do with these."

Popping the top, Mik groaned with pleasure. Inside were several martial arts stars, the tips of which were loaded with KMB. "Awesome."

Leaning over his shoulder, Arek looked at the stars. "So what? They're just stars."

"No, they aren't." Mik clipped the little box to the top of his pants. "They're loaded with explosive. When one point is detonated by impact, it sets off a chain reaction, igniting the KMB on each of the other points. They can do some major damage."

"Sounds gruesome."

"If you throw them at a body, they can be. I usually use them to clear a path."

Not for the first time, Arek wished he'd been born somewhere else in the universe. He would have enjoyed associating with such men. "We need to get going. The mess hall will begin serving in a quarter hour. There will only be a small window of opportunity before the first to eat begin to trickle back to the practice arena."

Mik tossed him an empty ammunition sack. "Then make yourself useful."

Arek felt the skin draw across his damaged cheek when he smiled and realized it had been a while since he felt like smiling. "Aye, Captain." He raked a shelf of Sonic grenades into the bag.

Callus chuckled. "I like him. He catches on fast."

***

Dev glanced at the timepiece again. "Showtime, boys." Aden and Aron knelt on the floor, hands behind their backs as if they were bound. Dev held a short sword in one hand and Aden's hair in the other, pulling his head back so she could look him in the face. Ewen and Tim stood by the door so they'd be out of sight when the door opened, as it did momentarily.

"By the Goddess, what's going on here?" The newly arrived guards burst into the room just as Dev had predicted.

"You tell me. You're supposed to be the ones in charge." Dev tightened her grip on her brother's hair, twisting his face toward the newcomers, prominently displaying his scarred face. "You're supposed to be protecting me from scum like this."

One woman stepped closer; the other remained in the doorway. "Where are the guards who were posted outside?"

"I suggest you ask them. I apprehended them when they snuck into my quarters."

"Believe me, we will." The second guard moved forward. Ewen slammed the door behind her. Tim struck her kneecap with the leg they'd removed from a chair. Well trained, she reached out, but Tim was no longer there. Instead he had danced away and brought the cudgel down again, this time on her outstretched arm. She cried out in pain.

When her partner spun to see what was happening, Dev struck, applying the butt of the sword to just the right spot on her head. The warrior collapsed.

Tim wasn't quick enough to escape this time. The uninjured hand of his opponent grabbed him by the leg, drawing him closer. "I'll kill you, you little bastard."

Dev's weapon was a blur of motion that ended in the middle of the woman's back. Slowly she released her grip on the child's leg. Tim scrambled away, undaunted by his brush with death. "Wow, Ewen, did you see that? Mom can throw a sword as good as she throws a knife."

"You nearly got yourself killed." Ewen closed in on his brother. "You weren't supposed to go back. You were supposed to hit her once and run away. You didn't obey orders."

"But I didn't get hurt." Tim still held the chunk of wood but never raised it toward the older boy who now loomed over him. "Mom got her." His voice had risen to a screech.

"That doesn't excuse what you did. We were supposed to protect her. We promised dad. She could have been hurt helping you." He took the stick and threw it across the room. "You never do what you're told."

Tim's bottom lip trembled, but he didn't cry. He looked toward his mother. "I'm sorry."

Dev wanted to grab him up and hug him, but Ewen was right. Failure to follow orders was a serious matter. "I accept your apology, Tim. But you can expect to hear more about this once we get home." She was so proud of her boys. Tim was impulsive but adept. And Ewen had great leadership qualities. She smiled inwardly imagining Kevnor and Miklus as boys. They hadn't been very different from these two.

"Okay boys, now comes the hard part." Dev faced her children. "Getting out of the palace."

"I've been thinking about that mother."

"And have you got any ideas, Ewen?"

"Yes, I have."

She raised an inquisitive brow.

"I think you should put on the armor of one of the guards and escort your prisoners to the guardhouse. Tim and I are never noticed. We'll go separately."

Aden and Aron had been busy securing one guard and wrapping the other in bedding to prevent a blood trail when they transported the bodies. "We'll be right back."

"Wait." Dev pointed to the now squirming guard. "Strip her." The woman bucked even harder, trying to talk around the gag they'd placed in her mouth.

"What?"

"You heard me. I'm going to be trading clothes with her."

Aden shrugged, punched the woman in the jaw, and then removed the clothing from her now acquiescent body. He'd always wondered what it would feel like to touch a woman, but he never imagined doing it in quite this manner.

Chapter Twenty-six

Dev and her brothers were the last to arrive. Kev was fit to be tied. "What took you so long, woman?" Crushing her in his arms he took a full minute to kiss the rebuttal out of her before releasing her. "I was worried," he whispered against her ear.

"Sucks, doesn't it? Being the one left behind to wonder."

Maybe he hadn't kissed her long enough.

"Let's move, kids. The clock's ticking."

"You won't be going anywhere." As one they spun to see Aldora in the doorway, flanked by a dozen or more of the palace guards. "Now that I'm queen, I'm taking the opportunity to reinstate the death penalty for spies."

Dev pushed her way past her husband and crewmates to confront her cousin. "Queen? Since when?"

"Oh, sorry. Your mother died several hours ago."

Despite the enmity between them, Dev didn't want her mother to die. She swayed slightly, but caught herself. "Nice of you to inform me."

"Oh, we went to inform you. But you weren't in your quarters. And your guards weren't at their post, either. Imagine our surprise when we discovered the new addition to the supply closet." She motioned her warriors into the room.

"Unless you want them all dead, I'd call them back." Kev's black eyes blazed with fury.

"We outnumber you by far, with reinforcements on the way," Aldora scoffed.

"Yeah, but they're armed with knives and spears and we're armed with these babies." The Bird's crew drew down on the warriors with phazers and pulse riffles.

Red suffused the queen's face. "My arsenal. You've raided my arsenal." She waved a hand dismissively. "But never mind. We'll just keep you pinned down here until I can send a contingent to the armory."

"Wouldn't do that if I were you," Callus warned.

Ignoring him, Aldora barked orders to her troops. Moments later the ground rocked with a massive explosion.

"Told you not to do that."

Screaming with rage, Aldora charged Devona, intent on at least taking out her nemesis. Kev rushed toward her but was engaged by two of the queen's guards, and the battle was on.

The crew of the Bird was at first reluctant to utilize their superior weapons, but found it necessary under the overwhelming assault. Arek and his brothers had no such compunctions, lobbing a barrage of grenades into the body wave that confronted them. One warrior was unlucky enough to laugh when Zoë stepped up to do battle. Moments later the warrior was on her back, staring in horror at Zoë as she drew a blade across her throat. "People keep underestimating me." Zoë spat at the woman and returned to the fray.

Dev and Aldora circled, looking for an opening in the other's defense. Aldora struck first, kicking at Dev's belly, but was blocked by a forearm. "Figures you'd stoop to such low tactics." Dev was disgusted.

"In battle, you use whatever means necessary to win." This time she punched at the protrusion.

Dev had hoped for an honorable resolution, but now she was seriously pissed. With deadly precision, she went to work on her cousin. Not as well balanced as normal, she eschewed her usual jumping kicks and settled on a less flamboyant style. She beat the shit out of Aldora, punching and jabbing, advancing and retreating, until Aldora sank to her knees on the floor. "I tried to leave this wretched place without incident," Dev gasped. "But you wouldn't let it happen." She ignored her bloody knuckles and gave into the desire to feel her fist smash the arrogant nose. Blood spurted and Dev smiled. "You just had to press the issue." This time she raised a knee under the royal chin. "You had to prove you were the best." She administered a left hook to the cheek. "Well guess what?" Reaching out with the index finger of her right hand, Dev pushed Aldora to the floor. "You can't beat me, bitch. Even if I am pregnant."

Out of breath but exhilarated, Dev looked around to see how they were doing. Much of the fighting had stopped when Aldora fell. Some of the Imani had even knelt in homage to Devona. Just what she needed.

A scream from Tim caused her to turn back to Aldora just in time to see her cousin raise a crossbow and aim it at her husband. "No-o-o-o!" Raw, bleeding agony rose from her throat as she sprinted toward Kevnor. Surprise crossed his face as the bolt from the bow cut through her body and propelled her into his arms.

His cry was not even human as he clutched Devona to him, begging whatever deity might be willing to bargain to take him, not her. To spare his woman.

Aldora's smirk morphed into a grimace when Aron stepped up behind her and snapped her neck with one deft move. It wouldn't bring his sister back, but it felt good just the same.

Kev's howling finally broke through the inertia. Mik helped him lower Dev to the ground. Callus cleared back the crowd. Zoë and Dugan took off for the palace in search of medical care, and the triplets surrounded their sister and her husband, a human wall between Devona and any threat. Ewen and Tim knelt on the floor, hugging each other and crying silent, desperate tears.

One by one, the warriors dropped their weapons and dispersed. In the silence that followed, Kev brushed back the wisps of hair that fell on his beloved's brow, murmuring endearments and ordering her to live. When her eyes fluttered and opened, Kev felt a new rush of unfamiliar moisture flood his eyes. He blinked rapidly, but the droplets splattered on her cheeks.

Dev raised a hand to run a finger down his cheek. "Hey, don't worry. I'll be fine." Her body convulsed as the first pains of childbirth ripped through her body. "Oh, God. Kev. The baby." Reaching down between her legs, she brought back her trembling hand to display bright red blood. "Not my baby. Kevnor, save our baby." The woman who faced battle with a cool head became hysterical over the impending loss of her child. Over and over she screamed for Kev to do something. Helpless he wept, sitting there on the cold floor of the practice arena.

Three days later, she opened her eyes again. The first thing she did was reach for the comforting bulge of her stomach, only to find it flat and sore. Silent agony slipped from the corners of her eyes to pool in her ears. She closed her eyes against the pain, and her mind against the desire to live.

Kev dozed beside her, three days growth of beard shadowing his face. Exhausted physically and emotionally he missed his wife's brief moment of consciousness, dreaming fitfully of the horror he'd experienced, seeing her throw her body between his and the crossbow's bolt, jerking awake with a cry of despair. Pacing to the window he looked without seeing out over the city. As a child, he'd thought the loss of his parents the most horrendous thing he could possibly endure. The pain he faced now far surpassed that. If he lost Devona, he could not go on living.

Zoë slipped into the gloomy room. "Kev," she said softly, "you need to eat."

"I don't want food. The very thought makes me ill."

"Then at least go take a shower. I'll sit with her."

"No." His voice cracked. "Thanks, but no. I don't want to leave her. She might need me." Zoë gasped when he turned to face her. His eyes were the red of a blazing supernova, puffy and without hope.

She ran her palm down his forearm. "You have to provide the strength for both of you. You can't allow yourself to get too run down."

He shook her off. "I said no." He didn't mean to yell at her, but he did.

Dev moaned, drawing their attention to the bed. Kev fell to his knees beside her, pulling her hand to his cheek. "Honey." His voice cracked. "Wake up and talk to me."

"No." Already she was withdrawing.

Zoë had a revelation. Slipping from the room, she went in search of Miklus. "Captain. Call a war council."

He couldn't have been more surprised if she'd told him to plan a party. "To what purpose?"

"Just do it."

He held his hands up in surrender. Sometimes she was a little termagant. "Okay."

When they'd all assembled, Zoë recapitulated the events in Dev's room. Blank faces stared back at her. "Don't you get it? Dev needs something to come back to. She has withdrawn into despair. If we don't reach her soon, she'll die of grief."

"What do you suggest?"

"She loves us. I suggest that we all go in her room, turn on the lights and talk. Her subconscious will react to the stimuli."

"And if it doesn't?"

"What do we have to lose?"

"Good point."

"Kev's not going to like this."

"I don't give a fuck what he likes. Dev is my friend, and I don't intend to give up on her." Taking a deep breath Zoë continued, "Kev is in almost as bad a shape as she is. And we need to bring the boys in. They'll reach her even if we don't. She's crazy about those kids."

Mik ran his fingers through his hair. "You're right. We have nothing to lose."

Kev came to his feet when the door opened. "Hey. What's this?" He stepped between Dev and his friends. "You're going to disturb her." Ewen and Tim darted around him to their mother's bedside. It was a testimony to his own deteriorated state that he seemed unable to stop them. His arms dropped to his sides as they passed.

The defeated demeanor of his best friends sat like a lead weight on Mik's chest. When he'd spoken to Shesshie the night before, he'd been unable to talk much about Dev and Kev. His throat had closed with emotion. But his wife hadn't pushed. Instead, she'd told him she loved him and missed him and encouraged him to take as much time as he needed to take care of them. She understood they were family in all the ways that counted.

"Mom," Ewen whispered. "Don't leave us. We never had a mother before. We need you."

"Yeah." Tim, for once, was speechless.

The older boy continued, stroking her arm as he talked, "I know we told you we'd look out for our baby sister, but we don't know how to without you to show us. She's so tiny we can't even touch her yet." Emotion almost overcame him, so he cleared his throat. "Please, mom."

Kev turned wild eyes on the boy. "What did you say, Ewen?"

Jumping guiltily, Ewen stepped back from the bedside. "I just told her to live. I promise I didn't upset her." Zoë had been emphatic about not upsetting his mother.

"But what else did you say?" His feet dragged as he walked. "About the baby?"

Tim stepped between them. "He didn't mean anything, dad...uh, Kev. He just thought she'd want to hear about the baby."

"What baby?" His voice seemed filled with gravel.

"Y-your baby, sir."

"Sh-she's alive?" His knees buckled. Tim and Ewen rushed forward, trying to stop his fall, but his knees crashed into the floor, taking them along. "Our baby is alive?"

"My God." Mik and Callus helped him into a chair. "We thought you knew."

Dugan hurried to explain, "King Jacton sent his own personal medical staff as soon as we notified him. The little one is in an incubator but seems to be doing well. Naturally, she's tiny, but her lungs were fully developed. Her prognosis is good."

Devona clinched the bedclothes. Her eyes sprang open.

"Kev, look." Zoë was staring at the bed.

She was crying openly now, taking loud, gulping breaths. Kev moved to sit on the bed beside her. Their eyes met, and in a moment, exchanged more emotion than a month of conversation could convey. He leaned down and gathered her into his arms. Everyone else left the room.

"I thought I'd lost you. I couldn't bear to lose you."

Dev had transferred her grip to his hair as she clung to him. "I'm sorry. I couldn't face life without our child."

"Oh, baby, don't apologize. I'm the one who needs to apologize. If I had taken better care of you, none of this would have happened. I thought I'd lost you both."

"How could you not know? How could you not know our daughter was still alive?"

"I never left your side. No one mentioned her. I just assumed..."

"The same thing I assumed."

He kissed her, drawing life from her even as he gave back the same.

"Go see her. Go see her and come back and tell me about her."

"I'm not sure I can. I don't know if I can leave you for that long right now." He smoothed her hair back. "I just have to look at you for a while."

"Kevnor, please. I have to know she's real."

"The other's said—"

Palsied fingers pressed against his lips. "It has to be you. I have to hear it from you."

Fighting his compulsion to stay, he reluctantly left the room. When he reappeared a few minutes later, his face was an open book, which Dev read with a joyful cry. "Tell me," she ordered.

"She's the most incredible thing I've ever seen. I thought Tessa was small when we found her, but our girl is even smaller. But Dev, she's a fighter. When I spoke to her, she screwed up her little nose and let out a wail that nearly shattered the windows."

"What does she look like?"

"Beautiful. Her eyes are brown like mine, but she has soft blonde fuzz on her head and a tiny little dimple in her chin."

"Did you count her fingers and toes? Are they all there?"

Mirth rumbled up from his chest. "No, I didn't. She had socks on her feet, but all her fingers were there, complete with minuscule fingernails. Amazing."

Dev threw back the covers and struggled up on her elbows.

"Draco. What do you think you're doing?" The desperate look was back in Kev's eyes.

"I'm going to see my baby."

"Defecating Darnuvian drayhorns! You aren't going anywhere. You almost died." A large calloused hand came to rest on her shoulder.

"If you don't let me out of this bed, I'm going to hurt you." Her teeth were clinched. A sure sign she was pissed.

"Now, Dev, be reasonable." It was a pitiful thing when a powerful man was reduced to begging.

"Okay." Her suddenly sweet tone made him nervous. "I'll be reasonable. You get out of my way and I won't break your arm." She smiled like a practiced courtesan. This was not good.

Laughter filtered in from the doorway. "Could I make a suggestion?" Mik asked.

Relief flooded Kev's features. "By all means."

"Why don't you carry her down the hall? That way she gets to see the baby and you don't have to worry about her falling on her face."

A man of action, Kev bundled the sheet around her and hefted her against his chest. "I knew that," he mumbled.

Chapter Twenty-seven

It took a full week to get the baby stabilized enough to travel. Dev was still arguing with her spouse over what to name their daughter. "We can't present her to Jacton unnamed." She tucked the blanket around the soft arm, allowing her finger to skim along the downy cheek. "She needs a name."

"I still don't see anything wrong with Kevnora." His grin belied his serious tone.

"Yes," she agreed dryly. "It's almost as attractive as Dev Junior."

"I thought it appropriate," Callus groused. "She looks just like you."

"No, she doesn't. She has her father's eyes, don't you, sweetheart?" No one could hold back a smile at the sound of Devona cooing to her child. Who'd have thought?

Frowning, she raised her head and swept the room with her gaze. "One word. One word out of any of you and you'll have to face me on the mat."

"Forget it. The doctor said you weren't to have any strenuous activity for a full month." Kev lowered his voice and added, "And I have plans for your first strenuous activities."

Still walking like she had a twelve pound Prima Lizard egg clutched between her knees, Dev blushed and pushed at her husband's chest. "Forget it. You're never coming at me with that thing again." The bridge erupted into laughter. "Unless." Her voice grew husky. "You make it worth my while."

"Honey, that's a promise."

"What was your mother's name?"

Mik shook his head. "That was out of left field, Dugan."

The Bauxite shrugged his broad shoulders. "I just thought they might want to name the baby after Kevnor's mother. Many Bauxite families hand down names from generation to generation."

"That's not a bad idea." Dev smiled at Kevnor. "It was Kabria, wasn't it?" Rubbing noses with her child she smiled. "It suits." She tried it out again. "Kabria." Brows raised she turned to ask, "What do you think, dad?"

Afraid to try to speak, Kev nodded and ran a knuckle across Dev's cheekbone.

"We're coming up on Baux." Zoë checked the readouts, adjusting the angle of approach. Dugan stood behind her, a proprietary look on his face. "Instructions, Captain?"

"Just contact central navigation and see where they want us."

Doing double duty while Kev stood around looking besotted, Zoë slipped on a headset and made arrangements with the Bauxite Aviation Authority. A brow rose as she listened to instructions. "Well, well, well. It seems we're instructed to dock on the royal substation and taxi down directly to the palace. Rooms have been prepared for us."

"Draco. I wanted to head straight home. Shesshie is becoming impatient."

Dev laughed. "Shesshie is or Miklus is? The last time I spoke to her she seemed to understand the delays."

Mik's cheeks took on a decidedly pink glow. "I admit it. I miss her." Turning to Kev he asked, "How long do you think this will take?"

"I have no idea. I never expected this."

Breaking off the impromptu neck rub he was administering to Zoë, Dugan offered, "He probably just wants to see that we're all okay and hear firsthand what happened on Iman. Reports are dull reading. Conversation over dinner is a lot more informative. Besides, he'll want to see little Kabria. Children are very important to Bauxite society."

Mik's shoulders relaxed. "That shouldn't take long then."

"I'll make a point of telling him I'm anxious to get the baby home and settled in," Dev promised.

***

Seeing Jacton holding Kabria brought tears to Devona's eyes. If not for his quick action in sending medical experts, they might have lost her. The midwives on Iman had been adept enough at delivery, but knew nothing of care for at-risk infants. On Iman, you either lived or died according to the will of the goddess. Well Dev didn't believe in their goddess and certainly didn't want her child's survival at the whim of such a deity. "What do you think, Your Highness?"

"Please. No formalities. You're family." He chucked Kabria under the chin. "I think she's perfect." He looked Dev square in the eyes. "Thank you for passing on the tradition of family names, even though you and Kev don't live on Baux."

"I wanted to. Honoring Kevnor's family is a privilege."

"Well, honoring your beautiful daughter is my privilege." Reaching to the table beside him, Jacton retrieved an official document and handed it to Dev. "Will you read it for everyone to hear?"

Taking the paper she skimmed the content. Tears welled up in her eyes. "This is too much. You can't."

Jacton chuckled. "I am the king. I can do whatever I want."

"What is it?" Kev crowded closer to get a glimpse.

"It's the deed to a new ship. The ship is to be christened after the baby and is presented to Kevnor and Devona until such time as our daughter reaches her majority." She gazed up at Kev. "Upon her twenty-fifth birthday, Kabria becomes sole owner of the cruiser."

"Perhaps it will help get your shipping business on its feet. By the time your daughter assumes command you should have acquired several other vessels."

Kev extended his hand to the king. "Thank you, Jacton. It is a generous gift and on behalf of our daughter we thank you."

Instead of taking the proffered hand, Jacton reached his free arm around Kev and hugged him. "I'm through with being at arms length. Our family has dwindled down practically to nothing. I don't intend to lose what I have left."

Dev kissed the king on the cheek. "I'm glad to hear that. And now that we have another ship, we'll be able to come and visit more often." The gleam in his eyes told her that was probably the real reason behind his extravagant gift. "And if you can ever steal away from your royal duties, you're always welcome at the Nest."

"Nest?"

"That's what we call our home and base of operations."

"All of our ships are named for birds," Mik added.

"Then the Kabria should fit right in."

"How so?"

Jacton looked over at his cousin. "Didn't you tell them?" When Kev shook his head, he continued. "Kabria is an ancient word for the Bauxite Goddess of Love. She is always depicted with wings, the theory being you have to be quick to keep up with human emotions."

Dev turned on her husband. "You knew that?"

"Well, yeah, I knew it, but I hadn't really thought about it till Jac mentioned it."

They were interrupted when the housekeeper entered the room. "Dinner is served, your majesty."

"We'll be right in." Turning to his guests he asked, "Anyone hungry? The staff has been working on this meal all day."

"I don't know about the rest of them, but I could eat an entire flock of those furry little critters you've got grazing up on the hill." Callus stretched and patted his stomach.

Kev burst out laughing. "I doubt you'll be tasting any of those, Callus. The Neebree are the official symbol of Baux. It's on all our official flags, stamps and seals. They are protected by the government."

Callus grumbled. "Well how was I to know?"

Jacton rose, transferring Kabria to his shoulder. "No harm done." He squinted. "But I'll be sure to have the shepherd count the flock before you leave."

Zoë hit Callus with her hip as she passed. "I see the king has you figured out already."

He took a halfhearted swing at her butt. Dugan glowered at him and tucked her under his arm as they went in to dinner. "Have you told them yet?" he asked her.

"Told us what?" Dev asked.

"Now you've done it. I was going to wait till after we finished eating. This discussion is liable to give us all indigestion."

"Might as well come clean now, Zoë." Mik held a chair out for her before Dugan could get to it. He, too, received a scowl. Mik bit the inside of his lip to keep from laughing.

Sliding into the seat beside her before anyone else took a notion to irritate him, Dugan announced, "Zoë won't be returning to Bright's with you."

"The hell you say." The news distracted Callus so much he took his eyes off the feast for all of five seconds. "Who will I torment if she's not around?"

"Don't worry, friend. I'll make sure to torment her every day." The promise in his voice had Kev's brows raised.

"How long will you be away?" Mik wanted to know.

"Well, I'm not exactly sure..."

"If all goes well, she won't be back. At least not to live." Dugan reached over to caress the nape of her neck, exposed by her upswept hairstyle. "I plan to do everything in my power to convince her to stay on Baux as my wife."

Zoë's jaw hung open. "What? That's news to me. I thought this was just about a month of hedonistic pleasure."

Dugan's hand slid off her shoulder to grasp her upper arm, his fingers burning into the side of her breast. "Don't worry, little girl. There'll be plenty of hedonistic pleasure. It's all part of my wicked plan to steal you away."

Mouth suddenly dry, Zoë ran her tongue over her bottom lip, leaving a glistening trail over the full temptation. Dugan didn't have the strength or inclination to suppress his desire to taste those lips. Leaning over he took control of them, enticing her to grant him entrance, twining his tongue with hers until both of them forgot where they were.

Jacton cleared his throat...several times. Still they kissed. "Well, I suggest we eat. It looks like those two have gone straight to dessert."

Everyone laughed, catching Dugan's attention. Reluctantly, he pulled back, adding one last chaste kiss to Zoë's mouth before settling back in his seat, a knowing smile on his face.

Chapter Twenty-eight

The sun had just risen over Bright's Planet, washing everything with a golden glow. Shesshie squinted, scanning the skies for a first glimpse of the Freebird. "I wonder what's keeping them?"

Jim Darner harrumphed. "They just radioed you. It takes more than three minutes to get here from that altitude." Tessa in his arms, he screwed up his features as the baby slapped both sides of her face with her chubby little hands and chanted, "Doc, Doc, Doc."

"How do I look?" Miranda arrived with a pirouette, showing off her new dress in a swirl of multicolored synthoweave.

"Fabulous." Shesshie approved of the change in her sister. A beautiful, confident woman was emerging, thanks to Callus' attentiveness. "Callus will be drooling."

Miranda smiled broadly and sassily flipped the ends of her hair. "That's the idea." Lowering her voice she moved closer to her sister. "You won't have your feelings hurt if we have our own private celebration tonight, will you?"

"Too much information." Jim pretended to scowl, but his twinkling eyes gave him away.

"Celebration?" Shesshie looked horrified. "I haven't planned a celebration."

Jim winked. "It appears both of you had the same idea about welcoming home your men. Better be careful, Miranda, or you'll end up in your sister's shape."

"There is nothing wrong with my shape. I haven't gained that much, have I?"

Rolling his eyes, Jim hurried to make amends. "Only your stomach has grown. I was just teasing your sister." He felt an ache deep in his chest as he recalled the mood swings his wife used to have when she was pregnant. "I promise, Mik will think you look ravishing."

"Da-da?" Tessa clapped her hands and pointed upward. Sure enough, the sun glinted off an incoming vessel.

Eb sauntered out of the office building. "Everyone's up early today. Does this mean you've made breakfast for everyone?" The teenager looked longingly at the hangar that had been converted into apartments.

Shesshie laughed and ruffled his hair. "I left biscuits and fried meat in the warmer. You'll have to cook your own eggs or wait on the rest of us." He was off like a shot.

"You've done such a fine job with him, Doc." Shesshie rubbed her stomach.

"He's done as much for me as I've done for him, believe me."

"Is that a second vessel?" Miranda squinted at the heavens.

"I believe you're right." Jim handed the baby over to her aunt and walked out toward the landing pad. "You ladies go inside till I check this out."

"Not on your life." Shesshie was rarely defiant, but when she took a stand she never backed down. "If there was danger, Mik would never have told me he was on the way. He'd have taken care of the problem first."

"What if he wasn't aware of the problem?" Jim took his job as protector seriously. He didn't want to screw it up at this late date. "Please just step inside until they debark."

Sighing heavily, Shesshie tugged on her sister's arm. "Let's back up a little, Miranda. Doc's probably right to be cautious."

They went as far as just outside the door, so they could retreat quickly if necessary. It wasn't necessary. The Freebird settled onto the tarmac just moments later, followed by a beautiful new cruiser. "Son of a bitch. Where'd they steal that?" Jim hurried over to where Mik was descending from the Bird.

Mik caught him up in a bear hug, but kept moving toward his wife and daughter. Callus didn't even acknowledge him in his headlong rush toward Miranda. Jim laughed. "Nice to see you, too, Callus." He slapped a broad shoulder as the younger man passed.

When Kev and Dev appeared in the doorway of the second ship, Jim rushed over. "Let me see her," he demanded.

"She's a beauty, isn't she?" Kev asked. "She made light speed in record time, her engines are the latest and—"

"Screw the ship," Jim interrupted. "I want to see the baby."

With an air of superiority, Dev shouldered her way past her spouse and presented Kabria to Doc. "Isn't she beautiful?"

"Let me hold her." Gently he took the baby, careful to support her head and back. "Dev, she is beautiful. I thought nothing could come up to our Tessa, but she surely does." The baby looked up at him and screwed up her face to cry. "Hear now." He jostled her gently up and down. "Don't be scared of old Doc." Lip still trembling, she did an about face and broke out into a grin. "There's my good girl." Tiny fists waved in the air.

"We ought to get her in out of the sun. Her skin is too delicate to be exposed." Dev glanced around the landing pad. "Where is everyone?"

Laughter rumbled from Kev's chest. "It didn't take either couple two minutes to disappear inside. I don't think they'll be joining us for breakfast."

"Maybe I should go get Little Bit." Jim took a step toward the family dwelling, but Kev stopped him.

"Naw. Tessa wants to see her daddy. Leave 'em be for now." He steered them toward the galley. "What say we get some chow? I'm starving."

"Aw, shit." Jim picked up his pace. "We left Eb alone with the food."

Laughing, Kev, Dev and Kabria followed him at a slower pace.

About the Author

Diane Merlin is a wife, mother and grandmother who never outgrew her love of the bizarre and the unusual. An avid reader since early childhood, it was a natural progression to weave tales of her own. Writing is an obsession she suppressed but never abandoned until her children were grown. She writes romance, but never the everyday garden variety. Her stories always contain a unique element be it futuristic worlds, vampires, or shape shifters. When time and deadlines allow, she enjoys movies (anything Sci-Fi), reading (tucked away in her loft), and time with her family.

She invites you to settle back and Enter the Fantasy...

Visit her website at: www.dianemerlin.com